The
Lost House
of Ireland

BOOKS BY SUSANNE O'LEARY

The Road Trip

A Holiday to Remember

SANDY COVE SERIES

Secrets of Willow House

Sisters of Willow House

Dreams of Willow House

Daughters of Wild Rose Bay

Memories of Wild Rose Bay

Miracles in Wild Rose Bay

STARLIGHT COTTAGES SERIES

The Lost Girls of Ireland

The Lost Secret of Ireland

The Lost Promise of Ireland

Susanne O'Leary

The
Lost House
of Ireland

bookouture

Published by Bookouture in 2022

An imprint of Storyfire Ltd.
Carmelite House
50 Victoria Embankment
London EC4Y 0DZ

www.bookouture.com

ISBN: 978-1-80314-444-3
eBook ISBN: 978-1-80314-443-6

This book is a work of fiction. Names, characters, businesses, organizations,
places and events other than those clearly in the public domain, are either the
product of the author's imagination or are used fictitiously. Any resemblance
to actual persons, living or dead, events or locales is entirely coincidental.

1

Allegra lay back on her beach blanket and closed her eyes to the sun. Finally, a moment to herself after a hectic morning trying to keep track of the children on this huge beach, packed with families on vacation after a long New England winter. She had always loved Cape Cod and the cottage in Chatham that had been the family vacation spot ever since her grandfather had bought it in the 1950s. She had played and swum here on Harding Beach since she was a small girl, and now she was watching her niece and nephew doing the same.

Her sister, Lucia, and brother-in-law, Phil, had taken over the cottage when their father died, buying Allegra's share for a sum she couldn't refuse. She no longer owned any part of the cottage, as she would never have been able to afford the upkeep, but she was happy it had stayed in the family. A project leader at an IT firm in Boston, her career was on the up, but her salary was quite modest. With Lucia and Phil as owners, she could still come here for a few weeks every year, which was lovely, even if this meant she would be a kind of nanny to their two wild kids while they had a well-earned break. What they meant by 'well earned' Allegra didn't quite know, as they had a full-time nanny in New York, where they now lived. But as this nanny never joined them on vacation, Allegra had to step in and fill the role. She could have refused and told them off for using her as unpaid help, but she adored the children and they adored her right back, as she was the 'cool aunt' who wore 'funky clothes' and played fun games and read stories at bedtime. It was mostly a great job, even if they wore her out and stretched her patience to the limit.

Right now, however, she could relax for a while as eight-year-old Emma and her ten-year-old brother, Joe, were being taken care of by the mother of one of their friends. Allegra looked at them with half-closed eyes as they tucked into sandwiches and shared cookies, and then gave herself up to the warmth of the sun and the sound of the waves. It was heaven to lie here and rest for a little while.

The past year had been hard as she had, while working, looked after her father, who had suffered a stroke earlier in the year and had needed to use a wheelchair. When her father finally passed away, Allegra was happy that she had spent this time with him. Lucia had tried her best to help, but living so far away in New York, with a family and a career in law and accountancy, she had little time to spare. Allegra was the only one who had the time and the patience to care for him, and she had seen it as a privilege rather than a chore. Now it was over, she could pick up her life again. But her grief was still so fresh, and it felt too soon to move on.

As the weeks passed, Allegra found Emma and Joe's company the only thing that cheered her up. She felt so lucky to have these two in her life, and she often went to New York to see them. But her therapist hadn't approved of her frequent visits to Lucia and Phil, calling them her 'surrogate family'.

'You need to try to stand on your own feet,' she said during one of the weekly sessions. 'Don't use your sister's family as a crutch. You should try to mix with people your own age, and perhaps get started on making a home for yourself in your new apartment. Then you'll be more independent and *that* will make you feel more positive.'

'But I don't want to be more independent,' Allegra argued. 'I need my family. They make me feel secure.'

'It's a false security, I think,' the therapist had said. 'You have to build your own life, your own stability, instead of leaning on them. Face your fears. That's the first step to recovery.'

Allegra bristled. She had always resented being told what to do and how to feel.

'Well,' she said, 'in that case I will take the first step towards that independence, and I'll stop coming here.' She got up from the chair and held out her hand. 'Thanks for your help. It's been – interesting.'

'But, but...' her therapist stammered, 'you can't walk out just like that. You need a lot more help.'

'I can work on what you just told me on my own,' Allegra countered. 'There is a lot I need to improve on, that's true, but I can do that better on my own from now on.'

Then she said goodbye, shook the woman's limp hand and walked out, feeling a wonderful sense of freedom. No more therapy. No more being told how to grieve and how to live her life. Lucia, Phil and the children were her only family right now and she was going to continue seeing them as often as she could. She was looking forward to the summer vacation with them on Cape Cod. That would be better than any therapy.

One day she would have a family of her own, but until then, she could enjoy her time with Emma and Joe and be the fun aunt who spoiled them. She was only thirty-five, after all, so there was plenty of time to find that special man, she felt. But busy looking after her father, she had not been on a date for nearly a year. After the funeral, her friends had invited her to join them when they went clubbing in Boston but she hadn't felt ready. 'Maybe in the fall,' she had said. 'When I've had a little time and space to myself.' And now, as the summer vacation was drawing to a close, she was beginning to feel ready to go out there and have a little fun again.

'Auntie Allie!' a voice called, pulling her out of her daydream. 'Come here and help us build a castle. You're so good at it.'

Allegra sat up, brushed back her long reddish-blonde hair and tied it up with a scrunchie. Then she scrambled to her feet and grabbed the bucket and spade beside her on the sand.

'Okay,' she shouted, 'start digging a moat and then we'll build the castle.'

As she stepped towards the edge of the water, she smiled at the two children, so alike with their strawberry-blonde hair and brown eyes. A mix of Italian and Irish, just like her. The huge brown eyes were from her Italian mother, who had died young, the reddish-blonde hair and smattering of freckles from her father, who had been so proud of his Irish heritage, even though it was a long time since the first Casey landed on America's shore and came to Boston to seek his fortune. Several generations later, Allegra's grandfather had married an Irish girl who had just arrived, and they had had Patrick – Allegra and Lucia's father – who had passed on his reddish-blond hair and freckles to his youngest daughter, Allegra. Where her nearly six-foot height and long limbs came from, nobody knew.

'Could be a throwback from some Viking ancestor,' her father had suggested, looking up at his tall daughter in awe when she had turned fifteen. 'But this way you can always look down on everyone,' he had joked.

But Allegra never felt like looking down on anyone. Her height had never fazed her either, as she was elected captain of the school basketball team and found herself very good at it. She was quite the heroine in the school as the team won nearly every match and soon became champions, which made her very popular. The few snide comments about her height never upset her and, as she didn't react, the jeering soon stopped. Her confidence was simply too strong, so any attempt at bullying was doomed to fail. This continued when she went to college and took up track and field sports, but by then being tall was an advantage rather than a liability.

Her older sister, Lucia, was darker, shorter and curvier, but her two children took after their aunt, which made their bond even stronger. And now as Allegra watched them, she felt a dart of happiness. She began to believe that maybe, very soon, she would come out of the gloom she had been in for so long. Life was for living, and you never knew what was around the corner.

'Come on,' Emma shouted, flicking her hair out of her eyes. 'Let's start building the castle.'

Allegra sank down on her knees and started digging a channel around the mound of sand the children had made. She handed Joe a bucket.

'Here, use this as a mould and make the turrets and towers. I'll keep digging the moat.'

'And then we have to have a bridge,' Emma said. 'But dig the moat really deep. Wouldn't it be fun if we had some fish in it?'

'I don't think that's going to happen,' Allegra said, laughing as she dug. She stopped as her spade hit something buried deep in the sand. 'Oh, I think there's a shell here. Or a stone.' She looked down and saw a small square object and started to dig around it. 'What is it?' she said to herself. 'Looks like some kind of ring.'

Emma looked at it over Allegra's shoulder. 'Buried treasure,' she squealed.

'Don't be silly,' Allegra said. 'It's probably just the ring from a can.' She dug with her nails and prised the object out of the hard-packed sand and peered at it. And then her eyes widened and her heartbeat quickened. 'It is a ring,' she said quietly. 'But not from a can. It has a stone.'

'Wow,' Emma said, staring at the ring encrusted with sand in Allegra's hand. 'Is it expensive, do you think?'

'Joe, get me some water in the bucket,' Allegra ordered. 'So we can wash it clean.'

Joe did as he was told and ran to the water's edge and filled the bucket, running back to Allegra. 'Here. Wash it clean and we can see what kind of stone it is.'

'Could be a sapphire like my mom's,' Emma suggested.

'Maybe it's worth millions,' Joe suggested while Allegra washed the ring in the bucket, swirling it around in the water to get all the sand out.

'There,' Allegra said at last and held the ring up. 'All clean. And look, it's a diamond, I think. It sparkles like one anyway.'

'Could be fake,' Joe said. 'Like those rings in the chewing-gum machine.'

'I don't think so,' Allegra said as she studied the square-cut diamond, surrounded by smaller diamond chips, on a band of gold. 'I think it's old. Diamonds are usually set on white gold or platinum these days.'

'I wonder who lost it?' Emma said. 'Maybe it's someone's granny's ring and they inherited it?'

'Or it's been down there in the sand a very long time,' Joe mused.

Allegra looked inside the ring. 'There's an inscription. Can't really see what it says. Can you?' she asked, handing the ring to Joe, who squinted inside the band of gold.

'I think there are two names here,' he said. 'I can see a D and an A and a V... I and N and an A...'

'Davina?' Allegra said. 'Anything else?'

'Yes,' Joe muttered. 'S and E and A and N.'

'Sean,' Allegra said, taking the ring from Joe. She looked inside the gold band again. 'There's a number, too, like a date...

one... slash, zero, five, and then... 1939. The fifth of January 1939. Or the first of May if you're European. Must be the date of someone's engagement.'

'Nineteen thirty-nine?' Joe said. 'That's like a hundred years ago.'

'Not quite, but nearly,' Allegra said, slipping the ring on the ring finger of her left hand, holding it up to the bright sunlight. 'It's a little tight, but it nearly fits me. Look how it glitters. I think it's a real diamond.'

'Maybe it's worth a *lot* of money,' Emma said, her eyes huge. 'We'll be millionaires!'

'Not so fast,' Allegra said with a grin. 'The ring is hardly worth that much. And in any case, I have to hand it in to the police station in case someone has reported it missing.'

'Or stolen,' Joe suggested. 'Maybe some burglar broke into a house around here and then dropped the ring when he was about to get away.'

'On the beach?' Emma said. 'That's stupid.'

'He might have tried to get away in a boat,' Joe retorted.

They were interrupted by one of the mothers in the group of children. 'Emma and Joe!' she called. 'We're getting ice cream from the van in the parking lot. Do you want to come?'

'Ice cream!' the children shouted in unison, the ring all but forgotten. 'Can we, Auntie Allie?'

'Of course,' Allegra said, getting to her feet. 'Come on back to our blanket. I'll give you money.'

When the children had gone, Allegra sat on the blanket, looking at the ring, still on her finger. She took it off and looked at the inscription again. *Davina and Sean*, she thought. *Who were they? And how did Davina lose her ring? She must have been devastated.* The diamond gleamed in the sunlight, and Allegra suddenly had a feeling that there was some kind of mystery attached to the ring. A story, in any case. She would probably never know. Once she had handed it in to the police, the owner would claim it and that would be it. But maybe if that happened, she could contact them and ask about its history?

It would be fascinating to find out about the original owner and what had happened to her. Davina, engaged to Sean in 1939. So long ago, just before the war; what could have happened to make the ring turn up here, on a beach on Cape Cod after all these years...

Allegra suddenly felt she couldn't wait to find out. The idea to do a little research and see if she could find out who these people were started to grow in her mind. It felt like a wonderful adventure, something that would turn her mind away from the sad time she had been through. She loved history and always watched documentaries about old houses and people who had lived a long time ago, and this would be a kind of historical sleuthing.

But first she had to hand it in to the police. She had heard in a news item on TV that if you found something of value, you could keep it if nobody had claimed it after ninety days. Three months was a long time to wait, and the rightful owner might turn up to claim the ring during that time. But whatever happened, Allegra wanted to know the story behind the ring. She couldn't shake off the idea. She just had to find out more and she decided to do a little research while she waited to hear. She felt a dart of excitement as it suddenly came to her exactly where she would start.

2

A few days after she handed the ring in to the local police station, Allegra went to the Eldredge public library, housed in an old red-brick building in the main street of Chatham. The little town had always been a delight to visit. Walking down the street with its quaint shops and restaurants that oozed old Cape Cod charm, Allegra gazed at the beautiful houses with their steep roofs, shingled exteriors, symmetrical façades and large chimneys in the middle. To her, these were the all-American houses that had always delighted her. This type of architecture had begun when the Puritans came to America in the seventeenth century – it was the way they'd built their houses. She had walked down this street all through her childhood, but strangely enough had never been in the library before. It was a Victorian house, different to the typical Cape Cod style.

The library was 125 years old, she learned from the plaque outside, and it had been built by Marcellus Eldredge, a successful businessman who had grown up in Chatham. She wondered fleetingly what it would be like to live here all through the year, instead of being a summer visitor, but she turned her attention to the librarian at the desk who was looking at her with a polite smile.

'Hi, how can I help you?' the woman said.

'Hi,' Allegra replied. 'I'm trying to find out... I mean, I'm doing some research and I'd like to look up the archives of the *Cape Cod Chronicle*. I believe I can find them here?'

'Of course you can,' the woman said. 'But we have recently put all the archives online. You can find them on our website. Easier than before.'

'Oh.' Allegra thought for a moment. 'I could look it all up on my phone, I suppose. I didn't bring my laptop when I came on vacation.'

'You can use one of our computers,' the woman offered. 'They're usually reserved for students, but in the summer anyone can use them. They're over there,' she added, pointing at a long table with three screens.

'That's great. Thank you,' Allegra said.

'If you want anything printed, we can do that for you. It's fifty cents a page.'

'I'll let you know.' Allegra smiled at the woman then walked over to the table and sat down in front of one of the screens.

It didn't take her long to find what she was looking for, and she quickly put 1939 into the search box. Then she scrolled down from January through to May and clicked on the link. She went through a series of pages, looking for the small ads in all of them, thinking she might see something like 'lost and found' or a small notification about someone having lost their engagement ring. Or perhaps even an announcement of Davina's engagement. But nothing came up. She went through the same routine for June of that year, again coming up with nothing. Her stomach started to rumble, and she realised she had been there for over three hours and now it was lunchtime, and she had promised Lucia to mind the kids for the afternoon.

Just one more issue, she thought and scrolled down to the

first of July 1939. And then... there it was. On the very last page, there was a short notice that seemed to stand out. Allegra held her breath as she read the text. *Has anyone found my ring?* the headline said under a small grainy photo of not a woman, as Allegra had expected, but a young man.

Allegra's heart beat faster as she read the story.

Sean Walsh, a young man from County Kerry in Ireland, has been looking all over Harding Beach for the ring his fiancée Davina Courtney lost while they were spending the day there before she went back to Ireland to organise their wedding. Sean Walsh had been working in Boston when he met Davina, also from Kerry, and they are planning to marry in the fall. Sean is offering a hundred dollars to anyone who finds the ring. As he has to go back very soon, to the village of Sandy Cove in County Kerry, where his parents live in the coastguard station, he hopes he can bring back the ring to his fiancée and put it on her finger before the wedding. If you should find it, please hand in the ring to either the police station in Chatham, or the office of this newspaper. Here is hoping there will be a happy ending for this sweet couple!

Allegra peered at the photo of the young man, but it was hard to make out what he actually looked like. She could see a shock of black hair, and a pair of brooding dark eyes, but that was all. But then, as she kept staring at the photo, his dark eyes seemed to speak to her, and there was nearly a physical pain as she imagined his feelings and desperation. *How sad*, she thought, *to lose your engagement ring like that, just before getting married. What happened then?* she wondered, still looking at the blurry photo. *Did this couple marry in the end? What were their lives like over there across the ocean during the war?* The story kept pulling at her heartstrings and she had an odd compulsion to know what happened to these people.

Sandy Cove, County Kerry in Ireland. And a coastguard station... It sounded so romantic. Allegra quickly googled the name of the village and looked at the photos that came up. Windswept, wild, magical and stunningly beautiful, Sandy Cove was situated in the south-west of Ireland, on the very edge of the Atlantic coast. The main street with its colourful houses, the lighthouse on top of a cliff, the beaches, the intense blue ocean, and then... the coastguard station, now renovated and renamed Starlight Cottages. It all looked like something from a fairy tale. Cape Cod was lovely, but this was more than that. The dramatic coastline, the beaches with the white sand, the bays and inlets, the mountains and rolling green hills...

Staring at the images, Allegra felt a sudden pull inside, a longing to see the country from where her ancestors had come. She just *had* to go there. Not only to find out about Davina and Sean, but to find herself, her past and her father's roots. Could this be what would finally heal her? She was sure nobody would come forward and claim the ring, simply because it had been buried in the sand for over eighty years, but discovering it suddenly seemed like a sign, an omen that might affect the rest of her life.

When her vacation was over, Allegra went back to Boston and her small apartment bought after the sale of her father's house. She tried to feel enthusiastic about picking up the strands of her life again, surrounded by boxes that still had to be unpacked, but she felt reluctant to even open them. The apartment was nice, with a bedroom, a big living room and a bright little kitchen off the hall. A good place to live in a great location. But Allegra couldn't settle in, couldn't get started on making this her home. She just unpacked her clothes and the crockery for the kitchen, leaving everything else stacked in a corner of her living room.

Everything seemed so hard, even going back to work and concentrating on the project she had been working on before her father died. She found herself constantly wishing she could get away, go somewhere different, somewhere that had no connection to the memories of these last few months. But that was an impossible dream. She knew she had to pull herself out of this way of thinking and she scolded herself for being such a wet blanket. The only thing that helped turn her mind away was the story about the lost ring she had seen in that old newspaper article. Those sad, dark eyes in the photo kept popping into her thoughts and she wished she could find out if the wedding had gone ahead, and if there had been a happy ending for the young couple after all.

There was still a month to go before she would get the ring, and the images of that lovely little village across the Atlantic Ocean haunted her thoughts and dreams. She constantly looked at the article she had had printed at the library, studied the Sandy Cove website and the pictures of the little village, read up about the history of Kerry and tried to search for people called Walsh or Courtney in the area, all without much success. Walsh was a common name in Ireland, and Courtney seemed to be more English than Irish. But she couldn't get Sean and Davina out of her mind and felt a growing compulsion to go to Ireland. Then she started to look at flights and hotels.

Of course, it was sheer madness to even contemplate going to a place like that in middle of October, the coast being battered by wind and rain at that time of year, she had read. And what about her job? She couldn't afford to take any kind of leave right now, when they were so busy developing a new gaming app that was to be launched just before Christmas. Could she simply quit and live on the inheritance from her father for a while? Allegra thought about it, and then dismissed the idea. She had come so far on the career ladder and taking a break would push her right down to the bottom again. There was no way she could go anywhere right now.

But still, at night, she dreamed of Ireland, and watched all the movies set there she could find. Right now going there was a dream, but she knew that one day, somehow, it would come true.

Because, she thought, *it is meant to happen; it's written in the stars.*

The ring came in a small package in the post in the middle of October with a note saying that, as nobody had claimed it, she was now entitled to have it. Allegra put it on her finger and looked at the diamond glittering in the early morning light. There was something about it that made her feel quite strange, as if the whisper of the past was softly blowing across the back of her neck. But it was a nice whisper, a greeting, maybe even a wish of good luck in her own quest for love, somewhere in the future.

She took it off and went to find a gold chain in her little jewellery box in the bedroom. Then she put the ring on the chain, deciding she would wear it around her neck as a talisman. Wearing it on her finger didn't seem right, somehow. Davina and Sean might look down from their heaven and smile, happy the ring had been found and was being taken care of. She touched the ring and knew that she had to go to Ireland to find out more about the couple and perhaps give the ring to their descendants, if they had any. It didn't seem right to keep it. She just *had* to go. But how?

A few days later, she took the bull by the horns and decided to talk to her boss, Annie.

'Would it be possible to change my way of working?'

Allegra asked, standing in front of Annie's desk in her small office.

'In what way?' Annie asked, as she stopped typing on her laptop and leaned back in her chair.

'Working remotely,' Allegra said. 'From somewhere else.'

Annie stared at her for a moment. 'From where?'

'Er... another country?' Allegra said, shifting from foot to foot.

Annie's eyebrows shot up. 'Like...?'

'Like Ireland,' Allegra said. 'I want to take a break for a bit and go away,' she babbled on. 'And I have always wanted to go to Ireland because my dad was constantly talking about it, and I thought I could work from there for a bit, and—'

'Stop for a moment,' Annie interrupted, swivelling in her chair. 'Let me think about this. I was actually just going to call you in to say that we're ahead of schedule on the new app. So it looks like you could take some time off, if you want. I really don't think working remotely would be possible. But if I give you a few weeks off, would that suit you?'

Allegra stared at Annie. 'Oh yes, it would suit me wonderfully,' she said, beaming Annie a wide smile.

'And then, when you come back, we'll talk about the next project that I have in mind,' Annie continued. 'You might be able to work on that online, but we can talk about it when the time comes. I know you've had a rough time, so I think going away will be good for you right now.'

'Oh, that's very kind of you, Annie.'

'Not really,' Annie said with a laugh. 'I wouldn't let you go if I needed you. But it's okay for you to go away right now.'

'Thank you,' Allegra said, feeling a dart of affection for her boss, who had been so kind and helpful during the difficult time she had been through.

'You're welcome,' Annie said. 'Enjoy your trip and take a lot of photos. It's a beautiful country, I've heard.'

'It sure is,' Allegra said and left the office to start making plans. It was finally happening. She was going to Ireland. All she needed to do now was book a flight and find accommodation, preferably in, or near, that little village called Sandy Cove. And then she had to tell her sister.

3

'Are you crazy?' Lucia cried down the phone from New York. 'Going to Ireland at this time of year? For what?'

'I need to get away,' Allegra said, sitting with her phone on the sofa in her small living room after arriving home from work. 'I haven't felt well ever since Dad died, you know. And I want to go to Ireland, because he always wanted to go back, but never had the chance. He and Mom spent their honeymoon in Kenmare, remember? They wanted to go there again, but then Mom died, and it was too late, and he was so sad about that. So I want to go partly for him. And another reason which I can't talk about right now,' she added. 'I think it'll help me to heal,' she tried to explain.

'But you were beginning to feel better this summer,' Lucia argued. 'And your therapist was a huge help, wasn't she? At least I thought so.'

'You might, but I didn't,' Allegra replied. 'She kept telling me how I was supposed to feel, and that I was using you and the kids as my surrogate family. I know she meant that I should go out there and date, and eventually have my own family, but that's not going to happen in a hurry. I couldn't bear going back and hearing all sorts of psychobabble that was supposed to make me feel better. It felt as if I was standing still and I wanted to move on, so I stopped going. That made me feel a lot better, believe me.'

'Typical,' Lucia said with a resigned sigh. 'Why did I think you would do something sensible?'

'I thought it was very sensible,' Allegra cut in. 'And now I feel the time is right to do something different.' She paused, wondering how she would explain to her sister that she felt as if the ring had put some kind of spell on her. A spell that could only be broken by going to Ireland now that her lucky break at work had suddenly made it possible. 'I just want to go,' she said to put a stop to Lucia's arguments.

'But what about your job? You can't take off just like that.'

'I can because of what happened today,' Allegra replied. 'My boss rearranged my work schedule in such a way that it's possible,' she continued, in order to put a positive spin on the situation. 'We're launching the new app next week, and then she gave me three weeks off as a bonus because of all the over-time I've put in. And she said I can work online after that if I want.' Allegra smiled as she thought about the conversation, and of how kind Annie had been.

'Well, that sounds okay, I suppose,' Lucia said, her voice calmer, even if she didn't seem quite convinced. 'But still... Ireland in late October? Who goes there at this time of year?'

'I do,' Allegra stated. 'I'm about to book my flight and then I'll be looking for some kind of accommodation. I'm going to Kerry,' she added. 'That's in the south-west.'

'I know where it is.' Lucia sighed. 'Okay. I give up. You have made up your mind, so it's useless to try to stop you. When are you going?'

'End of the week, I think.'

'Why don't you book a flight from Boston to here, and then fly to Ireland from JFK?' Lucia asked. 'Then you can stay here the night before you leave. The kids would love to see you. And we'll drive you to the airport.'

'That would be great,' Allegra said, her spirits rising at the thoughts of staying with Lucia and Phil in their plush apartment on the Upper East Side. 'I'll book my flight for Sunday evening. That way there'll be less traffic.'

'Make it a weekend, then,' Lucia suggested. 'Come to us on Friday. Phil will pick you up from the airport when you arrive from Boston. We can go to the theatre district for dinner, and we'll arrange a date for you. There's this great guy at Phil's office who's moving to Boston and—'

'No,' Allegra moaned. 'Please, Lucia, don't set me up with someone again. Remember what happened the last time?'

'You weren't trying hard enough to make him like you.'

'He spent the whole dinner texting his mother on his phone,' Allegra said, cringing at the memory. 'He didn't even look at me once. And I'd bought a new dress and all.'

'Oh, okay, but that was just bad luck. This guy is different. Really nice and fun and—'

'No, Lucia,' Allegra said, this time with feeling. 'I won't come if you do that. Please let me find my own men.'

Lucia gave up. 'Okay. Just the three of us on Friday night, and then we'll do something fun with the kids on Saturday. And brunch somewhere nice on Sunday morning before you leave. How's that?'

'What a send-off,' Allegra said with a laugh. 'Sounds fabulous. So yeah, I'd love all of that. I'll let you know when I've booked my flight.' She said goodbye and hung up with a smile.

Lucia, being the older sister, had always been a little overbearing, trying to look after Allegra ever since they lost their mother when Allegra was only ten years old, and Lucia just fifteen. This had continued into their adulthood, and Allegra had felt quite intimidated by her successful sister. Lucia's life seemed so perfect, with her high-profile job, gorgeous family, her apartment in New York and the cottage on Cape Cod. All this perfection was quite overwhelming and Allegra always felt inferior, even though she had done quite well herself. She was happy Lucia didn't live in the same city. If she did, she'd be constantly trying to set Allegra up with 'suitable' men. Living far apart was a good thing, even if Allegra missed having her sister nearby.

Allegra shrugged those thoughts away and turned her attention to booking a flight to Ireland and searching for somewhere to stay, which seemed a tougher nut to crack than she had thought. As she was planning to stay for three weeks, a hotel was too expensive. But most of the B&Bs she looked up were closed in the winter months.

Having given up on B&Bs, Allegra turned to the rental market, just to see if there were any small flats or even cottages for rent in or near Sandy Cove. And then, suddenly, she struck gold. Not only was there a cottage to rent in Sandy Cove, but one in the coastguard station! Wasn't that where Sean Walsh had been from? The man whose fiancée had lost the ring... She found the printout of the old newspaper article and read it yet again. Yes, she had been right. She looked at the grainy photo of the young man and the few lines that said he hailed from Sandy Cove, County Kerry, and that he had grown up in a coastguard station.

Excited, Allegra read the description of the house that was being let: *House for rent in Starlight Cottages, a former coastguard station in a charming village.* The photo showed a row of cottages perched high up on a cliff with incredible views of the ocean and the headlands. What an enchanting place. As she looked at the photos of the interior, she saw that it had been extensively renovated and now had central heating, a modern bathroom and a state-of-the-art kitchen. It was a little disappointing, as she had hoped to find something old-fashioned and cosy, but it would still be amazing to stay in the place where Sean had actually grown up. She was sure she would find out more about Sean and Davina's story if she went to this village. In any case, it looked so beautiful and adventurous. What did she have to lose? The off-season rent was quite reasonable, and she would book it for the minimum period of a month, even though she'd have to leave after three weeks.

Having booked the cottage and then the flight, Allegra quickly sent a text message to Lucia to confirm all was going to plan. Her heartbeat quickened as she thought of her trip, and she jumped up and went into her bedroom to start sorting out clothes. Warm sweaters were soon piling up on her bed, along with jeans, socks, a raincoat and a down jacket for chilly days. She hugged a cashmere pullover to her chest and closed her eyes for a moment, knowing her dream was coming true. She really was going to Ireland.

The weekend at Lucia's home in New York was fun and hectic, as the children wanted Allegra to join them in practically all their activities. The morning after a late-night dinner with Lucia and Phil, Allegra was woken up at the crack of dawn by Emma and Joe carrying a tray with coffee, orange juice and a plate of croissants and Danish pastries, delivered by the bakery down the street.

Allegra yawned and sat up in the big guest bed, piling pillows behind her. 'Hey, you two. Come and sit with me and help me eat these pastries. I can't finish them all by myself.'

Emma climbed up and sat beside her aunt, grabbing one of the croissants. 'Yummy.'

Joe sat on Allegra's other side and took a Danish pastry. 'There are loads. Dad made a double order for the weekend because he said we have to spoil you so you don't forget to come back.'

'I'd never forget to come back,' Allegra said and took a croissant from the plate. 'But maybe I should pretend so you keep spoiling me?'

Emma laughed. 'Yeah, you should. But we won't tell on you. Will we, Joe?'

'Not if you share the food with us,' Joe mumbled through a huge mouthful of pastry.

'Of course I will.' Allegra sipped the coffee that was a little too strong. It tasted good all the same because Emma and Joe had made it especially for her.

'Tell us about Ireland,' Joe said. 'And why you're going there.'

'Mom says you're crazy to go right now,' Emma piped up. 'But I think it's great. It's the best time of year to see the spooky castles and ruins and everything.'

Allegra smiled. 'Yeah, I know, but that's not why I'm going. Please don't tell anyone. It's a secret.'

'We swear,' Joe said and held up his hand. 'So help me God.'

'That's about telling the truth,' Emma argued, pushing at Joe. 'We have to swear to keep it a secret, cross our hearts and hope to die if we tell.'

'We swear,' Joe said again. 'Tell us the secret now.'

'It's about the ring we found, and who should have it,' Allegra said. 'I don't feel right keeping it when maybe that couple might have had children and grandchildren. I want to give it back to them.'

'If you find them,' Joe said. 'But you found out a little bit when you looked up that newspaper, so maybe you'll find out more over there.'

'I'm sure I will,' Allegra said. 'Ireland is a small country and people know each other in a way that we don't over here. That's what my grandma used to say, anyway.'

'Are you going to the place she was from?' Emma asked.

'No. She was from somewhere in County Kildare, which is south of Dublin. But the farm was sold and the family moved away, so there's nobody left there. I'm going to the south-west, to County Kerry. That's where your grandparents spent their honeymoon. So it will be nice to see that too. But first of all, I'm going to a small village called Sandy Cove, which is on the Atlantic coast.'

'Opposite Cape Cod?' Joe asked.

'Not quite, but nearly,' Allegra said. She sat back against the pillows and ate her croissant, looking out the window at the clear blue New York sky. She could hear traffic and police sirens in the street ten floors below them and knew she had to get out of the city and into some soothing countryside. 'Can't wait to get there. It seems like such a romantic place.'

'Maybe you'll meet a handsome man there who you'll marry,' Emma said. Her face fell and she put her head against Allegra's shoulder. 'And then you'll stay over there and we'll never see you again.'

'Of course not,' Allegra said and stroked Emma's cheek. 'I'll never want to be away from you two for long.'

'When you come back it will be nearly Thanksgiving,' Joe said. 'And we've been invited to stay at the farm in Vermont with our cousins. Are you coming too?'

'Yes, I wouldn't miss that for the world,' Allegra declared as the image of her uncle's farm popped into her mind. It was a lovely place, now owned by their cousins after their uncle's death ten years ago. She had spent all her Thanksgiving and Christmases there with Lucia and their father. 'I'll be back in plenty of time. We might even be able to go together.'

'That'll be fun,' Emma said. She wriggled out of bed. 'I want to go and watch a Harry Potter movie on the TV in the den.'

'Me too,' Joe said and jumped onto the floor. 'Do you want to watch it with us, Auntie Allie?'

'Thanks, but I'll just stay here and finish my lovely breakfast,' Allegra said. 'And then we'll plan the day.'

When the children had left, Allegra finished her pastry while she thought about her trip. She'd be arriving in Ireland on Monday morning. She had seen that the weather would be bad, but that didn't scare her in the slightest. Ireland was wild and wet in the fall, but she knew it was the place she needed to go in order to heal and to connect with people she had yet to meet, and that it might change her whole life in some way. And then she would be back for Thanksgiving and spend time with her family, who meant so much to her.

But first, Ireland. She began to feel a tiny dart of excitement at the thought of her adventure. What was waiting for her over there at the other side of the Atlantic? Whatever it was, she was sure it would shake her out of her sorrow and make her feel alive again.

I need this trip, she thought. *Whatever happens, good or bad, I'm ready to face it. Adventure, romance, new friends, tears and laughter... Bring it on.*

4

Allegra was woken with a start by a loud voice above her head.

'This is the captain speaking. We are about to land at Shannon airport but, because of high winds, it might be a little bumpy. Nothing to worry about, I can assure you, just the usual autumn storms our country treats us to at this time of year. Fasten your seatbelts, hang on to your seats and get ready. There are sick bags in the pocket in front of you, but hopefully you won't have to use them. Sorry about not being able to serve breakfast, but I'm afraid it was too wild out there for our staff to stand upright. Have a nice stay in Ireland. *Céad míle fáilte* and all that.'

'Typical,' the chubby dark-haired woman in the seat beside Allegra said with a snort. She had introduced herself as Eileen Murphy from County Limerick and had gone to sleep just after dinner. 'And I was hoping we'd get some nice weather for my dad's birthday. I'm only here for a week and then I have to get back to the States and my job at the consulate in New York.' She peered curiously at Allegra. 'You're here for work?'

'No, I'm on vacation for three weeks,' Allegra replied, sitting up and removing her sleep mask from the top of her head.

'Vacation?' Eileen asked. 'At this time of year? Are you mad?'

'Probably,' Allegra said with a smile that died on her lips as the plane suddenly seemed to rise and then plunge several hundred feet. 'Oh God,' she gasped.

'Yeah,' Eileen said. 'That's what we were told to expect. But don't worry. We'll be on the ground soon.'

'I hope so,' Allegra said, hanging on to the armrest as the plane lurched and swung and plunged downwards only to rise again.

She felt sick, both with fear and the motion, and she glanced at the bag sticking out of the pocket of the seat in front of her, wondering if she should grab it before it was too late. But then she saw green fields and little houses through the window and realised they were close to landing, so she screwed her eyes shut and held on to the armrest for dear life until the plane hit the ground with a series of rough bumps. She opened her eyes and looked at her neighbour with a smile.

'Phew. We're here.'

'And still alive, thank God,' Eileen said and crossed herself. 'Jesus, Mary and Joseph, that was one rough landing.'

'AAAand we're down!' the pilot's triumphant voice said on the loudspeaker. 'It got a little bumpy, but we're here on the ground safe and sound. Welcome to Ireland, you brave souls who have come here at this time of year. The weather here is a little wild, that's true. But hey, it's not boring. Hang on to your hats when you get out. We don't have a bridge today, so you have to climb down the steps and walk across the tarmac to the terminal. Good luck to ye all!'

'That pilot should get an Oscar for comedy,' Eileen remarked. 'But he managed to make us all feel less terrified. Flying Aer Lingus sure has its benefits.'

Allegra laughed. 'I love Ireland already.'

Eileen peered at her. 'Is this your first visit?'

'Yes,' Allegra said. 'My father's family are Irish and my grandmother was born in Ireland. Her family's farm was in County Kildare, but there is no one left there.'

'So you're not here to visit family?'

'No,' Allegra replied. 'It's a kind of fall vacation. I know it might be better to arrive in the spring or summer, but I have three weeks' leave from work, so I decided to come anyway. Wrong season, I know, but I'm really looking forward to it.'

Eileen shrugged and started to gather up her things as the plane came to a stop. 'We don't really have seasons in Ireland. Only weather. When this storm has gone, you might get a great stretch of warm sunshine.'

'Even at the end of October?'

'Absolutely. Here, you could get a summer's day in January and winter storms in July. Especially on the Atlantic coast. That's the charm of the unexpected.'

'The charm of the unexpected,' Allegra repeated. 'I love that. Not just about the weather. I have a feeling I'm about to experience a lot of the unexpected during my stay here.' She got up as the passengers started to file out of the plane. 'By the way,' she asked Eileen, who was ahead of her in the queue. 'What did those words the pilot said mean? The cad mile thing? I think I've heard it before.'

'*Céad míle fáilte?*' Eileen asked. 'That's the very cliché Irish greeting. It means *a hundred thousand welcomes*. Which is something nobody ever says in real life.'

Allegra smiled. 'I see what you mean. Well, I do feel welcome all the same, even if the weather is rough.'

'Where in Ireland are you going?'

'Kerry,' Allegra replied. 'A small village called Sandy Cove. I think it's on the Ring of Kerry, actually. Near a place called Waterville.'

'Oh, I know Waterville,' Eileen said. 'And Sandy Cove is a

lovely little place. One of those hidden gems of Kerry. But how are you going to get there?'

'I was planning to rent a car and drive there,' Allegra said. 'I'm picking it up at the airport.'

'In this weather? Driving on the left-hand side in a strange country?' Eileen asked, sounding doubtful.

'Yeah, well, I thought it would be okay on a Monday morning.' Allegra felt a tight knot in her stomach as she considered what Eileen had said.

'Not from around here,' Eileen stated as they slowly eased forward toward the exit door. 'You'll be heading straight into rush-hour traffic with trucks and buses driving like lunatics. Probably just about okay in calm weather, but in this... I'd rethink the plan if I were you.'

'How?' Allegra asked as they stood at the door of the plane, ready to go down the stairway that was swaying precariously in the strong wind.

'Let's get into the terminal and we'll think of something,' Eileen said as she went outside, her hair whipping around her face.

Happy that Eileen had taken her under her wing, Allegra followed her down the steps and across the tarmac, leaning into the wind, the rain lashing against her. She had put on her raincoat, so she wasn't too wet when they finally made it inside the doors of the terminal. They walked the short distance to the passport control, and then on to the baggage hall, before retrieving their luggage and exiting through the door to the arrivals' hall.

Eileen turned to Allegra. 'I've had an idea. Why don't you come with me as far as Adare where I'm going? My brother is picking me up. It's on the way to Kerry and you can stay the night there. Plenty of nice B&Bs that are still open. And then, tomorrow morning, take the bus to Killarney and pick up your rental car there. It's a nice drive to Waterville and that place you're going to from there. Country roads with not much traffic, except for flocks of sheep. What do you say?'

Allegra thought for a moment while people came in and out of the terminal, the wind howling outside as the doors opened. She could see the trees swaying in the wind and heavy rain beating against the windows, making her realise that driving anywhere wouldn't be wise for someone like her who didn't know her way around. 'Thank you so much, Eileen. That would be great,' she said. 'But I've booked the car from here. Do you think I can change the booking just like that?'

'Of course you can,' Eileen assured her. 'I'm sure they don't want to send tourists out in weather like this.' She pointed at a row of desks at the other end of the arrivals' hall. 'You'll find all the car rentals over there. Go and have a chat with the one you booked with and I'll find my brother.'

It proved quite easy to rebook the car from Killarney the following day and, as soon as that was organised, Allegra joined Eileen, who was talking to a tall man dressed in a waterproof anorak and wellies. With his dark hair and warm smile, he was very like his sister.

'All fixed,' Allegra said. 'They seemed relieved that I wasn't going to drive one of their cars in this weather.'

'I bet they were,' Eileen said and gestured at the man. 'This is Garret, my brother who has come to pick me up. He came in the Land Rover, so there's plenty of room for you and your suitcase. Garret, say hello to Allegra.'

'Hi, Allegra,' Garret said and held out his hand. 'Welcome to Ireland.'

'Hi, Garret,' Allegra said and shook hands with the pleasant-looking man. 'I'm so grateful for all your help.'

'Ah sure, that's no problem,' Garret replied. 'Happy to help a stranded woman.'

'Especially if she's as pretty as this one,' Eileen said with a wink.

'That adds to the pleasure,' Garret said and grabbed Allegra's suitcase. 'I'll take this one for you. Come on, then, we'd better get going. The storm is going to get a lot worse before it dies down.'

'What a happy thought,' Eileen said and started to roll her suitcase behind her as she followed Garret. 'And we're jetlagged and had no breakfast. I thought we'd have something here before setting off.'

'Nah, let's get something at a petrol station,' Garret said over his shoulder. 'Come on, will ya? I'm parked quite near, so we should soon be on the road.'

He proved to be right and, with Allegra in the front seat, and Eileen in the back, they were soon driving down the motorway to Limerick. Allegra looked out the window and tried to catch a glimpse of the landscape through the driving rain but there wasn't much to see until a huge castle with grey stone walls came into view.

'Bunratty,' Eileen shouted. 'Fifteenth-century pile. Great hit with tourists. They do medieval banquets there and you can eat food from that time and listen to harp music. Good fun if you like that kind of thing.'

'Sounds great,' Allegra said, staring at the stone walls of the castle as they drove past. 'Such an old building.'

'Old?' Garret said with a snort over the noise of the rain. 'That's modern compared to most historical buildings in Ireland. We have stuff from the fifth century and earlier all over the place. Just wait till you start driving around.'

'I'm looking forward to that,' Allegra said.

Garret slowed the car as they came to a layby with a small petrol station. 'We'll get something for you to eat here.'

'I'll go,' Eileen said and opened the door when the car had come to a stop. 'What do you want, Allegra? I think they have a coffee machine.'

'Coffee and some kind of pastry would be great,' Allegra replied.

'I'll see what they have. Garret, do you want anything?'

'Same here,' he replied. 'But I'll get it. You must be wrecked after that long flight.'

'No, I managed to sleep,' Eileen said. 'And I need to move around after sitting for so long.'

Garret turned to Allegra when Eileen had gone into the little shop. 'So tell me. What are you going to do here in Ireland? Just a quick visit with family?'

'No,' Allegra replied. 'I have no family here. But I'm going to do some research into the history of another family – or families, I suppose.'

'I see,' Garret said. 'That sounds interesting. What families are you looking into?'

His eyes were so sympathetic and Allegra instantly warmed to him. Before she could stop herself, she found herself telling him about the ring and what her research had revealed.

'I couldn't get the story out of my mind,' she continued. 'I felt such an urge to come over here and find out more. And then my boss gave me three weeks off as I had worked so much over-time. And I really needed a break, so I decided to get over here. Just to see...' she ended vaguely.

Garret nodded. 'I know what you mean. And why not? It sounds like a fascinating story to be discovered. And who knows? You could write a book about it in the end.' He leaned towards her, a strange gleam in his dark eyes. 'Did you say that woman was called Davina Courtney?'

'That's right.'

'Who lived near Sandy Cove in Kerry?'

'That's what it said in that newspaper clip.'

'Could be the Courtneys of Strawberry Hill.'

Allegra stared at him. 'Strawberry Hill? What's that?'

'It's a big old house near Sandy Cove,' Garret said. 'Owned

by three cousins. One of them, Gwen Courtney, runs a yard there.'

'A yard?' Allegra asked. 'What's that?'

'Horses,' Eileen said, having just arrived with a box with three steaming paper cups and three croissants. 'Garret, give me a hand with these.'

Once Eileen had got back into the car, and they were drinking coffee and eating croissants, she continued. 'Garret must be talking about someone who runs the same kind of outfit as him. Training and breeding horses for show jumping and eventing. Did I hear you mention Gwen Courtney?'

'That's right,' Garret said. 'Allegra is looking to find out about someone related to her family.'

'I wouldn't have anything to do with that crowd,' Eileen said as she sipped her coffee. 'Especially that Gwen woman. Lives in two rooms in that old house that's nearly falling down. Old pile from the seventeenth century. It's been in the same family since then. Must have been an amazing house when it was built, but now it's nearly a ruin. I've only met Gwen once, but that was enough. Talk about eccentric.'

'She has amazing horses, though,' Garret countered. 'I bought that bay gelding from her two years ago and he's won a heap of prizes since I sold him on to the eventing team. Should have held on to him a bit longer.'

Eileen rolled her eyes. 'Horses. They'll break both your heart and your bank account. I'll never understand the obsession some people have with them.'

'That would he half the population of Ireland,' Garret remarked. He drained his cup and handed it to Eileen. 'Let's get a move on. I need to get back to check on the stables. Storms always unsettle horses, and I have a mare about to foal.'

'And I want to get home to Mum and Dad. The party is on Thursday, but they'll be preparing for it already.'

Garret started the engine. 'Let's get going, then. We'll be in Adare in about an hour if we step on it.'

'I'll find a B&B for Allegra,' Eileen said and picked up her phone. 'I'd invite you to stay with us, but there isn't much room in my parents' bungalow, and Garret's house is a mess. Better to be near the bus station, anyway, I think.'

'That'd be great,' Allegra said, grateful she didn't have to stay with either of them. They were both very nice and had been amazingly kind to her, but she'd prefer to be on her own and get her bearings in this country that, except for the weather, was so welcoming.

As the car drove on, she stared into the driving rain and thought about what Garret and Eileen had said. Strawberry Hill... it sounded like a strange place. But instead of putting her off, what Eileen had said about the place made her want to go there as soon as she could. Those Courtneys had to be part of the same family as Davina, who had lost her ring, and then... she'd be staying in the coastguard station where Sean had lived. Even though it had been extensively renovated, there must be something left of what it was like in the old days.

Allegra suddenly felt a strange buzz of excitement. Meeting Eileen and Garret, who knew about the Courtneys, might not be some random good luck, but more like something that was meant to happen and would lead to an exciting adventure. She touched the ring that hung on the gold chain around her neck, and looked through the windscreen at the storm with both trepidation and hope.

She couldn't wait to get started on this journey of discovery.

5

Allegra woke up to brilliant sunshine the following day. She had slept so deeply it had felt like falling into a black hole, and when she checked the time on her phone, she saw it was eight o'clock and realised she had been out for the count since nine o'clock the previous evening. Eleven hours' sleep. Amazing. She stretched and started to get out of the comfortable bed of the charming little B&B Eileen had found for her. Once installed, she had walked around Adare, a picturesque village on the road to Kerry.

Chocolate-box thatched cottages housing cute boutiques and quaint pubs lined the main street, Allegra had discovered, but she secretly thought the village was a little like a theme park, and it didn't feel quite genuine. Eileen had called it a real tourist trap and told Allegra that her parents lived a few miles away and didn't visit it often. Garret had laughed and said it was a great place to bring clients from abroad to butter them up before they went to his yard to inspect a horse. But the B&B just off the main street was lovely, and the hostess so welcoming and kind, that Allegra didn't mind it being a bit touristy. It was only for one night, in any case.

Eileen and Garret had said their goodbyes after exchanging phone numbers with Allegra and giving her a few tips on how to manoeuvre herself around the Irish way of living. The tip about getting an Irish account for her phone had been excellent, and it wasn't too complicated to get a new SIM card and an Irish phone number, which would cut down on her costs. She went on WhatsApp immediately to connect with Lucia and some of her friends back home, promising to keep in touch. That done, she had gone back to the B&B as it was still raining heavily and spent the evening in her room watching TV until she fell into that deep hole of sleep. And now she was refreshed, and ready for the first day of her Irish adventure.

The bus trip to Killarney was uneventful and Allegra spent a pleasant hour gazing out over the sunlit landscape with rolling green hills, looking at fallen branches and bins that had been blown over by the storm last night. She silently blessed Eileen and Garret for rescuing her, knowing she would never have managed to drive through the high winds and heavy rain. She had liked both Eileen and Garret instantly. They had proved to be great company and had been extraordinarily kind. Garret had a cheeky glint in his eyes that she found very appealing and that, when combined with his Irish good looks and the lilt in his voice, reminded her of her father and his warm voice and Irish sense of humour.

The bustling town of Killarney seemed like a fun place to visit, but Allegra didn't want to linger. Once she had found the car rental company and signed all the papers, she drove away in the small car, having bought a sandwich to eat on the way. She didn't want to delay her arrival at Sandy Cove any longer.

The picture of the coastguard station she had seen online was stuck in her mind and she couldn't wait to get there and start her vacation, and her research into the lives of Davina and

Sean and to find their relations. She was sure that the woman called Gwen Courtney who Garret had mentioned must be related to Davina. And that house with the name Strawberry Hill sounded like something from a romantic novel. She simply had to find it and to talk to this Gwen woman, whoever she was.

But what about Sean Walsh? How would she find out anything about him? There just had to be something to go on in the coastguard station – but what? The cottages in the row seemed all to have been extensively renovated, and there wasn't any way to find out which one he had lived in. The best option was to go there and start asking questions once she had settled in. Someone had to know something, even if it was just a faint memory. In any case, Eileen had told Allegra that Ireland was a small country and that people generally knew each other's families, 'or they know someone who knows someone,' she had added, laughing. 'It's hard to keep a secret in rural Ireland.'

Allegra smiled as she remembered those words, hoping it would also apply to people who had lived in a place long ago. Maybe she would find someone who knew someone who knew Sean and Davina back then, if she asked around. But how would the people of Sandy Cove react to a stranger asking questions? She knew from what Garret had told her, that Irish people often clammed up when asked personal questions. They didn't like telling just anyone about other people as it might make them 'tell-tales'. This was a remnant from the war of independence, he had said. 'You will have to be a good spy and ask questions without appearing to do it,' he said with a wink. 'Let me know how you get on.'

She suddenly felt, as she drove through this enchanting landscape, that it had been a good decision to come here, where the hills and lakes and mountains were just as her grandmother had described when she talked about the old country and its peace and tranquillity.

Her grandmother had always been slightly homesick, even

though her life in America had been happy. She often sang songs in Irish to her grandchildren and showed them photos of the family farm south of Dublin, where she had grown up. But as there was nobody of the family left in the area, neither their father nor Lucia and Allegra had felt they wanted to visit.

'Go to the south-west, if you ever go to Ireland,' her father had told her. 'That part of the country is so lovely.'

And here she was, finally following his advice.

There was a brief, heavy shower just as she reached the turn-off to Sandy Cove, but it ended as she drove down the main street. She slowed the car, looking at the houses with their neat, well-tended gardens, some adorned with Halloween decorations in the shape of white ghosts, plastic skulls and spiders hanging from trees and bushes. Allegra knew Halloween had been celebrated in Ireland since pagan times, and that the traditions had been brought to America from here. So she reasoned this would be an important date in the Irish calendar.

It wasn't difficult to find Starlight Cottages, and Allegra pulled up at the one she had booked in the middle of the row. They were all the same, except for the front doors being different colours. Hers was painted a bright red. She had been told the key would be in a box beside the window, and she had been sent the code to the lock when she had paid the deposit.

Allegra got out of the car and tapped the code into the small box and released it, finding the key inside. Shivering with excitement, she unlocked the door and opened it, carefully stepping inside a small hall with a coat rack and an umbrella stand. Then she continued down a short corridor, glancing into the modern kitchen with gleaming appliances, and then through the door to a large, bright living room that had a glass door leading to a sunroom.

Allegra crossed the wooden floor to the sunroom and then

went out onto the terrace, where she stood, stunned, looking at the panoramic views of the bay and the ocean beyond. She had known there would be nice views from here, but this was more than that – it was spectacular. As the ocean met the sky at the horizon, she could see the undulating shapes of dolphins playing far out in the bay. And the air... Even though it was chilly, the breeze brought with it the tang of salt and seaweed.

Allegra closed her eyes, feeling as if she could float up into the blue sky and fly over the ocean like a bird. 'Oh, this is heaven,' she murmured to herself.

'Isn't it?' a voice said.

Allegra gave a start and turned to her right, discovering a tall, white-haired woman on the terrace of the house next door. 'Oh,' she said. 'I thought I was alone.'

'Sorry to frighten you,' the woman said. 'But I had to agree when you stood here, mesmerised.' She looked curiously at Allegra. 'Just arrived and seeing this view for the first time?'

'Yes,' Allegra replied with a laugh. 'I knew it would be beautiful, but not like this. It's overwhelming.'

'I know what you mean,' the woman said. She held her hand across the hedge that separated the terraces. 'I'm Lucille Kennedy. Not living here, just keeping an eye on things and tidying away the garden furniture for the lady who lives here. She's spending the winter in her native Amsterdam, looking after her grandchildren.'

Allegra shook hands, looking more closely at the woman. Attractive now at around eighty or so, she would have been even lovelier when she was young. 'Hello. My name is Allegra Casey. I'm from Boston and I've come to spend a few weeks here.'

'Lovely name,' Lucille said. 'And you're very tall and very pretty. You could have been a wonderful Bluebell girl.'

'Bluebell girl?' Allegra asked.

'They were a dance troupe in the Lido in Paris when I was

young,' Lucille explained. 'Had to be at least five foot seven to qualify. And I did, then.' She sighed and withdrew her hand. 'Those were the days. But hey, today isn't too bad either, even though I'm not as young as I was.'

'It's a beautiful day,' Allegra said, looking back over the ocean. 'I can't take my eyes off this view.'

'Quite distracting,' Lucille agreed. 'Especially at first. So,' she continued, 'you're here for a holiday? A lovely autumn break, perhaps?'

'In a way,' Allegra said. 'I'm also trying to find out about someone who used to live here a long time ago.'

Lucille's eyes lit up. 'How long ago would that be?'

'Eighty years or so. I think he lived here in the late 1930s.'

'Here? In the coastguard station?'

'That's right,' Allegra said, wondering why the old woman looked suddenly so excited.

'And you're related to this person?' Lucille asked.

'No. But I feel connected...' Allegra stopped. 'It's a long story.'

'Hmm,' Lucille said, looking thoughtful. 'Eighty years you say?'

Allegra nodded. 'Yes. Around 1939 or later.'

'A little modern for me,' Lucille said. 'Not the period I'm really interested in at the moment.'

'Why is that?'

'I'm into something a little earlier right now in my research. But we can talk about that later.'

'Yes,' Allegra agreed, her gaze drifting back to the ocean. 'I'm a little distracted by all this right now.'

'Seeing this view for the first time would distract anyone. And you've just arrived and haven't even unpacked, I suppose,' Lucille said.

'Exactly.'

'Well, in that case, you should get settled in. But before you go, I'd like to tell you that I might be able to help you in your research about this person you were talking about.'

'Really? How?' Allegra asked, intrigued.

'I'm quite the historian, you see,' Lucille explained with a proud glint in her blue eyes. 'One of my ancestors lived here in the 1800s, and I wrote a book about him which was published two years ago. And now I'm in the middle of writing another one about the history of the people in this village. So I would know where to look if you need any help. When I get to the twenty-first century, I mean.'

'Oh, that would be amazing,' Allegra said, smiling warmly at Lucille across the hedge. 'The man I'm looking for was called Sean Walsh.'

Lucille frowned. 'Never heard that name, I have to say. But maybe your neighbour on the other side would know more. Lydia, I mean. Her great-aunt lived here when she was young and would have been around at that time. Do you know anything at all about this person you're researching?'

'Just that he was engaged to a woman called Davina Court-ney, who also lived in this area.'

Lucille looked startled. 'Courtney? One of the Strawberry Hill Courtneys?'

'I think so. Where is Strawberry Hill?'

'Up there in the hinterland,' Lucille said, pointing towards the village. 'Huge wreck of a house. Not a place I like to visit. They're not very welcoming, to say the least. Especially that Gwen woman. But the cousins are even worse.'

'How do you mean?' Allegra asked, intrigued by the dark look in Lucille's eyes.

'Too long to explain.' Lucille moved away across the terrace. 'I'll go now and leave you to settle in. I have to see to the other house here too,' she said, pointing at the house next door, the last house in the row. 'My son and daughter-in-law live there and they're away in Paris until the end of the week. I have to water the plants and feed the cat. So much to look after,' she muttered. 'How would they manage without me, I wonder?'

She waved and disappeared into the house before Allegra had a chance to ask where she could get in touch. But it didn't really matter. They'd meet again, she was sure. This was a small village, and they would bump into each other sooner or later.

Allegra went inside, both amused and intrigued by her conversation with this interesting old woman, so sharp and knowledgeable. But what had she meant by what she'd said about Strawberry Hill? Allegra suddenly felt an urge to find that old house and meet the people who lived there, despite all the negative things she had heard about them. They were sure to know who Davina was and what had happened to her and Sean. But she could hardly just arrive there and start asking questions, could she?

Allegra stopped on her way to the car to get her bags and thought for a moment. She had always acted on impulse, which had sometimes landed her in trouble. *I only have three weeks,* she thought, touching the ring on the gold chain around her neck. *And during those weeks, I have to find out about the woman who lost her ring and give it back to her family. What do I have to lose?* She nodded and continued outside, making a mental list of the things she had to do today. First, unpack and make her bed. Then, go to the little supermarket she had seen on the main street and buy food.

Then, tomorrow, she would find the house that was called Strawberry Hill. She couldn't wait to see it.

6

Lulled to sleep by the sound of the waves, Allegra dreamed she was walking on the beach below the cottages, in another time, another dimension. She saw a couple in the distance, walking hand in hand, smiling at each other, before they disappeared into the mist. It wasn't a sad dream, more like looking into an image of long ago, or maybe into the future. Something to do with love that lasted until the end of time.

Allegra woke up feeling strange but happy as the wisps of sleep and the memory of the dream slowly faded. She gazed at the window, at the curtains moving softly in the light breeze, and slowly got up, stretched, then padded across the carpet and pulled the curtains back. The view of the sea in the early morning light was enchanting, and the day felt as if it would be full of adventure. Allegra knew instantly that she would do what she had planned earlier: find Strawberry Hill, the old house where she might get some clues to the owner of the ring. She stood for a while, planning her visit and wondering how she would explain the reason she was there. But the breeze felt chilly and she closed the window, fished out her dressing gown from the half-unpacked suitcase and went downstairs to make breakfast.

The underfloor heating made the rooms feel cosy and warm, and Allegra found she didn't mind this aspect of modernity at all, even if she silently lamented the removal of every period detail in the house. The kitchen was state-of-the-art, with an induction hob, built-in oven, stainless-steel fridge-freezer and a dishwasher discreetly hidden behind a panel under the ceramic sink.

After making a large mug of coffee and a pile of toasted soda bread, she had a proper look at the living room as she carried her breakfast tray through. This room had a beautifully laid parquet floor, and a modern fireplace with a piece of driftwood as a mantelpiece. In front of it was a large blue velvet sofa, which looked like the perfect place to relax and watch TV on the wall-mounted flat screen. There was a round table at the far side of the room, with six chairs, a sideboard and a bookcase, all in the same bleached wood. The walls were hung with a few seascapes and a framed print of a sailing boat riding a storm somewhere. A nice room, bright and welcoming.

But it was the sunroom that Allegra liked the most. With its wicker chairs and table, a telescope, and the windowsills decorated with seashells, pieces of driftwood and polished pebbles, it had that maritime feel she loved. The light through the windows was wonderful, and she sat down in one of the chairs to enjoy her breakfast while gazing out at the view of the ocean, and the constantly changing light, as the clouds drifted across the sun.

Deep in thought, she gave a start as someone knocked on the glass door leading to the terrace. She could see a woman with pale blonde hair dressed in jeans and a red jacket, smiling at her. Allegra got up to let her in.

'Hi,' the woman said, holding out her hand. 'I'm Lydia O'Callaghan, your neighbour.'

'Hi,' Allegra said as they shook hands. 'I'm Allegra Casey. You must be Jason's wife, then.'

'That's right. Jason just left for work, so I thought I'd look in and say hello and welcome. Hope you didn't have any trouble finding the key.'

'No, that was really easy,' Allegra replied.

'Oh great,' Lydia said. Then she paused and took in Allegra's dressing gown and breakfast tray on the table. 'Oh God, I barged in on you in the middle of your breakfast. I keep forgetting that people generally don't get up as early as we do.'

'Well, I usually do,' Allegra said. 'But as I'm on vacation, I slept in. And I'm still a little jetlagged.'

'I know the feeling,' Lydia said. 'But sit down and have your breakfast. I won't disturb you anymore.'

'You're not disturbing me at all,' Allegra said. 'Why don't you join me and I'll make some more coffee? Or tea if you prefer?'

'Oh.' Lydia hesitated. 'Well, that would be great. I have an appointment in Waterville but that's at eleven, so yes, please, I'd love a coffee.' She took off her jacket and pulled out one of the chairs.

'Okay,' Allegra said, walking to the kitchen. 'It won't be long. That super modern machine spits out coffee in seconds.'

Lydia laughed. 'I know. Jason put in all the mod cons when we did up this cottage. He loves anything new and shiny in the kitchen.'

'Do you want some toast, too? I got some of that delicious Irish soda bread at the shop yesterday.'

'That'll be perfect.' Lydia plumped up one of the cushions in a chair and sat down. 'Lovely to take a break, I have to say.'

It didn't take Allegra long to make another cup of coffee and toast a slice of the soda bread that she spread with butter. She arrived back in the sunroom within a few minutes, and put the mug and plate in front of Lydia. 'Oh, I forgot to ask if you take milk or sugar in your coffee?'

'I take it black, so this is grand,' Lydia said and grabbed the mug while Allegra sat down. 'So,' she continued after taking a sip, 'what brings you here? I take it you're from somewhere in America? By your accent, I mean. The rental agency didn't give us any details, only that someone had booked the cottage for four weeks.'

'I'm from Boston,' Allegra said.

'Really?' Lydia said. 'That's a coincidence. My husband is from there, too. What part?'

'Brookline,' Allegra replied. 'But now I live more centrally. I bought a small apartment near my office recently.'

'And you have Irish roots?' Lydia wanted to know. 'From around here?'

'No, not here. My Irish family, on my father's side, came from somewhere south of Dublin. But there is nobody of that family left.'

'And your mother's family?' Lydia enquired.

'My mother's family came from Italy several generations ago. I'm the typical American, I guess,' Allegra stated with a smile. 'With roots from all kinds of places.'

'Which resulted in a lovely mix,' Lydia said. 'I'm also a bit of a hotch-potch. My mother's family came from Norway.'

'I thought you looked a bit Scandinavian,' Allegra said.

'And you look more Irish than anything else,' Lydia said, studying Allegra while she took a bite of soda bread. 'But your beautiful eyes are Italian.' She stopped and smiled. 'Gosh, this is getting a little personal when we've just met! I didn't mean to comment on your looks like that.'

Allegra smiled and sipped her coffee. 'I don't mind when the comments are so positive.'

'Great.' Lydia paused. 'Don't tell me if you don't want to.

But is there any particular reason why you've come here at this time of year? It's the low season, even though we're in the middle of the mid-term break and Halloween is only a few days away. But we don't get that many people renting the cottage at this time.'

'I came on an impulse really,' Allegra replied. 'I had three weeks off work and thought I'd go somewhere different. My father died recently, and the time after his death was so stress-ful, sorting out his things and selling the house and moving to a new place, and...' She stopped as a pang of sadness hit her.

'I'm so sorry,' Lydia said, her eyes full of sympathy. 'That sounds like it was hugely traumatic. Losing a parent is always horrific. And then all that comes with it afterwards is so hard, isn't it?'

'Yes. Very hard,' Allegra said quietly. She sipped her coffee to hide how sad she felt suddenly.

'So then you decided to go away for a bit and thought Ireland would be a nice place to come to?' Lydia suggested.

Allegra nodded. 'Yes. My parents spent their honeymoon in Kenmare, and my dad always wanted to go back, but never did. And then, recently something happened to give me a push to travel.' Allegra stopped, not quite knowing how to explain the rest. But she had clicked with Lydia instantly and now she felt like someone who could be a good friend. 'There is a reason why I wanted to come to Sandy Cove especially, you see,' she started. 'It's a bit complicated actually.' As she spoke, her hand went to the chain around her neck.

'Oh, please,' Lydia said. 'Don't tell me anything at all for now. I'm not the curious type. When I came here first, I was so raw and hurt after some horrible things that had happened to me. My first husband had died and left me with a pile of debts.'

'How awful,' Allegra exclaimed. 'That must have been such a shock.'

'It was. The only thing I had left was my great-aunt's

cottage next door, where I still live today. But to cut a long story short, I didn't want anyone to know what I had been through and then I had my daughter to think of. But here, in a small village, everyone knows everything about everybody. Not in a nasty way, just in that small rural village way, if you see what I mean. I was really paranoid about it. But then, as time went on, they accepted me on face value and I turned from being the strange woman from Dublin with a secret to being just Lydia and part of the furniture, so to speak.'

'That's wonderful. Tell me about your daughter,' Allegra continued. 'How old is she?'

'All grown up now and doing a degree in environmental science in Dublin,' Lydia said with a proud smile.

'Oh, wow. You must be so proud of her. Does she ever come here?'

'Oh yes, she'll be here at Christmas.'

'I'll be back in Boston by then.' Allegra finished her toast and drank some coffee. Then she looked at Lydia, knowing that she would have to tell her story in order to find anything out. 'To go back to why I'm here in this village,' she began. 'I don't mind telling you, because it isn't my story, it's someone else's. It's something that happened a long time ago, and it's connected to these cottages, and also to another place nearby.'

'Oh?' Lydia looked intrigued. 'In that case, do tell me. I love stories from long ago.'

Allegra touched the chain around her neck again. 'I found this ring in the sand on a beach on Cape Cod in the summer.' She took the ring off the chain and handed it to Lydia. 'It says *Davina and Sean, 1939* on the inside.'

'So it does.' Lydia studied the ring. 'It's beautiful. But how is that connected to here?'

'I did some research at the local library,' Allegra explained, and went on to tell Lydia the whole story.

'How amazing,' Lydia said when Allegra had finished. 'Sean

Walsh?' she mused. 'Hmm. Never heard that name. My great-aunt would have been here around then, too. She grew up in the cottage next door. But there is nothing I can think of that will tell me if they knew each other. I wonder which one was Sean's house?'

'No idea,' Allegra said. 'I met a nice elderly lady yesterday who said she was doing some research into the history of the village and she promised to look into it. Such a fun, lively woman. I can imagine that she would have been even more amazing in her youth.'

'Sounds like Lucille,' Lydia said.

Allegra nodded. 'That's right. Lucille Kennedy, she said her name was. She was on the terrace when I arrived and we had a chat. Awesome old woman.'

'Oh yes,' Lydia agreed. 'She's incredible. Eighty-six years old but still going strong in body and mind. Can be a bit force-ful, if you know what I mean, but that's what keeps her young and fit.'

'I'd say it is,' Allegra agreed. 'I think this Davina of my story lived at a place called Strawberry Hill. Do you know anything about that house?'

Lydia nodded and handed back the ring. 'Of course, everyone does. It's a big old wreck of a house further inland. About twenty minutes' drive from here. It must have been a wonderful house a long time ago.' She stopped and put her hand to her mouth. 'Davina? Is that what you said?'

'Yes,' Allegra said, puzzled by Lydia's shocked expression.

'Davina Courtney?'

'I think so.'

'That must be Gwen's great-aunt,' Lydia said. 'A very old woman called Davina.'

'What?' Allegra exclaimed, her heart beating faster. 'Is she still alive?'

'No, I'm afraid she died only about a month ago at the age of over a hundred. But that would fit, wouldn't it?'

'It would,' Allegra said. 'She would have been in her twenties eighty or so years ago. Did you know her?'

'No, but I've met Gwen,' Lydia replied. 'A bit brusque in that horsey way, but nice enough. She runs a yard and gives private riding lessons to people who want to compete in show jumping and eventing. I think there are other relatives who own the house together, but I have never met them. I think they have something against this village, whatever that might be. And there's some kind of conflict with the will since their great-aunt Davina's death, I've heard. I'm guessing that they want to sell and Gwen is trying to stop them. No idea what's going on really. Family rows are always bitter and hurtful. Better not to get involved at all.'

'Of course not. Except I'd love to find out more about Davina,' Allegra remarked. 'There must be someone there who can tell me more.'

Lydia smiled. 'I have a feeling you want to go there and find out.'

'I really do,' Allegra said. 'But I don't know how I can just arrive and start asking questions. Especially after a bereavement.'

'I suppose not. But she was very old, and in a nursing home the last few years, so maybe it wasn't really a tragedy.' Lydia thought for a moment. 'I know,' she said, looking suddenly excited. 'I'll come with you. I've met Gwen, and I could pretend I'm looking for a venue. I'm a fundraiser, and my business partner and I are always looking for unusual places for our events. In fact, now that I think of it, that old house would make a perfect place for a treasure hunt for children.' Her face fell. 'Pity I didn't think of it earlier, it could have been ideal for Halloween.'

'Maybe not a good time anyway, considering their recent

bereavement,' Allegra suggested. 'But you could do something
for Christmas,' she continued, thinking that Emma and Joe
would have loved a treasure hunt in an old mansion like that.
'Maybe Santa's grotto or something like that? And then an
Easter egg hunt in the spring? And you could develop an app
for the kids to use for just that occasion. Like a game app or
something.'

'Goodness,' Lydia exclaimed, looking at Allegra with
respect. 'You're amazing. That would be incredible. But where
do we get something like that?'

'I could do it for you. I'm project leader at an IT firm, you
see. We make programs like that all the time.'

'Gosh,' Lydia said. 'That's hugely impressive. I'm quite good
at computers and stuff like that, but this is way out of my
league.' She gave a start as a phone pinged. 'That's mine. My
business partner is probably looking for me. I have to go.' She
got up and put on her jacket. 'So lovely to meet you, Allegra.
Sorry for barging in on you on your first morning while you
were having breakfast.'

'That's okay,' Allegra said. 'I was really happy to meet you.'

'Me too,' Lydia said, beaming Allegra a huge smile. 'Come
for dinner tonight. I know Jason will love meeting you as much
as I have. And then we can make plans to go to Strawberry Hill
and talk to Gwen. You could be my assistant. In fact, come to
think of it, I'd love you to help with this new event we have just
dreamed up together. We need new, fresh ideas, actually. What
do you say?'

'Oh,' Allegra said, her spirits rising at the thought of helping
this friendly woman with her project. It would give her something to do and introduce her to the people in the village who
might know something about Sean and Davina. 'I'd love to.'

Lydia hesitated at the door. 'Are you sure? I mean, you're on
holiday, so maybe you want to relax and just do nothing for a
while.'

'No, that would be boring,' Allegra declared. 'I'm here to find out about that couple and see who I should give the ring to. So this project would give me a reason to look around that old house and meet the Courtney family.'

'Fabulous,' Lydia said. 'This'll inject some new blood into the old fundraising formula. I'm getting a little tired of doing lunches in posh hotels in Killarney for ladies wearing hats and chatting about the latest fashions, and who has done what kind of plastic surgery.'

'I can imagine,' Allegra said with a laugh. 'Must be getting a bit boring.'

'Yeah! We've done that to death. But now I really have to run. Just give me your phone number and I'll be in touch when I've spoken to Helen.'

When Lydia had left, Allegra stayed in the sunroom, staring out at the view, thinking about their conversation. Lydia looked to be in her forties, but could be older. They had clicked nearly immediately, which felt lovely. The way the conversation had so easily drifted to Allegra's reason to be here, and her quest to find out about the couple, gave her a strange feeling this was meant to happen. Now Lydia was going to come with her to Strawberry Hill and they would have a real, concrete reason to be there, which was a lot more reassuring than her own vague idea of simply arriving and telling the story. Much better this way, she decided. And the idea of the app had just come to her, but it would be fun to do. It would give her visit a purpose and still leave plenty of time to enjoy this magical place. And today looked like a perfect day to explore.

Allegra tidied up the breakfast things and went upstairs to get dressed, thinking about the plan to visit that old house. She felt a buzz as she thought of seeing Davina's home, the place she had gone back to after saying goodbye to Sean in order to organise their wedding. But had that wedding taken place? Or had they left each other never to meet again as the war in Europe broke out and travel was suddenly impossible?

If that was the case, Davina's family should have the ring, Allegra decided. But first, she had to find out what had really happened. She suddenly had an eerie feeling the answer to her questions were waiting for her at Strawberry Hill.

Later, as Allegra was walking on the little private beach below the cottages, enjoying the salt-laden breeze, her phone rang. She pulled it out of her pocket and answered, hearing Lydia's excited voice at the other end.

'Hi, there. Guess what?' Lydia said. 'I talked to Helen – my business partner – about the ideas and she thought they were brilliant. So I immediately phoned Gwen Courtney and asked if she'd agree to meet us. I didn't tell her the details, only that we wanted to ask about organising an event at her house. She was a bit grumpy but then said that it would be okay, if that meant a bit of money would come her way. I said of course we'd pay if it went ahead. Then she said we could come over this afternoon, because she's going to deliver a horse somewhere tomorrow and might be gone for a while. Would that be okay? Short notice, I know, but if you want we could head off around three?'

'That would be amazing,' Allegra said, feeling a buzz of excitement. How fantastic. She would see the house where Davina had lived today.

'It's kind of sudden, but I thought I'd jump at the chance before she changed her mind,' Lydia explained. 'Hope this is okay for you, even though you've just landed here.'

'I was hoping we could go there soon,' Allegra said. 'I'm dying to see the place.'

'Fabulous. I'll toot outside when I'm ready to go. Put on warm clothes and sturdy shoes. We'll be walking around the grounds and it could be wet and windy.'

'Okay. I'll dress for the occasion,' Allegra promised.

'Grand. See you later so.' Lydia hung up.

Giddy with excitement, Allegra sat down on a rock and stared out to sea, the wind now growing in strength, whipping her hair around her face.

Strawberry Hill, she thought, *a house full of history and secrets. Will I find Davina's spirit there?*

7

The road wound itself through an enchanting countryside with green fields flanked by trees in blazing autumn colours. The sun was already dipping towards the west when they turned into a narrow road full of potholes.

'Drat,' Lydia said as the car wobbled and bounced over the holes. 'I should have asked Jason for his Land Rover. My little car is too lightweight for this kind of road. But we'll be there shortly, so try not to get too carsick.'

Allegra laughed as the car lurched. 'I never get carsick.'

'That's a good thing,' Lydia remarked, and soon they came to a pair of rusty gates set between two pillars, each topped with a stone eagle. 'Here we are. Grand entrance, don't you think?'

Allegra looked up at the eagles. 'Must have been a long time ago.'

'A very long time,' Lydia agreed. 'Could you hop out and open the gates, please?'

Allegra got out and pushed against the gates that opened slowly with a loud creak. Then she let the car through, closed them again, and got back in. They continued past a deserted gatehouse, up a long avenue flanked by tall beech trees with leaves in a riot of yellow, gold and orange. Green fields stretched on each side, and Allegra could see horses grazing in the distance. Then the avenue curved around shrubs and a rose garden, ragged and bare except for a few stray blooms. Lydia drove onto a circular driveway and they could finally see the house.

'Oh my God, it's huge!' Allegra exclaimed, staring at the building in front of them. The low autumn sun was reflected in the many tall windows and it looked for a moment as if the rooms inside were on fire. But then clouds drifted in and she could see the building clearly. Built of granite in the Palladian style, it was three storeys high with wide steps that led to a pillared portico.

'I think there are something like ten bedrooms,' Lydia said, 'and a number of reception rooms downstairs. All very dilapidated, though. And freezing.' She turned off the engine. 'Let's go and ring the doorbell.'

They got out of the car and walked up the steps to the massive front door of carved oak with a coat of arms on a brass plaque. Lydia grabbed the old-fashioned bell pull and gave it a good tug, which resulted in faint ringing inside. 'It might take her a while to get to the front door from wherever she is,' Lydia said.

'It's like something out of *Downton Abbey*,' Allegra said, looking up at all the windows. 'They must have had a lot of servants in the old days.'

'A butler, two footmen, a number of housemaids, a cook and a scullery maid,' a voice said behind them.

Allegra turned around and discovered a man in riding clothes standing just below the steps. He was tall, with shaggy light brown hair and she could see, even from a distance, that his eyes were bright blue. He looked to be in his late thirties. 'That's what my great-aunt always told us, anyway,' he said, studying them with a slightly arrogant air. 'Have you come to see Gwen?'

'Yes,' Lydia said. 'We rang the doorbell, but nobody seems to be in.'

'Try around the back. We don't ever use the front door anymore. Not since the last butler died, anyway,' he added with a smile. 'Which was a long time before I was born. So now we live around the back. Trekking to the front door from the kitchen is a bit of a chore.' His clipped way of speaking sounded more British than Irish to Allegra.

'Oh,' Lydia said, walking down the steps to his side. 'We had no idea.'

'Why would you if you've never been here before?' he drawled. 'Have you?'

'No, we haven't,' Allegra said. 'At least I haven't.' On closer inspection she noticed his straight nose, clean-cut jaw and those blue eyes, fringed by long black lashes.

'I've been here once, a long time ago,' Lydia said. 'But then I met Gwen at the stables.' She held out her hand. 'I'm Lydia O'Callaghan. And this is my assistant, Allegra Casey.'

'Hello,' the man said and shook Lydia's hand. 'I'm Max Courtney-Smythe, part owner of this pile.' He held out his hand to Allegra as she descended the steps, breaking into a dazzling smile. 'And you, if I'm not mistaken, are from somewhere across the pond.'

'That's right,' Allegra said, shaking his hand. 'How did you guess?'

'Your accent is quite a giveaway.' He studied her so intently it made her blush. He was just a little taller than her which meant she could look straight into his eyes, which felt slightly unnerving.

She steeled herself to look unperturbed and returned his amused gaze. 'You have quite an accent yourself, which makes me think you're not from around here either,' she retorted.

'Oh but I am,' he said. 'It's just that I spent my formative years in an English boarding school, thanks to my mother. But that's a very long and boring story. Let's go and see if we can find Gwen. Follow me.' He started to walk to the corner of the house, the gravel crunching under his riding boots as Lydia and Allegra followed behind him.

'Who is he?' Allegra whispered to Lydia as they fell in behind Max.

'Never met him before,' Lydia whispered back. 'Must be one of the cousins. Handsome man, though,' she added, looking at Max's broad shoulders and long legs in riding boots.

'Um, yes.' Allegra had to agree as she contemplated the effect those lazy blue eyes had had on her. 'But a bit stuck-up, I think.'

Lydia's reply froze in the air as two huge black Labradors came around the corner, barking and growling.

'Help,' Allegra squealed and grabbed Lydia's arm. They stood stock-still, terrified, as the dogs came towards them, still barking.

'Oh, bloody hell,' Max exclaimed. 'Those dogs are such a pain. SIT!' he shouted. The dogs immediately stopped barking and sat down. Max shot an apologetic look over his shoulder. 'Sorry about that. They're really quite nice, but get excited when they see someone coming to the house.'

One of the dogs approached Allegra and sniffed at her.

'It's okay. You can pat him,' Max said. 'That's Buster and the other one is Lola. Gwen's precious darlings.'

'They're gorgeous.' Allegra touched the dog's head and when he wagged his tail, continued to stroke him. 'He's sweet,' she said as he looked at her with his sad doggy eyes. She crouched down and contained to stroke his head, which earned her a lick on her face, which made her laugh.

'He likes pretty girls,' Max said with a grin.

'I love dogs,' Allegra said, ignoring his flirtatious look as Lola joined Buster. She put her arms around both of them. 'You're a lovely pair.' The dogs wagged their tails furiously as Allegra got up, and they stayed by her side as they walked around the corner and into a courtyard paved with flagstones to a door which flew open before they had a chance to knock. A woman with short dark hair streaked with grey dressed in a wax jacket and jeans peered out.

'Oh, hi,' she said. 'You're here already. Do come in. I just have to get out of my jacket and boots. Max, put the kettle on and we'll have some tea. Leave the dogs outside, they're filthy.'

'Yes, ma'am,' Max said and held the door open. 'After you, ladies.'

They entered a small room that seemed to be a kind of utility space, with coats and jackets hanging from hooks under which boots, wellies and muddy shoes stood in ragged lines on a mat. There were two dog beds under the window and a sink piled with bowls and bags of dog food. The room smelled of horse and dogs, which to Allegra wasn't at all unpleasant. It reminded her of her father's cousin's farm in Vermont that they used to visit when they were children. It was nice to be in such a house again, where animals were part of life.

'Should we take off our shoes?' she asked as Max and Gwen came in behind them.

'Not at all,' Gwen assured her. 'Your shoes look clean.'

'Unlike mine,' Max grunted as he pulled off his boots with the help of a bootjack. Then he took off his jacket and hung it up, stuck his feet into a pair of scuffed loafers and disappeared through the door at the far side of the room.

'Follow Max,' Gwen said. 'He'll put the kettle on and then we'll have tea and a bit of a chat.' Her voice was quite deep, but her tone friendly. Allegra found herself wondering why Garret and Eileen had talked about her in such negative terms, but maybe she was difficult to deal with when it came to horses.

They hung up their jackets and went through the door into

a large kitchen, where a huge beige Aga radiated heat. An enormous pine table with a number of chairs around it took up a lot of the space on the flagstoned floor and two huge Belfast sinks sat under tall windows through which the sun cast a warm light into the room. There was a smell of apples and newly baked bread. Allegra felt oddly at home in this big messy room that had to be several centuries old.

'What a gorgeous kitchen,' Lydia said behind Allegra. 'It's like stepping back in time.'

'The only warm room in the whole house,' Max said from the sink, where he was filling the kettle. He put it on the worktop beside the stove and plugged it in. 'There. Kettle on.' He took a teapot from a dresser crammed with plates and cups and various bits of crockery opposite the windows and placed four mugs on the table. He glanced at Gwen. 'Meant to tell you that horse is a bit fresh and needs a lot more work, if you ask me. Nearly had me off at the river.'

'Maybe you need to be more assertive with him,' Gwen said.

'If I were more assertive, you'd have me for animal cruelty,' Max retorted. 'He calmed down after a bit, but he was hard work.'

'Well, ride him a bit more often, then,' Gwen said as she opened a packet of ginger biscuits she had taken from a cupboard and put them on a plate. 'Didn't bake you a cake, so these will have to do.'

'That's absolutely fine,' Lydia said. 'We're not here to eat cake, but to talk to you.'

'More often?' Max said with a snort. 'I don't have the time. He's lazy as sin and then when he feels like it, he tries to buck you off. He needs to be worked hard every day and I'm not always here to do it.' He glanced at Allegra. 'I don't live here, you see. I'm only here for a few days' break and to oversee a building site nearby.' He took a tea caddy from the dresser and brought it and the teapot to the kettle that had just stopped boiling.

'Max is an architect,' Gwen explained. 'But please, sit down.'

They all sat while Max busied himself making tea. He joined them when he had put the teapot, mugs and a small milk jug on the table. 'There. Tea made.' He took a biscuit from the plate and looked at Allegra and Lydia. 'What is this business you've come to discuss with Gwen?'

'It's about a fundraising project,' Lydia said. 'I'm with O'Dwyer and Callaghan.' She took a card from her shoulder bag and handed it to Gwen. 'We've been hosting events for charities for a few years now. We did a big lunch at the golf club in Waterville for Concern last summer and raised over ten thousand euros. And now we're looking for a different venue for our next fundraiser. We were thinking this place would be ideal for a Christmas event for children.'

Gwen looked at the card. 'Lydia O'Callaghan,' she said. Then she looked at Allegra. 'And where do you come in? Does this outfit have a branch in America?'

'Uh, no.' Allegra squirmed as Max shot her an amused look which made her blush. 'I have actually just arrived and I rent the cottage next door to Lydia. Starlight Cottages,' she explained. 'The old coastguard station. I'm here on a different errand, but I'm also helping Lydia with the event she is planning. If it goes ahead, I mean.'

'I see,' Gwen said, looking slightly suspicious. 'The old coastguard station, eh? I've heard it's been tarted up. But all this seems a little complicated, if you don't mind my saying so.'

Max lifted the teapot. 'Tea, anyone, while we sort all this out?'

'Please,' Lydia said and pushed her mug towards Max.

Max filled the mugs, took one for himself and put some milk into it. 'Right,' he said when he had drunk some tea and finished his biscuit. 'This different errand,' he said, looking at Allegra. 'Would you care to tell me what that's about?'

'Why do you want to know?' Allegra asked, sticking out her chin in an attempt to hide her nervousness.

'Because it might concern my family and this house,' he replied. 'You wouldn't be here if it didn't, would you?'

'No, but—' Allegra started.

'Maybe we should discuss the charity event first,' Lydia interrupted.

'Yes,' Gwen said and poured milk into her mug. 'Let's hear what you're planning to do.'

'A Christmas fair, or something similar,' Lydia said. 'It would involve a lot of people from Sandy Cove walking all over the house and the grounds. If that's not something you'd be happy with, please tell me now before we go any further.'

Gwen looked at Lydia for a moment. 'We don't usually like mixing with people from Sandy Cove, but maybe I should start to make an effort. The past is the past, and it's better not to carry grudges and to live in the present,' she said cryptically.

'Of course it is,' Lydia agreed. 'Not that I have any idea at all why you'd carry grudges... But let's not start digging up old conflicts.'

Gwen nodded. 'Absolutely. So, if you organise some kind of event here, I suppose you will pay me for the use of the house and grounds? And meet the cost of insurance?'

'Yes,' Lydia said, picking up a biscuit. 'We will have all that ironed out beforehand and sign an agreement with you.'

'With *all* of us,' Max said. 'Gwen is only part owner of this estate. Or will be when the probate after our great-aunt Davina's death is over. There is me and then there is also Edwina, my sister. We all have to agree. And then the money has to be split between us.'

Gwen let out an exasperated sigh. 'Please, Max. Don't be

difficult. Neither you nor Edwina need more money than you have already. Whatever we're paid should go into the house.'

'Into this bottomless money pit, you mean,' Max said, his voice dripping with irony. He shot Lydia an annoyed look. 'We're in the middle of a dispute, you see. We only just inherited this pile after our great-aunt passed away. She was our grandfather's sister and was a hundred and three and fully fit, when she dropped dead suddenly. She hadn't made a will, so the three of us are now the happy heirs of a house that will cost several millions to restore, not to mention the death duties. The probate is still going on, and her solicitor is looking to see if there are any other heirs, but that's just a formality. She wasn't married and had no children, so I don't think they'll find anyone else. But the law says they have to try. I'd pull it down, but that's not possible because it's a listed building and can't be demolished because of its historical and cultural value.'

'It's my home,' Gwen said. 'Aunt Davina wanted me to have it, but she hadn't got around to making a will. She thought she would live forever.'

'Davina?' Saying the name out loud made Allegra shiver. 'Davina Courtney? Was that your great-aunt's name?' Her heart suddenly started to beat so fast she was sure everyone could hear it.

Aunt Davina, she thought, *now I'll find out if she is the woman I'm looking for. The young girl who lost her ring and then went on to be over a hundred years old, and lived until quite recently here in this huge, cold house?*

8

'Yes.' Max looked curiously at Allegra. 'You seem a little shaken suddenly. And you're very pale.'

'Yes, well...' Allegra touched her neck where the gold chain seemed to burn her skin. 'I was so surprised to hear that name.'

'Why is that?' Gwen asked.

'It's a strange story,' Allegra said. 'Something I came across recently by accident.'

'And it has something to do with us?' Gwen asked. 'And this house?'

Allegra looked at Lydia for support.

Lydia nodded. 'Go on. Tell them the story.'

'It's not about the house, really,' Allegra said. 'But the woman. That woman, I mean. Davina Courtney.'

'Aunt Davina?' Max asked.

'I think it's the same woman.' Allegra pulled the gold chain up to show the ring. 'I found this on a beach on Cape Cod in the summer.' She took off the chain, removed the ring and handed it to Max. 'It says *Davina and Sean, 1939* inside.'

'So it does,' Max said, holding the ring to the light and peering inside it. He passed it to Gwen. 'See for yourself.'

'Yes,' Gwen said after having looked inside the ring. 'The names are barely visible, but that's what it says. It also says *Tiffany* with a tiny number.'

'Oh,' Allegra said. 'I missed that. Must have been expensive, then.'

'Possibly. Lovely ring, but the cut of the diamond is old-fashioned.' Gwen turned it in her hand, then slipped it on her finger. 'It fits. Auntie Davina and I had the same sized fingers, actually. But that doesn't prove anything.' She handed the ring back to Allegra. 'What makes you think the Davina who owned the ring is – was – our great-aunt? I mean, Cape Cod... I don't think she was ever there. Was she?' she asked, looking at Max.

Max shrugged. 'No idea. I think she was in the States some-time before the war.' He smiled at Allegra. 'This is fascinating. So, tell us what led you to this house. I have a feeling you must have found some kind of connection to here.'

'Yes,' Allegra replied. 'There was a newspaper article in the *Cape Cod Chronicle* published in June 1939 about a young man looking for the ring his fiancée had lost on the beach. His name was Sean Walsh, and his fiancée was called Davina Courtney. It said that Sean Walsh lived in the coastguard station in Sandy Cove, and that Davina was also from the same area.'

'What?' Gwen exclaimed. She shot a look at Max. 'Coast-guard station? This woman was engaged to someone from there? It can't be our Davina. Can it?'

Max shrugged. 'Who knows? Maybe Auntie Davina was a dark horse and had an exciting life before she came here after her travels. I believe she and our great-grandad had some rip-roaring rows during that time, according to family legend. Maybe he was angry about her falling for a pauper.'

'Could have been about something else,' Gwen argued. She turned her attention to Allegra. 'Go on with your story.'

Allegra squirmed under the woman's cold gaze. 'That's all I could find out. But the story seemed so romantic to me and I wanted to find out what had happened to this couple. And then...'

She stopped, not knowing quite how she could explain her decision to travel to Kerry to look for two people who were no longer alive. To her it had been an escape, a fantasy, something to occupy her mind and pull her out of her grief for her father. But now, sitting here, looking at these people, and seeing how startling the story was to them, she realised the reality was a lot less romantic than she had imagined.

'And then you started dreaming about those two?' Max suggested, his voice oddly soft. 'And you looked up the village on the web and saw what a beautiful place it was.'

Allegra nodded, surprised by the sudden empathy in his eyes. His earlier arrogance was gone as if it had never existed.

'Exactly,' she said. 'And as I had a few weeks off, I thought I'd come here and find out more. And to see this part of the world too. Kerry always had a special part in my late father's heart. My parents spent their honeymoon in Kenmare.'

'That explains your trip here, then,' Max remarked. 'You always wanted to come here, didn't you? And the story of the ring gave you a push to finally do it, I suppose.'

'In a way,' Allegra said. 'I wanted to find its true owner. It doesn't feel right to keep it, when it might have belonged to someone's grandmother or aunt or something.'

'But we don't know if our great-aunt was the Davina whose name is in the ring,' Gwen cut in. 'I never heard her say anything about being engaged or talk about someone called Sean.'

'Maybe it was a secret engagement?' Lydia suggested. 'It occurs to me that the Courtney family of Strawberry Hill would hardly have thought a young man from the coastguard station was a great catch for their daughter. In those days, I mean.'

'You're right,' Gwen agreed. 'There was such a class difference then. Our lot never mixed with your lot, if you know what I mean.'

Lydia nodded. 'Oh yes. My mother told me it was very much "us and them" in those days.'

'Even when I was young, those old traditions lived on,' Gwen continued. 'And my God, Davina would certainly not have been allowed to even go into a pub in the village, or mix with anyone her own age in the 1930s.' She looked thoughtful. 'I wonder if our auntie Davina had a love affair she never told anyone about? She was a bit of a tearabout, I've heard. It's quite possible she might have fallen in love with some handsome young man at some stage. And if that happened, did those two run away to America, maybe? Or meet over there and...' She stopped. 'This makes me dizzy. It's not possible. Is it?' She looked at Max as if he had the answer.

'Anything is possible. Auntie Davina was a feisty old girl. And very pretty in her youth, judging by some old photos I've seen. You should try to find this Sean fellow,' Max said to Allegra. 'I mean, try to find out who he was and what he did.'

Allegra nodded. 'Yes. I have someone to help me with that.'

'Good,' Gwen said. She put her empty mug on the table with a bang. 'Right, then, back to the fundraiser. A Christmas event, you said?'

'That's right,' Lydia replied. 'I thought we might have a Santa's grotto in one of the old buildings, and then maybe a Christmas fair with arts and crafts somewhere in the house. Maybe serve tea and cakes, too.'

'For what charity?' Gwen asked.

Lydia thought for a moment. 'I think we should give the main part of the money to Unicef and then a bit to help restore this house. Maybe set up a restoration fund? I haven't seen the inside, but it seems to me it could be included in the heritage programme of Ireland or whatever it is the National Trust does.'

Gwen brightened. 'That's a terrific idea.'

'But we'll have to take a look around first to see if it's suitable,' Lydia warned.

'Of course.' Gwen got up from the chair. 'Let's have a tour. Maybe we can split up? Max could take one of you around outside and I'll show the other the house, and then we'll compare notes in a little while.'

'Good idea,' Max said, getting to his feet. 'I can check on the horses at the same time. Allegra, do you want to come with me?'

Torn between her longing to explore the house where Davina had lived, and seeing the grounds and stables with Max, Allegra hesitated. Then she looked into those blue eyes and felt an odd tug at her heart.

'I'd love to see the horses,' she said, and got up from her chair. 'In any case, Lydia has to see the house first.'

'Great. See you later, then,' Lydia said as she drained her mug. 'Can't wait to see the rest of the house, Gwen.'

'Come this way.' Gwen opened a door at the far side of the room. 'Be careful and follow me. It's a bit dark in places and easy to get lost and fall over the furniture or a loose floorboard.'

'I'll be careful,' Lydia said and followed Gwen through the door.

Max looked at Allegra. 'Sure you don't want to go with them?'

'I'm sure,' Allegra replied. 'The grounds must be very interesting, too.'

'Yes, they are. There are some ruins and an old tower from the fourteenth century and the stables are actually quite beautiful, built in early Georgian times.' He opened the door to the utility room. 'Let's get our jackets and get going. I'll put on a pair of wellies as the grass is wet.' He eyed Allegra's hiking shoes. 'Are those waterproof?'

'Yes.' She lifted her foot for him to see. 'They're lined with Gore-Tex.'

'Perfect. You came well prepared.'

'Thanks to Lydia,' Allegra said. 'She said to dress for mud.'

'She was right.' In the utility room, Max took Allegra's jacket from the peg and helped her on with it.

'Thank you,' Allegra said, unused to such gallantry. Their eyes met for a split second before Allegra looked away, feeling oddly shy.

Max put on his own jacket and pulled on a pair of green wellies. Then he held the door open for Allegra and they went outside, breathing in the chilly autumn air. The sun cast a golden light through the leaves of the trees and there was a smell of woodsmoke from the kitchen chimney. Max walked on, across the gravel at the front of the house and around the other corner, and continued down a path that ran along a wooden fence at the end of which rose a big square tower, its jagged outline silhouetted against the late-afternoon sky.

Allegra stopped and looked up at the wall of the tower, partly covered in ivy. 'Wow. This does look old. Who built it?'

'Some of our Norman ancestors,' Max replied. 'They were called Fitzmaurice. They built this in the fifteenth century.'

'That Fitz prefix is so Irish,' Allegra remarked. 'I've met people called Fitzgerald and Fitzpatrick and all kinds of other Fitzes in Boston.'

'It's really not Irish at all,' Max said. 'It's a Norman prefix. Fitz is from *fils de* in French, meaning *son of.*'

'So Fitzmaurice really means *son of Maurice*?' Allegra asked. 'And Fitzgerald, *son of Gerald*?'

'Exactly,' Max said. 'You learn fast.'

'Amazing,' Allegra said, looking up at the tower. She started to walk around it and looked in through a half-open iron door that led to a large room. She stepped inside and looked up at the rough stone walls trying to imagine what it had been like when it was lived in over five hundred years ago. She was standing in what must have been a great hall and she could see the remnants of a large fireplace where she could picture a blazing fire. 'I think this is the oldest building I've ever seen,' she said when she stepped back outside.

'If this is your first trip to Europe, it would be,' Max remarked. They stood there looking out over the fields that sloped down to the river where the setting sun cast a golden glow on the water. 'But there are buildings around here that are older still,' he remarked. 'Like the round towers you might have seen dotted around the landscape. The monks built those to defend themselves against the Vikings. They would shin up the towers as soon as they spotted one of those wild Norse men. A bit mean to leave the peasants to fend for themselves, I've always thought.'

'I agree,' Allegra said. 'Not very Christian of them, I have to say.'

'Not at all. But I suppose they saw themselves as very superior and worth saving.'

'Like your lot?' Allegra said in a cheeky tone.

Max looked startled but then he laughed. 'Hmm, yes. Maybe you have a point there. Let's press on, shall we?'

'Interesting about the meaning of Fitz,' Allegra said as they continued walking along the path towards a group of houses in the distance. '*Son of*, huh? I didn't know that.'

'There are a lot of hidden meanings in Irish names,' Max replied. 'But of course, the Courtneys' roots are also very much from England. A long and very dramatic history, which left a lot of people with family history in two different countries. We're still struggling a little with the identity crisis.'

'You're talking about how the English came here and conquered Ireland?'

'That's right. And then they were forced to leave a little over a hundred years ago. After the war of independence, or the Rising, as it was called. After that, we intermingled and intermarried and it all became quite confused.' Max smiled. 'But I'm sure you've read up on Irish history, so you know what I'm talking about.'

'Oh, yes. My father made us read books on the subject. I found it fascinating. The English families were the landed gentry in the old days, weren't they?'

Max nodded. 'That's right, and then we became the stranded gentry,' he said with a grin. 'We all stayed and became part of the new, multifaceted Ireland. It's much better this way. All good friends and part of this amazing country.'

'Do you feel Irish or English?' Allegra asked.

'Oh, I'm Irish,' Max declared with feeling. 'My roots are here in this soil, in this part of Ireland, despite my mother trying to turn me into an English gentleman. She insisted we take her name as well, hence the Smythe addition. Didn't go down well with my old pater –

it tore their marriage apart,' he ended with a touch of bitterness. 'But that's another story and not one I want to dwell on. Upwards and onwards, as the saying goes. Moving on is better than staying stuck. Don't you agree?'

Allegra returned his earnest gaze and nodded. 'Absolutely,' she said, intrigued by all he had told her.

There was a lot more to this man than good looks and arrogance. She had a feeling there were hidden depths, with a history of conflicts and sadness, despite his flippant tone.

They had come to an archway with an iron gate through which Allegra glimpsed a cobbled courtyard with a trough in the middle, surrounded by planters with red geraniums.

'Here we are,' Max said. 'Gwen's haven and favourite place in the whole world.' He pushed at the gate which opened smoothly without a sound. 'Step into the Shangri-la of the horsey world,' he said with a sweeping gesture.

Allegra entered the courtyard and smiled as she saw the horses sticking their heads out of the stalls that lined the yard.

'Wow,' she said, amazed. She stepped closer to a chestnut

horse and touched his soft muzzle. 'Hello there, handsome fellow,' she whispered into his ear as he bent his head towards her. She stroked his silky coat and instantly knew this was a top-quality horse.

'The star of the show,' Max said, coming to her side. 'His name is Stanley and he's nearly all thoroughbred apart from a little draught horse through his mother. He will one day be on the Irish Olympic show-jumping team once Gwen has finished his schooling.'

'He's beautiful,' Allegra said.

'And he knows it,' Max said, giving the horse a pat on the neck. 'Come, I'll introduce you to the others. I can see you like horses.'

'I love them,' Allegra said, breathing in the smell of horse and hay that took her back to her childhood and the visits to the farm.

'Do you ride?'

'Not really,' she said. 'I rode a bit when I was younger. My dad's cousin had a farm in Vermont and he had an old horse we used to trot around on, but that's all.'

'Summer holidays?'

'No, mostly in the fall and at Christmas. Summers were always on Cape Cod where we had a cottage.'

'You had a happy childhood, I gather,' Max said.

'Yes. Until I was ten,' Allegra said quietly.

'What happened then?'

'My mother died.'

'Oh.' Max's eyes were suddenly full of empathy. 'I'm so sorry. That's so sad for a child. And now you've had another sadness.'

'Yes.' Allegra looked at Stanley and rubbed his face. It felt so comforting to be near this big animal somehow. 'It's so soothing to be with animals, I find,' she said to get away from the subject of her loss. 'Especially this gorgeous fellow.'

'Horses are a great balm to the soul,' Max said. He tugged at her arm. 'But there are others. Here, next door is my favourite,' he said and patted the neck of a big bay horse. 'His name is Pat and I always ride him when I come here. He was a bit hot today, that's why I had to complain to Gwen. He needs to be worked hard and often. Don't you, old chap?'

The horse let out a little grunt and nibbled at Max's face.

'He likes you,' Allegra said.

'Because I spoil him,' Max said. He picked up a carrot from a bucket beside the door of the box and gave it to Pat, who grabbed it with his big teeth.

With the sound of munching in her ears, Allegra looked around the stable yard and noted that there were around twenty stalls. An open door revealed a tack room with saddles and bridles. 'It's quite a big yard,' she said as a young man came in through the gate leading two skittish young horses which he proceeded to put into their respective stables.

'That's the last of them, Max,' he called across the yard. 'I'll do the hay nets now and then we'll give them their feed.'

'Great,' Max replied. 'Thanks, Connor. Oh, and this is Allegra from America who's come here for a visit.'

The young man waved. 'Hi, Allegra. Nice to meet ya.'

'Hi there, Connor. Nice to meet you, too,' Allegra called back before Connor disappeared through a smaller gate at the far side.

'Hey, why don't we give the horses their feed to help Connor?' Max suggested. 'It's only some oats and easy to do.'

'Great,' Allegra said and followed Max into the tack room where he started putting oats from a big bin into a bucket. Then he took a plastic scoop and set it on top. 'If I carry the bucket, you could put a scoop of oats into each feeding bowl that hangs on the wall of each box.'

'You mean I'll go in to the horses?' Allegra said, slightly nervous at the thought.

'They won't bite. Just open the door and put in a scoop,' Max urged. 'They'll love you for it. Come on,' he said and started to walk along the row of boxes. He opened a door to the stall where a grey horse whinnied as it spotted the bucket. 'Put a scoopful into his feeder.'

'Okay.' Allegra scooped some oats and put them into the feeder, then quickly went out again while Max closed the door.

They continued along the row and when all the horses had been fed, Max put the bucket back in the tack room and shot Allegra a wide smile. 'Well done. That wasn't so hard, was it?'

'No, it was great,' Allegra said as they left the tack room. 'And I love hearing the horses chomping.'

'Lovely sound,' Max agreed. 'Thanks for your help.'

'But we'd better get back. It's nearly dark,' Allegra said, suddenly noticing that dusk had fallen and lights had come on around the yard.

'Yes. I'll take you around the other side where there are some ruined cottages that would be great for the Christmas event, like a Santa's grotto. The tower is quite good, too. The steps inside are safe and the whole structure is solid, so no danger there.'

'That's good.' Allegra had nearly forgotten the Christmas event. 'I'll tell Lydia.'

They met Connor carrying two hay nets on their way out through the gate and Max told him what they had done. Then they continued down another path, past some ruins that Max said would also make good spots for the Christmas event and then they were nearly back at the house, its dark shape looming before them.

Allegra looked up at the windows. 'It seems brooding and a little spooky.'

'From this angle, maybe,' Max replied, following her gaze. 'But it's really a beautiful house waiting to be woken up out of its sleep and lived in and loved again.'

Allegra looked at him through the gloom. 'I thought you wanted to pull it down.'

'I said that to annoy Gwen. I would love to have the means to do it up. Can you see the roof from here?'

'Just about.'

'Well, in daylight, you'll see it's in good nick. Auntie Davina had the roof repaired about twenty years ago when she sold a horse for a lot of money.'

'That was a good thing to do.'

'Yes.' Max looked thoughtfully at Allegra. 'You know, you really set the cat among the pigeons with your story about the ring.'

'How do you mean?' Allegra asked, startled by his slightly annoyed tone.

'Because now we have the possibility of Aunt Davina having been married in the past.'

'Gwen didn't seem to believe that.'

'Oh, I think she did. And it really rattled her.'

'But why would that be so awful?' Allegra asked. 'Sean Walsh has to be long dead as well.'

'Yeah, but he might have had siblings and nieces and nephews. If Sean and Davina were married and there was no prenup, he would have been part owner of this estate. So it's possible that there are more heirs. And maybe they even had a child?' Max shook his head. 'Nah, that's not possible. She wouldn't have abandoned her child. But she might have married this Sean guy in secret.'

Allegra pulled up the collar of her jacket against the chilly wind. 'Why would they have married in secret?'

Max started walking again. 'Because their families would have been against it. He would have been a Catholic, she a Protestant. That was a huge no-no in those days, especially in rural Ireland where religion and class were so important.'

'But it said in the article she was going home to prepare for the wedding,' Allegra argued as she tried to keep up with his brisk pace across the grass.

'To arrange a secret wedding, if it ever took place, would be my guess.'

'Oh.' Allegra suddenly shivered, both from the cold and the feeling of sadness Max's comment had instilled. 'How hard it must have been for them. I didn't think of that. I had no idea this would have been so important in those days.'

'It certainly was in Ireland,' Max said with a grim expression. 'Awful snobbery and prejudice among families such as mine, and a lot of suspicion and resentment with Catholic families. Hard to imagine these days.'

'Yes, it is.' Allegra looked at the house again. 'But what about your great-aunt's belongings? Did any of you find letters or a diary, or anything like that?'

'We haven't been in her rooms since she passed away. She spent the last few years in a nursing home and Gwen went to get her things from there. But we didn't want to start sorting out her possessions or private papers that are still in her room here until the probate was finished.'

'I see. But will that take long?'

'It shouldn't, except... Your story opens up a lot of possibilities. I think...' He paused. 'We have to find out who this Sean Walsh was and what happened to him.'

'This old lady I talked to said she would do some research. She's writing a book about the history of Sandy Cove and the coastguard station will be an important part.' Allegra suddenly shivered as the wind increased.

'But you're cold,' Max said and took her arm. 'Come, let's go inside and get warm. I'm sure your friend will be wondering where you've got to.'

They walked around the corner of the house and into the courtyard, where the light from the kitchen threw a warm glow on the gravel. Then they went inside and took off their jackets and footwear.

Allegra could hear Lydia and Gwen talking in the kitchen, but before they went in, she grabbed Max's arm.

'Wait a minute,' she said. 'I just wanted to say to you, before we go in, that I didn't mean to cause any trouble by coming here with the ring. I just wanted to find out about Davina and Sean and their story, and maybe work out who should have the ring. I'm sorry if it's upset you and Gwen.' She stopped and looked at him, trying to gauge his feelings, her mind in turmoil.

He looked at her for a long time, then he took a deep breath. 'No need to apologise. I don't think that you have caused trouble at all, even if we're a little shaken by your story. But if you hadn't arrived it might have popped up later with someone else who might claim heritage. Better to do thorough research at this early stage, and find out if there is anyone out there who should be contacted.' He suddenly laughed. 'Some inheritance, eh? A large lump of a house that will only cost money to do anything with.'

'But it could be sold to someone with a lot of money who'd love to restore it and turn it into a hotel or something like that.'

'Oh yes, I know. There's a lot of land with this property, too. Five hundred acres of good farmland, which is, apart from fifty acres, let out to farmers for grazing and growing crops. That brings in some money, of course. Plus, the yard which is quite a good source of income for Gwen. So yeah, it's not all hopeless. But despite all that, the house is the biggest problem.' He shrugged and opened the door to the kitchen. 'We'll have to contact the solicitor in any case.'

'I see,' Allegra said as she followed Max.

'See what?' Lydia said from her place at the kitchen table.

'Oh, just something to do with the probate,' Max replied. 'We'll talk about it later, Gwen.'

'Fine,' Gwen replied from the stove where she was putting in some logs.

Lydia got up from the table. 'I think we've seen enough for today. We'll compare notes on the way home, Allegra. I have to get back to catch up on some work and to report back to my partner, Helen O'Dwyer. I'll give you a shout a little later in the week, Gwen, and we can talk some more?'

'Perfect,' Gwen said.

'Thanks for showing us around,' Lydia said, moving toward the door. 'I'm sure it's going to be a great event that will raise a lot of money for both our causes.'

'I certainly hope so,' Gwen said.

'The inside of the tower would be a great place for Santa's grotto,' Allegra remarked.

'Good idea,' Lydia said. 'And thanks for your help, Max.'

'Nice to meet you both,' Max said, looking at Allegra.

They said goodbye and put on their shoes and jackets in the utility room, where the dogs were snoring in their baskets, and emerged into the cold, starlit evening.

The wind had dropped and the still air was crisp. Allegra looked up at the stars and tried to sort everything that had happened. Her revelation about the ring and the possibility that Davina had been married had obviously shocked both Gwen and Max. She had apologised for upsetting him, but had been cheered by Max's reaction. Despite the fact that this could upset things for Davina Courtney's heirs, he wanted to do the right thing. So she could go on with her research and find out more about Davina and Sean, whose love story now seemed even more romantic. The work on the charity event would give her an excuse to go back to the house and explore it, and perhaps even see Max again.

The weeks ahead suddenly seemed full of possibilities.

9

'That went well,' Lydia said as she settled into the driver's seat. 'Gwen seemed very positive to my suggestions, which surprised me. I had heard that she wasn't easy to get on with, but she was really quite friendly, if a little reserved. Could be that her bark is worse than her bite.'

'I think you're right,' Allegra said. 'I heard the same kind of thing from some people I met on the way here.'

'Might be that she's a bit tricky when it comes to buying and selling horses.' Lydia glanced at Allegra before she drove off. 'How about you? How did you get on with Max?'

'We got on great,' Allegra said, turning away so Lydia wouldn't see how even hearing his name affected her. She had never felt such an immediate attraction to a man before, and it shook her up.

'I'll bet.' Lydia smiled. 'He's very handsome. I couldn't help noticing some sparks flying between you.'

'Yeah, uh, maybe,' Allegra mumbled, grateful that the darkness hid her expression and her hot cheeks. Then she laughed at herself as they drove through the gates. 'Of course I found him drop-dead gorgeous,' she admitted. 'Who wouldn't?'

'Oh yeah. Robert Redford meets Brad Pitt. What's not to like?'

'Not quite but, yes, something like that. I'm not going to fall for him, though.'

'Well, he certainly seemed impressed with you.'

'Oh, I'm not sure about that,' Allegra mumbled. 'But I'm only here for three weeks, so that's a no-go. I wouldn't want to start anything in such a short time and then have to leave and...'

'I know,' Lydia soothed. 'You're right. Pity, though. I think the two of you looked so good together. But I shouldn't let my love of romance get in the way of practicalities. The visit went really well and the house is amazing, despite its dilapidated state. The hall would be perfect for the Christmas fair. And you said the tower was quite impressive.'

'Yes,' Allegra agreed. 'The tower was great. The kids would love the magical atmosphere, and it would be easy to make it very Christmassy. But I don't think they want anyone near the stables.'

'No, that's what Gwen said. Those horses are worth a lot of money and could get spooked and start to panic, which might result in injuries. So we'll keep well away from them. I hope they won't be upset by a lot of people walking around.'

'I don't think that'll be a problem. There are fences and gates and they can put all the horses in their stables during the event.'

'Brilliant. Maybe you can get going on that app?'

'Sure,' Allegra said, tearing her mind away from Max's beautiful blue eyes and the way he had looked at her. 'In fact, I was thinking I might get my firm in on it. They might like a bit of exposure over here. Annie, my boss, is always open to suggestions. This way we can get my team to work on it and have it ready really fast.'

'Perfect,' Lydia said, her voice warm. 'We can talk some more over dinner. I'll call Lucille and see if she wants to join us.

She's at a loose end as Rory and Ella are still away. Her son and daughter-in-law,' she added.

'I know,' Allegra said. 'She told me when we met on the terrace.'

'Of course she did,' Lydia said as she turned into the main road to Sandy Cove. 'She'll be happy to talk to you some more, I'm sure.'

'How amazing,' Allegra said. 'I mean, I've just arrived, and now I'm already having dinner with my neighbours. And I met two really nice people on the way here who were incredibly helpful as well. A woman I met on the plane whose brother met her at the airport. They knew Gwen, actually. The brother runs a yard a bit like the one at Strawberry Hill. They were the ones who told me about the house and the Courtneys there. What a weird coincidence, don't you think?'

'Ireland is a small country,' Lydia said. 'And if you're in horsey business, you'd probably know everyone. It's a very tight-knit world.'

'The Courtneys don't seem to be part of the Sandy Cove community,' Allegra said. 'As far as I understood anyway. But I've only just met them, so I could be wrong.'

'No, you're right,' Lydia said as she turned into the main street of the village. 'I think that, in the past, they kind of turned their backs on the sea and led a more inland life with farming and their horses and so on. And in the old days, they would only have socialised with other people from the big houses. But that was years ago, of course. Now they seem more open to mixing with everyone in the village. But traditions take a long time to change. In rural Ireland,' she continued, 'owner-ship of land is very important. There is no longer a division when it comes to religion, but land is still king around here. I also have a feeling that the Courtneys find it hard to break with tradition and that they're afraid the people in the village look at them with suspicion. They are farmers and horse breeders. Not fishermen or people with a knowledge of the ocean. Worlds apart, even if there is only a distance of a few miles.'

'That explains it,' Allegra said. 'And Max told me all about the differences between Catholics and Protestants in the past, too: class, culture, religion all those years ago, and how it has changed since then. Now there is complete equality, of course. Except for what you just said. Two different worlds. Interesting.'

'And complicated. Thank God that's changed,' Lydia remarked. She pointed out the window. 'Look at all the Halloween decorations in this light. Aren't they amazing?'

'Oh wow,' Allegra exclaimed as she looked at the ghosts, skeletons and witches hanging from bushes and trees, eerily illuminated by the street lights. They looked even more spectacular in the dark. The wind made some of the figures sway which made them seem as if they were floating in the air. Spiders and skulls were pasted onto some of the windows and doors were swathed in what looked like spiders' webs. 'They take Halloween seriously here.'

'They certainly do,' Lydia said. 'And as it falls on a Saturday this year, there'll be a lot of partying and trick-or-treating all night long. The library is doing a fancy-dress evening with a buffet and wine. You should come along, it's always great fun.'

'Do I have to dress up in a costume?' Allegra asked.

'Yes, but that's easy. Just cut holes in a sheet and you're done.'

'Sounds easy enough,' Allegra said, excited at the thought of the fancy-dress party. 'I love those kinds of parties. Emma and Joe, my niece and nephew, love Halloween and fancy dress, just like me. Then you can hide behind a mask and feel free to say and do what you normally wouldn't dare.'

Lydia shot her a puzzled look. 'Why would you want to hide? You're a gorgeous young woman, with that hair and the long legs and the huge brown eyes. Don't tell me you lack confidence.'

'It's not about confidence,' Allegra tried to explain. 'It's more to do with all the things that have happened to me. I feel like I need to be in someone else's skin sometimes. Someone who has a different life and is not afraid to say exactly what she thinks.'

'Oh,' Lydia said as they arrived at the coastguard station. 'I think I know what you mean. I've felt like that sometimes. Especially when I first came here. I wanted to be someone else and not the sad woman who had lost her husband and all her money. But you know what my grandmother always said? People generally are too taken up with their own problems to notice other people. Nobody is really looking at you and wondering what's going on in your life.'

Allegra nodded. 'Yes, I think that's true. I tend to worry too much what people think when, in reality, they don't think much about me at all.'

'Exactly. I was going through all that angst when I met Jason.'

'How did you meet?'

'Right behind my house, I heard this voice in the dark saying hello. I said hello back and then we started to talk. Strange, but we used to have these long chats across the hedge in the dark for weeks before we met in daylight. It was like having an online friend I couldn't see. And because of that, I could say what I felt without having to look him in the eyes. Sounds weird, I know, but that's how it was.'

'That doesn't sound weird to me at all,' Allegra said, touched by the emotion in Lydia's voice. 'It sounds quite magical, really.'

'It was,' Lydia said dreamily. 'And sometimes I wish I was back at that moment, when we were talking in the dark and sharing our deepest thoughts with each other.' She shook her head. 'But now, I'm being silly. Wait till you meet Jason, he's such a special man.'

'You're very lucky,' Allegra said softly.

'Yes, I know I am.'

'Was it love at first sight?'

Lydia looked out the window of the car, her hands still on the steering wheel. 'I'm not sure. Not really. It kind of grew out of a mutual understanding of each other.'

'You don't believe in that, then?' Allegra asked.

'Love at first sight?' Lydia turned to look at Allegra, her face illuminated by the lights from the dashboard. 'I'm not sure. I don't think you can love someone before you truly know them. But I do believe you can meet someone and feel that you connect with them in a way you never have with anyone before. And of course, there is that instant physical attraction, that little shiver you feel when your eyes meet or your hands touch.'

'And then you build on that, you mean?'

'I think so.' Lydia turned off the engine. 'That's enough philosophy for now. We'd better get ready for dinner. I think I can smell Jason's Irish stew.'

'Me too,' Allegra said, her stomach rumbling. 'But I need to change.'

'So do I. But when you're ready, just walk in. Our door is always open. Jason will be in the kitchen.'

They got out of the car and Allegra went into her house to change out of her mud-spattered jeans and hiking shoes. After putting on a pair of clean corduroy slacks and a black polo neck, she went next door and entered the hall, breathing in the delicious smell of Irish stew. Further inside she found a tall grey-haired man standing by the stove in the kitchen, wearing a large apron over his jeans and sweater. He turned around and shot her a warm smile.

'Hi. Allegra, isn't it?' He held out his hand. 'I'm Jason. Welcome to our house.'

'Thank you for inviting me.' Allegra shook his hand, feeling even more at home as she heard his Boston accent.

'A fellow Bostonian is always welcome,' Jason said. 'We have to stick together against these wild Irish people.'

'Or maybe they have to beware of us wild Irish Bostonians?' Allegra retorted.

'Maybe they do,' Jason replied and turned to the stove. 'I made Irish stew. Should have been a Boston chowder to make you feel at home, I suppose. But after the storm, the fish was a little scarce today.'

'I love Irish stew,' Allegra said. 'Some people might say it's just lamb, onions and carrots, but it's much more than that.'

'It certainly is,' Jason said. 'I add barley and herbs, too, and let it simmer for several hours.'

'It smells divine.'

'I hope you'll have a happy time here in Sandy Cove,' he said and turned back to the stove.

'Thank you,' Allegra said. 'I feel very much at home here already, even after just one day.'

'That's good.' Jason put the lid on the casserole. 'This is ready, but we'll leave it to simmer for a bit longer. Let's go into the living room. I think Lydia has lit the fire and poured us a glass of wine, and I think Lucille will be here soon.'

Lydia, dressed in a red wool skirt and white cashmere sweater, had lit the fire and poured red wine into four glasses set out on the coffee table between the two red sofas that flanked the fireplace. But there was no sign of Lucille.

'I wonder what's keeping her?' Lydia said and checked her watch. 'It's nearly eight o'clock.'

Jason handed Allegra a glass of red wine. 'Let's take a sip of this while we wait. Lucille won't mind.' He took a glass and lifted it, smiling. 'Cheers, Allegra, and welcome to our village.'

Lydia lifted her glass in a toast. 'I second that. Lovely to meet you and to share our latest project with you.'

'Oh, yes, Lydia told me about that,' Jason said. 'Sounds like a lot of fun.'

'It will be,' Lydia declared. 'I think it will be hugely popular.'

They were interrupted by the front door banging and a breathless Lucille, dressed in a bright red raincoat, rushing into the room.

'I'm so sorry,' she panted, 'but I was stuck in the presbytery after evening mass with Father O'Malley. I mean, I was after some information and then he insisted on me having tea and looking at his stamp collection. I couldn't refuse as I was trying to make him look into the parish records from the 1920s for that Walsh family the new girl was looking for and...' She stopped as she caught sight of Allegra. 'But there you are! What a coincidence. You will be *very* interested in what I found out.'

'About Sean Walsh?' Allegra said, her heart beating faster as she said the name. 'Did he live here in this village?'

'He did,' Lucille stated.

'You think he's *my* Sean Walsh?' Allegra asked, staring at her.

'Yes, indeed,' Lucille said. 'Everything fits.'

10

'Calm down, Lucille,' Lydia said, laughing. 'You can tell us everything over dinner. Jason, take Lucille's coat and give her a glass of wine.'

'Okay,' Lucille said impatiently. She wrenched off her coat and handed it to Jason. 'Sorry about not dressing up, but I rushed straight here as I was so late.' She straightened her red-and-white checked sweater that she wore with a pair of wide-legged black culottes and black lace-up boots.

'You look great,' Lydia assured her.

'Thanks.' Lucile smoothed her short white curls. 'A bit windblown but all right, I suppose.' She took the glass from Jason and drank a little wine. Then she looked at Allegra. 'I can see that you want to hear what I found out.'

'I can't wait,' Allegra said.

'Then I'll tell you right now as it was quite tricky to get it out of the good father. Anyway, after I had admired the 1916 memorial stamps and the royal collection, I finally got him to look up those records. That man is not easily led, I have to say. But I suppose that's a good thing in a priest. So... where was I?'

'The parish records and the Walsh family,' Lydia prompted.

'Yes, of course. Sorry. Anyway, my dear, you'll be happy to hear that I found out that a Walsh family lived here in the coastguard station in the early part of last century. They had six children...' Lucille stopped. 'Imagine living in one of these cottages with six children!'

'Must have been a little snug,' Jason remarked.

'To put it mildly,' Lucille said. 'But to go on, their youngest child was called Sean and he was born in 1918.'

'Oh,' Allegra said, excited. 'That fits. He was twenty-one in 1939, then...'

'Would have been, yes,' Lucille replied. 'But I'm afraid that's all I can tell you for now.'

'There was no record of his death?' Lydia asked, sitting down on the sofa.

'No. Nor a marriage with anyone. The parish records have births, christenings, marriages and deaths,' Lucille said, sitting down beside Lydia.

'Why don't you sit down here, Allegra,' Jason said and pointed at the other sofa. 'I'll go and check the stew and warm some bread rolls.'

Her eyes still on Lucille, Allegra sat down. 'And that's it?' she asked.

'For now, yes,' Lucille said. 'But we have only started.' She rubbed her hands together. 'Now, we should go to the library and find out more. There'll be old newspaper articles and brochures and mementoes in the archives marked Sandy Cove. I only just skimmed the surface when I was looking for my ancestor who was convicted of a minor crime in the 1830s and sent to Australia. And I'm researching the late 1800s for my general history book on Sandy Cove. But now I will jump forward and get stuck into the years before the war.'

'But what about Davina Courtney?' Allegra asked. 'Were there no records of her family?'

'Not in the Catholic parish records,' Lydia replied. 'We'd

have to go to the Protestant church for that. And I think they were moved to Killarney when the rectory was sold. It's now the doctor's surgery and our Dr Kate lives there. Don't think there's anything left of the parish there, though.'

'No, there wouldn't be,' Lucille said. She drained her glass and put it on the coffee table. 'Lovely wine. Anyhow,' she continued, 'as it wasn't that long ago, I'm sure there'll be some older people around who might remember something. Like Dominic Foley, who runs the Wednesday bingo in the church hall. I seem to remember he said his father was the last butler at Strawberry Hill sometime before the war. I'll see if he'd like to come for tea at my house during the week.'

'Good idea,' Lydia agreed. 'And I'll ask Helen if she knows anything. Her father was the last vicar here and her mother or grandmother might have known the Courtneys.'

'Excellent,' Lucille said. 'I'll see what I can find out from the vicarage in Killarney, too.'

'It's so kind of you to go to all this trouble,' Allegra said.

Lucille laughed. 'Trouble? I love this kind of detective work. And you have to find out who should have that ring.'

'Most people would just have kept it,' Lydia said. 'It's a beautiful thing, and you're the legal owner.'

'Yes, but it doesn't seem right somehow,' Allegra argued. 'I don't feel I should have it. It's not giving me much pleasure like my other jewellery. There's no memory attached to it or anything.'

Lucille nodded. 'I know what you mean. As it's someone's else's engagement ring, it has a history that's not yours.'

'You're so wise,' Jason said, coming into the room with a casserole that he placed on the table. 'Dinner's ready, folks.'

'Wonderful,' Lucille said and got up. 'I'm hungry after all that talking.'

They all sat down around the table and enjoyed Jason's excellent stew with lamb flavoured with rosemary and thyme that melted in the mouth, along with more wine and some home-made bread. The conversation drifted from one subject to another, mostly about life in Sandy Cove, which Allegra found fascinating. Then suddenly, after about an hour and a half, she felt so sleepy she nearly nodded off.

Lydia glanced at her. 'I think jetlag is setting in.'

'Oh God, yes, it is.' Allegra blinked and tried to sit up straighter. 'I thought I was over it, but I feel completely whacked.'

'Then you must go home and get some sleep,' Lucille said. 'Right this moment, young lady. Do you want me to come with you?'

'No, I'll be fine,' Allegra assured her. 'If you don't think I'm being rude?'

'Of course we don't,' Lydia assured her, getting up. 'Come on, I'll see you to your door.'

Allegra got up. 'I'll say good night then,' she said, feeling sheepish. 'Sorry about this. Didn't mean to ruin the evening.'

'You didn't,' Jason said and stood up. 'We all know what jetlag feels like. It can take several days to wear off. Thanks for coming. It was great to meet you.'

'Lovely to meet you, too,' Allegra said with a wan smile. Then she waved at Lucille. 'Thanks for helping me with the research, Lucille.'

'You're very welcome,' Lucille replied. 'You'll forgive me for not getting up. The old knees don't like it when I bob up and down. I'll be in touch when I have more news. I'm going to find out all I can about that old bird. Davina Courtney, I mean. I'm sure her story is very interesting.'

'I'm looking forward to finding out more,' Allegra said before she followed Lydia through the house and across the little garden to her own front door, where she had left the light on. There she stopped and smiled sleepily at Lydia. 'I'll be fine now. Can't keep my eyes open so I'll crawl up the stairs to bed.'

Lydia smiled and patted Allegra's arm. 'Yes, go on. Off to bed. I'll get in touch tomorrow.'

'Thanks for everything,' Allegra said. 'It was an awesome day.'

'For me too. Sleep tight.'

Allegra smiled and nodded, too tired to say or do anything else. Then she went inside and managed to get upstairs and into bed before she collapsed. She laid her head on the soft pillow, pulled the duvet to her chin, put out the light and closed her eyes. All the impressions of what had happened that day whirled through her tired brain. The old house, Max, Gwen, their great-aunt who might or might not be the Davina she was searching for, and finally the horses and the stars shining brightly in the night sky above the roof of Strawberry Hill.

11

Allegra had barely opened her eyes when her phone rang. She blinked and sat up, momentarily disoriented. *Where am I?* she thought, looking around the bright room where the sun shone in through a slit in the sage-green curtains that billowed in the breeze. She spotted her phone on the cream carpet beside the bed and picked it up.

'Hello?' she croaked.

'Good morning,' a cheery voice said. 'This is Lucille, your personal historian. I hope I didn't wake you?'

Allegra cleared her throat. 'Well, yes,' she said, as the memory of the day before drifted into her mind. 'What time is it?' She tried to get out of bed and suddenly realised she had slept all night fully dressed.

'Nine thirty,' Lucille said. 'Is this too early for you? I could call later.'

'No, it's fine,' Allegra said. 'I don't usually wake up this late, but the jetlag must still be affecting me.'

'I hope you feel better today,' Lucille said.

'Yes, I do. Much better.' Allegra pulled back the curtains and stared out across the deep blue sunlit ocean. 'My God, what a gorgeous day,' she exclaimed. 'I'm just looking at the view from my window. Could be a summer's day.'

'Not if you go outside,' Lucille countered. 'It's quite chilly really. But I didn't call you to discuss the weather. It's about Dominic Foley and the amazing thing he told me. I think we have a lead on the Sean and Davina saga.'

'Who's Dominic Foley?' Allegra asked, smiling at the excitement in Lucille's voice.

'His father was the last butler at Strawberry Hill. I told you about him at dinner yesterday.'

'Oh, yes,' Allegra said, as she remembered the conversation. 'So he knew something about Davina?'

'And Sean. He only told me a bit of what he knows, but he's coming for coffee at my house at eleven to tell me all of it. Maybe you'd like to come, too, and talk to him?'

'Of course I would,' Allegra replied, her heart beating faster at the prospect of meeting someone whose father had worked at Strawberry Hill. He might have been told stories about Davina as a young woman.

'Thought so,' Lucille said. 'He said he had his father's diary and some other bits of paper from his days at the big house. I'm just going to give the house a bit of a flick with the duster and get some nice little treats from the bakery.'

'I can get those on my way,' Allegra offered. 'Just tell me where it is and how I'll find your house.'

'Oh, thank you, that would be very kind,' Lucille said. 'The bakery is on the main street next door to Sorcha's grocery shop. Get some of the little tea cakes and half a dozen ginger snaps. And my house is just a little bit further up the street opposite the pharmacy. I'll see you at eleven, then,' Lucille said and hung up.

Allegra smiled to herself as she hung up. It seemed to her that Lucille was treating this as a mission and would turn every stone in order to find clues to the mystery of Davina and Sean.

And who knew? Maybe they would find an additional heir or two to Davina's estate? But that could stir things up among the Courtney family and perhaps cause them a lot of problems. They might not like that at all, especially not Gwen.

Allegra suddenly felt as if she had landed in a hornets' nest of conflicts and that her arrival with the ring and the newspaper article was going to change not only the lives of the Courtneys but hers as well. But she was here, and the story was out there, so now all she could do was to see it to its conclusion, whatever it was. Allegra shivered at the odd feeling that something inevitable was about to happen. But she pushed it away and had a shower before she changed into fresh clothes and had her breakfast. She was looking forward to her walk up the street and to meeting this old man who might hold the key to the story that was about to unfold.

Allegra spent the next hour settling into the house, which she hadn't had time to do the day before with everything that had happened. After putting the rest of her clothes into the large wardrobe in her bedroom, she sat down with her laptop in the sunroom and wrote a long email to Lucia, telling her all that had happened since she arrived, and what she had found out about the ring. Even though she had told Emma and Joe to keep it a secret, she now felt she could tell Lucia everything as it was too late for her to stop Allegra going ahead with her plan.

She went on to describe the previous day, not holding back on her description of Max and the effect he had had on her. *Drop-dead gorgeous*, she wrote. *But he seems a little too arrogant for my taste and he is certainly very aware of his looks and his effect on women.* Allegra thought for a moment before she went on to describe Gwen and the old house and the sense that it held many secrets and memories that might be painful and sad. Writing it all down put her feelings into perspective and, as she sent off the email, Allegra felt calmer and more hopeful.

The wind was indeed very chilly and Allegra tightened her collar around her neck as she walked up the main street, grateful that she had brought her Canada Goose jacket which could withstand even the coldest weather. The sun was high in the sky but any heat it provided was whipped away by the Arctic breeze that blew down the street. The houses and their Halloween decorations cheered her up, and she smiled at the pumpkins and the spiders' webs draped all over the display in the grocery shop window. The bakery was next door and Allegra was happy to step into the warm shop where the smell of freshly baked bread, laced with vanilla from the cookies just out the oven, made her mouth water. The shop assistant greeted Allegra with a smile and a cheery 'hello', and offered her one of the cookies as a sample.

'We've only just tried this recipe,' she said. 'What do you think?'

'Fantastic,' Allegra said, when she had swallowed the first bite. 'It tastes very buttery with a touch of honey and vanilla. I'd give it five out of five stars.'

'That's lovely to hear,' the woman said. 'I think we can say it's a hit, then.'

'Absolutely,' Allegra replied. 'I'll take a dozen. And then four of the tea cakes. It's for a morning coffee at Lucille's house,' she added.

'I know,' the woman said as she filled a paper bag. 'And you're the visitor from America who'll be staying at Starlight Cottages for a few weeks.' The woman held out her hand. 'Welcome to Sandy Cove. I hope you'll have a lovely time despite the weather. I'm Carmel, by the way.'

Allegra shook the woman's hand. 'And my name is Allegra. So nice to meet you, Carmel.'

'Lovely to meet you, too,' Carmel said. She closed the bag and handed it to Allegra. 'Say hello to Lucille and tell her to let me know how she likes the new recipe.'

'I will,' Allegra promised. She paid the bill and said goodbye, promising to come back soon to taste their famous muffins.

It didn't take her long to find Lucille's house with the green door. Allegra didn't even have to knock as the door flew open the minute she stepped inside the neat front garden.

'There you are,' Lucille exclaimed. 'I was wondering if you had got lost.'

'I was chatting to Carmel in the bakery.' Allegra handed Lucille the bag. 'She had some tasty cookies that I couldn't help buying instead of the ginger snaps. She said to let her know what you think.'

'Wonderful.' Lucille took the bag. 'Come inside. Dominic is already here and I've made coffee. Go into the living room,' she urged as Allegra took off her jacket and hung it on a peg in the hall. 'The door on the left. I'll be back in a minute with the cookies and tea cakes.'

Lucille's living room was furnished in a chintzy country house style, with a sofa and matching chairs in a William Morris fabric arranged in front of a blazing fire. There was a deep red Indian carpet on the floor and the walls were hung with some beautiful oil paintings and watercolours that gave the room a vibrant air. But Allegra didn't have a chance to look around as an older man with thinning white hair rose stiffly from one of the chairs as she came in.

'Hello there,' he said. 'You must be the young lady from America. I'm Dominic Foley.'

Allegra shook his hand. 'Hi, Dominic. I'm Allegra. So nice to meet you.'

'Delighted,' Dominic said. His eyes were warm as he smiled at her.

'Sit down, the two of you,' Lucille ordered as she entered with a tray laden with a silver coffee pot, three china cups and a plate with cookies and buttered tea cakes which she put on the mahogany coffee table in front of the sofa. 'I forgot the milk and sugar,' she said, looking concerned.

'I take it black,' Dominic assured her.

'Me too,' Allegra said.

'Grand. Please sit down, so,' Lucille ordered.

Allegra sat down on the sofa. 'I love this room,' she said. 'So bright and cheerful.'

'Thank you.' Lucille busied herself with pouring coffee into cups. 'It's a little shabby-chic, I suppose. But I like it. Most of the stuff in here is from my former life as the wife of a country squire. Remnants of old decency, as my father would say.'

Dominic laughed. 'Yes, Lucille, that's exactly what I was thinking myself, but was afraid to say it.'

Lucille handed Allegra a cup of coffee. 'Why were you afraid?'

'I thought you might think I was making fun of you.'

'And what if you were?' Lucille asked as she gave Dominic his cup. 'Would I care? Not at all. If it makes you laugh, go for it, I say.' She sat down beside Allegra and passed the plate to Dominic. 'Here, dig in. I believe the new recipe is a huge hit.'

There was a brief silence while they all sampled the cookies.

'Yummy, aren't they?' Allegra said.

'Indeed,' Dominic replied, when he had swallowed.

'Delicious.' Lucille finished her cookie, put her cup on the table and looked at Dominic. 'Do you want to be typically Irish and talk about the weather, the latest news and maybe what the government is up to, or can we get straight to the reason I asked you here today?'

'I thought it might be a ploy to chat me up,' Dominic said with a glint of mischief in his pale blue eyes. 'And that maybe Allegra here was the chaperone.'

'Don't be silly,' Lucille said sternly. 'I told you what I wanted to know, so dish, as they say in the movies.'

Dominic chuckled. 'You certainly don't take any prisoners, Lucille.' He fished out a small leatherbound notebook and a few bits of paper from his inside pocket. 'But enough banter. Here are a few things from my father's desk. Things from his time as a butler up at the big house, I mean.' He handed the notebook to Lucille. 'This is just some notes about people who worked on the estate. My father was butler there until just before I was born in 1940. I think the family lost a lot of money during the war and had to cut down on staff. In any case, nobody entertained anymore, so there was no need for butlers or housemaids. I think they also shut part of the house and only lived in a few rooms because of the shortage of coal and turf. Then my father went to work as a clerk in a solicitor's office here in the village. All gone now, but they were quite busy in those days.'

Lucille flicked through the notebook and gave it to Allegra. 'Here, this is your story, so you must do most of the research.'

'You'll find a mention of a Sean Walsh there,' Dominic said. 'He was working as both groom and chauffeur at the house until the end of 1938.'

'Oh yes,' Allegra said as she saw the name on the very first page. 'He's listed here as having collected his monthly salary in December. And then there is a note about him getting a new uniform.' She turned the pages and discovered a few more mentions. 'S. *Walsh – day off for father's funeral*,' she read out loud. 'That's very sad.'

'Oh yes, his father died quite young,' Dominic said. 'My own father mentioned that when we talked about the people who lived in the coastguard station. Sean's mother stayed on with some of his siblings in the cottage for a while. And then

Sean went to America and started working over there, sending money home to his mother.'

'And Davina?' Allegra asked. 'Did your father say anything about her when he talked about the old days?'

'Oh yes.' Dominic passed the bits of paper to Allegra. 'He was very fond of her. A feisty girl. Very pretty. Wonderful rider. But stubborn and strong-willed. She and her father often had rows. He was fond of her but didn't like how she went her own way. She was supposed to go to London to be a debutante, but she refused. Said it was all silly and she would choose her own husband if she ever wanted to get married.'

Allegra looked at one of the pieces of paper. 'This is a letter to someone called Liam.'

'My father,' Dominic said. 'As the butler he was called Mr Foley, but Davina called him by his first name. That's just the way she was.'

Allegra felt a shiver up her spine as she held the letter written by Davina.

Dear Liam,

Just a little note to say thank you for your discretion concerning what happened this morning. I know you respect my privacy and will not breathe a word to anyone. It will all work out in the end to everyone's satisfaction, but, for now, I want to keep it under my hat, so to speak, and yours, too, if you know what I mean. Fond regards to your lovely wife, Mary, and the family.

Davina

'What was that about?' Allegra asked.

Dominic shrugged. 'No idea. I have a feeling he accidentally saw or heard something that she wanted to keep secret.'

'Could it be that he saw Sean and Davina cuddling somewhere?' Lucille suggested.

'That's possible,' Dominic agreed.

'Do you know if Davina went to America around that time?' Allegra asked.

'No idea,' Dominic said again. 'I only know that Sean went there but came back just as war was declared in Europe. He wanted to look after his family. His mother was very poor after her husband died. She had to leave the coastguard cottage around then and she had nowhere to live. But then it appears that Sean came into quite a lot of money just after that happened and he bought a house for her in Dingle town because he had found work there. No idea where that money came from. I believe the descendants of his family still live in that house. It's a shop or something now that they run together.'

Lucille's face brightened. 'Really? Then we must go there and talk to them, Allegra. What do you say?'

'Of course,' Allegra exclaimed. 'That's obvious. We could maybe see if we can contact them first.'

'Why?' Lucille asked. 'Isn't it better to surprise them? Maybe they'll be delighted to see the ring and hear your story. And they'll know a lot more than we have managed to find out today, even if that has been very useful,' she added, smiling at Dominic.

'Well, that's a relief,' Dominic said. He finished his coffee and put the cup on the table. 'Is there anything else I can help you with?'

'Not unless you have anything further to tell us about Sean and Davina, or if they were ever engaged,' Allegra said.

Dominic looked surprised. 'Engaged? I doubt that very much. That wouldn't have been acceptable in either of their families, you see.'

'So I've heard.' Allegra thought for a moment. 'But that letter she wrote to your father suggests he had come across her doing something she shouldn't. As Lucille suggested, he could have seen the two of them together.'

'That is a likely explanation,' Dominic said. 'But there is no way of knowing.'

'But they must have been on Cape Cod together in May or June 1939,' Allegra insisted. 'The ring, and what it said in the article...' She paused, feeling a growing frustration. She had hoped this old man with his connections to Strawberry Hill would have had more information. But all he had were little bits that didn't add up She looked at him while she tried to put it all together. 'Sean Walsh worked as a groom and chauffeur at the house,' she started. 'And then he left to go to America, but he came back when his father died.'

Dominic nodded. 'That's right.'

'Then he came into a lot of money somehow a while later,' Allegra continued. 'And bought his mother a house in Dingle. So that's all you can tell me about him. But what about Davina? Where does she fit into the story?'

'I have a feeling she's a very important ingredient,' Lucille cut in. 'We just have to keep looking.' She turned to Allegra. 'But I think you should also try to let it go a bit. Relax, enjoy your holiday and get to know this area. No need to get obsessed.'

'I know,' Allegra said, touched by Lucille's empathy. 'But it's too late. I am obsessed already.' She sighed and drained her cup. 'I thought it would be good for me to turn my mind to something else after all the sadness.' She looked at Dominic. 'I recently lost my father, you see. We were very close. And now I'm trying to live again.'

Dominic reached across the coffee table and patted her hand. 'I'm so sorry, my dear. I know how hard it is to let go of someone you loved. My wife passed away a few years ago and it took me quite a while to accept it and move on.'

'It can take years,' Lucille said. 'I think moving here was what helped me. A new life, new friends and a lot of new activities and hobbies. Just like you, Dominic. I know you're very active in the garden club as well as Wednesday bingo.'

'That's the only club you don't run,' Dominic countered. 'So I thought I'd have a go there. I could hardly join the ladies who knit, could I?'

'We crochet,' Lucille corrected. 'And we do other crafts as well.' She turned to Allegra. 'Are you good at things like that?'

'Not at all,' Allegra protested. 'I never did any kind of sewing or crocheting. My sister, Lucia, used to do crewel work, though, but she doesn't have the time anymore.'

Dominic rose stiffly. 'I'm sorry, ladies, but I have to go. My daughter is coming to lunch, so I have to tidy up my house.'

Lucille got up. 'I'll see you out, Dominic. Thank you so much for coming and for trying to help us with our research.'

'I hope it was helpful,' Dominic said. 'Delighted to meet you, young lady. I'll let you know if I come across anything else I might have overlooked.'

'That would be great,' Allegra replied.

Lucille saw Dominic to the door, and came back a few minutes later, her cheeks pink. 'That old fox asked me for a date,' she said and sat down.

'Did you accept?' Allegra asked, trying not to laugh at Lucille's expression.

'More fool me, but I did.' Lucille patted the back of her hair. 'It's not every day this old gal gets an offer of dinner in a posh place. I'll have to dig out my best frock, the only one I have, but it will be lovely to dress up and go out with a nice man, even if we're both past our sell-by date.'

'I don't think you're ever too old to date,' Allegra stated.

'I'm glad to hear a young thing like you say that.' Lucille leaned forward and looked intently at her. 'And what about you? Have you been on any fancy dates lately?'

'No,' Allegra said. 'There's no one in my life right now. But I will try to go out more when I get back home.'

'You should,' Lucille said and sat back, picking up a cookie from the plate and taking a bite. 'Life is so short. You must go out there and live a little.'

'I know,' Allegra said, smiling at Lucille's zest for life. 'And I will.'

'Don't wait too long,' Lucille said. 'But now we have to work out a plan. I was just thinking that we should split up. I'll go to Dingle and you should go back to Strawberry Hill and see if you can look around the house. I'm sure you could pick up something there.'

'How do I do that?' Allegra asked.

'Call that Gwen woman and ask if you could see the estate. Say that you're taking notes for the Christmas event. You're supposed to be Lydia's assistant, aren't you?'

'Yeah, well...' Allegra hesitated while she thought of Gwen's forbidding face. 'She seems a little stern. But that could be just the way she looks. She was quite friendly once we got talking. All the same, I'd hate to intrude.

'Don't worry about that. If you want to find things out, you have to ask people and do things that might seem pushy,' Lucille stated. 'But in this case, you have the perfect excuse. No need to rush into it, though. We can do it all at the weekend. I don't have the time until then anyway.'

'I'll ask Lydia for Gwen's number,' Allegra promised.

Lucille nodded. 'Good. But now I'm going upstairs for my nap. And I think you should go for a walk. You haven't seen much of the area since you came. There are some wonderful places just a stone's throw from here. Like the walk out to the headland, where you can see the Skelligs. That *Star Wars* movie was shot at Skellig Michael, you know.'

'Oh, I read about that somewhere,' Allegra said. She got up from the sofa. 'I'll go straight away and I'll take photos to send to my niece and nephew back home. They'll be so excited that I'm so close to that island. Thanks for reminding me.'

'Today is a good day to see it as it's so bright.' Lucille started to tidy up the cups and plates. 'I'd better put these away before I go for my nap. Then I'm having tea this afternoon at Mrs O'Dea's house. It's the first time she's ever invited me.' Lucille looked at Allegra with a rebellious expression. 'She's one of those domineering types. Thinks she can run this village as if it's her own little kingdom. She's mellowed lately, but I have to keep an eye on her so she doesn't start muscling in on my projects. We're both on the committee for the library Halloween party on Saturday. I think she's going to try to butter me up so I'll agree to all her suggestions. But if that's her plan, she has another think coming.'

Allegra had to laugh. 'That sounds scary. I wouldn't want to argue with you about something like that.'

'Indeed,' Lucille said. 'Nobody would be foolish enough. But that woman is a bit of a daredevil. Nice enough, but you have to keep her in her box. I bet she'll be serving me her barm brack and then telling me that it will be served at the party instead of mine – which has already been decided. But that's not going to happen.'

'What's a barm brack?' Allegra asked.

'It's a kind of fruit cake that's served at Halloween. It usually has an item or two inside, like a ring and a coin and even a pea. Whoever gets one of those things in their slice will have good or bad luck or get married within the year. Just superstition, really, but good fun.' Lucille paused. 'Have you bought a ticket to the party? It's twenty euros and the proceeds will go to St Vincent de Paul.'

'No. Where can I buy one?'

'Usually at the library. But you can buy it from me right now.' Lucille picked up a large handbag from the small side table beside the sofa and started to rummage around in it. 'Here they are,' she said and pulled out a stack of tickets. She tore one off and handed it to Allegra. 'There you go. You can pay me later if you like.'

'It's okay, I can do it now. Hold on.' Allegra went to find her jacket in the hall and took her wallet from the inside pocket. She gave a twenty-euro bill to Lucille, who had followed her out. 'There. Not sure I'll go, though. I won't know anyone. And isn't it fancy dress or something?'

'Yes. We'll all be wearing some strange costume or other. But do come,' Lucille urged. 'You might not know anyone when you arrive, but by the time you leave you'll have a whole lot of new friends, I promise.' She lowered her voice and winked. 'Mrs O'Dea is going to be the Queen of Hearts, I've heard. That alone is a spectacle not to be missed.'

'What about you?' Allegra asked.

'That's a secret,' Lucille said mysteriously. 'Oh, do come, Allegra. It'll cheer you up. I'll think of a costume for you. You could be a zombie or a ghost or a witch or...' Lucille stopped and laughed. 'I'm getting carried away. Off you go on your walk and don't worry. We have several days to think of your outfit. And if you meet anyone who'd like to go...' Lucille stopped. 'I just had another one of my brilliant ideas.' She handed Allegra the book of tickets. 'Here, sell them a ticket. Tell them it'll be the most fun they'll have this side of Christmas. You never know who you'll meet in the next few days.'

Allegra took the tickets. 'I'll do my best. But don't hold your breath. I might not meet anyone at all.'

'That would be impossible around here,' Lucille stated. 'Except if you locked yourself into your bedroom for days, and even then, someone might break down the door and ask if you want a bowl of their mammy's home-made chicken soup. That's the way it is around here. Anyone with plans to be a hermit has come to the wrong place.'

'That sounds nice,' Allegra said, thinking what a contrast it was to the anonymity of Boston or New York.

'Can be a nuisance, but it's mostly quite comforting,' Lucille said and made a shooing gesture. 'Off you go for your walk before it rains. I'll be in touch about what to do next and how we can find out more about Sean and Davina.'

Allegra said goodbye and left Lucille standing on the doorstep waving. As she made her way back down the street, onto the path that led out to the headland where the outline of the Skelligs shimmered in the distance, she went through what she had learned from Dominic. It was strange that Davina didn't figure much in the tale of Sean's life after he came back from America.

It was as if there was a piece missing in a jigsaw – a key one that would reveal the whole picture. She had to find that bit somehow. She was suddenly sure it would be found at Strawberry Hill.

12

'Allegra?' a man's voice asked.

'Uh, yes?' Allegra replied, the phone to her ear while she switched off her laptop.

She was sitting on the big sofa in front of the fire and had been looking at the Sandy Cove website to see if there was anything on the history page about the years during and just after the Second World War that would give her some kind of clue. 'Who's this?'

'This is Max Courtney-Smythe. We met yesterday at Strawberry Hill.'

'Oh yes, of course,' Allegra said, trying to appear as if she had forgotten, even though he had been on her mind ever since. 'How did you get my number?'

'Gwen gave it to me after I asked her to get it from that nice friend of yours.'

'Oh, I see.' Allegra paused, suddenly tongue-tied. His voice was like a summer breeze in her ear, melodious and sweet with a slight lilt. She could listen to it for hours. 'So why did you call me? Just to say hi?' she asked in a flippant tone in an effort to appear cool.

'I wanted to ask you if you want to come for a ride with me tomorrow morning? And then I could take you through the house afterwards, if you want to see it. We could look for clues about Auntie Davina.'

Allegra sat up. This was a stroke of luck. Here was a chance to do what Lucille had suggested and she didn't even have to ring up and ask. But it seemed to involve getting up on a horse.

'Ride?' she said just to make sure she had heard correctly. 'You mean on a horse?'

'No, a donkey,' he said.

'What?'

'I was joking,' he said with a throaty laugh. 'Of course I meant a horse. Or horseback riding as you call it over there in the States.'

'But I don't know how to ride,' Allegra protested.

'Of course you do. You said you used to trot around on an old horse at a farm in Vermont,' he reminded her.

'Yes, but that was years ago when I was a child. And I really don't call that proper riding.'

'I'm sure you're just being modest,' he argued. 'The forecast is great for tomorrow morning so it'll be lovely to be outside. Blue skies, the trees blazing, the green grass, the mountains and the blue waters of the river. Inland Kerry is just as nice as the seaside, you know.'

'Don't you have to work?' she asked to gain time to think. While the prospect of a morning with Max was enticing, getting up on one of those horses was not.

'Not tomorrow. I was at the site for a few hours yesterday, and I did some work on the plans, but I don't want to waste a beautiful day. I want to ride around the estate, and then I thought of you, and how you seemed to love the horses.'

'I do love them,' Allegra said softly. 'But I don't think I could actually ride them.'

'I think you could,' he argued. 'We have a lovely mare here

called Betsy. She's nearly twenty years old and as gentle as a lamb. I'd put my granny on her without fear. She used to be a brilliant event horse but is now retired. We love her so much and we treat her like the lady she always was. Don't you think you could trot around on her with me for a bit? We'll take it nice and slow, of course.'

'*Weeelll,*' Allegra said, her sense of adventure winning over her fears. 'I suppose I could try.'

'Good girl,' Max said approvingly. 'Could you be here at ten? I'll tack up the horses and I'll be ready to go when you get here.'

'I could. But what do I wear?'

'A warm jacket and jeans would be fine,' Max replied. 'You could borrow Gwen's boots if your feet aren't bigger than hers. If they are, I think my sister Edwina might have left a pair here. Her feet are huge. And we have plenty of helmets in all sizes in the tack room.'

'Great,' Allegra said, her spirits soaring at the thought of seeing Max the following morning. Getting up on an actual horse would be a challenge she wasn't sure she could meet, but she'd worry about that later. 'I'll be there in the morning as soon as I've had breakfast.'

'Splendid,' Max said. 'See you tomorrow, then. Bye for now.'

'Bye, Max,' Allegra said, her voice wobbly with excitement.

She hung up, hoping she hadn't sounded too eager. But what did it matter? She was hugely excited at the prospect of riding a horse, even if that part was scary, and looking through that house – with him. It would be wonderful to find out more about Davina and establish if she was the young woman who had been engaged to Sean Walsh and then lost her ring. Allegra was now sure this was the case, but she needed confirmation. But how could she find out? Maybe, as Max had said, there would be clues in the house, even if they couldn't go into her room and search her belongings before the probate was over.

All those thoughts swirled through Allegra's mind the next morning as she showered, dressed and had a quick mug of tea and a slice of toast. Her mind was still on Davina and Sean during her drive up the narrow country road to Strawberry Hill. But when she drove up to the gates and glanced at the stone eagles, she thought of riding a horse with a lot more than trepidation. Why had she agreed to this mad scheme? She would probably end up in a ditch with a broken leg. Would her travel insurance cover such an injury? And if she had to stay longer than three weeks, would Annie be so annoyed she'd get fired? What if...

The results of a potential fall grew to a crescendo in her head and, by the time she arrived around the back of the house and parked the car at the entrance to the courtyard, she was planning her own funeral. Allegra sat there staring into space, trying to calm down before she pulled herself together and got out of the car.

Max, dressed in a dark green polo neck and tan breeches, opened the door to the utility room and smiled at Allegra. She was about to say he looked like something out of *Horse & Hound*, but stopped herself. No need to sound sarcastic. He couldn't help being so ridiculously good-looking.

'Hello there,' she said cheerily.

'Hi and welcome,' he said. 'Come in and we'll sort out the boot situation. Gwen has to take a horse to somewhere in Limerick but she's on the phone to our solicitor before she leaves. We decided to tell him about your story and now he's going to try to find out if Davina was married and had additional heirs. It appears we can go through her belongings provided we make sure it all stays here. But Gwen is trying to get written permission from him just to be on the safe side.'

'Oh,' Allegra said on her way inside. 'That'll be interesting.' The two dogs, who had been sleeping on their beds, got up and padded towards her, their tails wagging. Allegra crouched down to pat them. 'Hi there,' she said, stroking the soft heads. 'No barking this time?'

'They know you're a friend,' Max said.

'That's good. They're lovely dogs.' Allegra got up. 'I hope it won't make you too sad to go through Davina's stuff.'

'I think it might be sad for Gwen. She was the one who was closest to Auntie Davina. I wasn't really here that much during her last years. And I was a little lax about visiting her in the nursing home,' he said, looking slightly guilty. 'But by then she was quite ill and didn't seem to be that aware of what was going on.'

'I'm sure it made no difference,' Allegra said, trying to comfort him. 'She was probably in her own world by then and thinking about other things. My father was like that during his last months. Not really in this world, but drifting off into the next one.'

'I'm sure you're only saying that to cheer me up,' Max replied. 'But thank you for making me feel a little less guilty.' He moved away from the door and lifted a pair of leather riding boots from a shelf crammed with all kinds of footwear for riding. 'Here, see if these fit you.' He glanced at her feet. 'I'd say they should.'

Allegra pulled off her shoes, put her foot into one of the boots and gave it a tug. Her foot slid easily down into it and felt surprisingly comfortable. 'They fit fine,' she said. She ran her hand over the butter-soft leather. 'Lovely. I hope Gwen won't mind me using them.'

'Handmade in England,' Max said. 'And they're not Gwen's but Davina's.'

Allegra froze, her foot halfway into the other one. 'They were Davina's?' she whispered, feeling an odd vibe.

'Yes. Do you feel weird wearing them?'

Allegra pulled on the other boot. 'No,' she said after the initial shock had died down. The boots were beautiful, if a little scratched here and there, and felt as if they were made for her. 'I feel honoured.'

'I thought it was right somehow,' Max said softly. 'Considering you found her ring and came all the way here to give it back.'

'If she was that Davina,' Allegra filled in.

'I think she was,' Max said. 'Gwen isn't so sure, but I am. I don't know why, but that ring spoke to me when I saw it.'

'Yes, me too. Isn't that strange?'

'Very,' he said, looking at her with an odd expression. He gestured at her feet. 'Do they fit?'

'Nearly perfectly,' Allegra said and wriggled her toes. 'A tiny bit big in the toes but that's a good thing.'

'True,' Max said as he pulled on his own boots and took a waxed jacket from one of the hooks.

The door to the kitchen opened and Gwen stuck her head out. 'Hi there, Allegra. Do the boots fit okay?'

'Nearly perfectly,' Allegra replied. 'Thanks for letting me use them.'

'You're welcome. And remember that you're doing this at your own risk.'

'Of course,' Allegra replied, meeting Gwen's stern eyes. 'It's my decision to ride and nobody else's. I take full responsibility should anything happen.'

'Good.' Gwen shot a look at Max. 'I got the confirmation email. So it's okay to go into Davina's room and look at her letters and stuff. Only—' She stopped as a shadow seemed to fall over her eyes. 'I don't think I can do it quite yet. It's too soon.'

'It's okay,' Max said. 'I know how hard it must be for you. I'll go in and see if there's anything important. If there's a diary or letters, we have to look at them. They could contain information about her early life and maybe establish if there's anything to the notion that she might have been married to this Sean fellow.'

Gwen nodded. 'Yes. We have to find out if it's true. Thanks for understanding, Max. Enjoy your ride. I'll be off to Limerick in a while.' She closed the door without any further comments.

'She looked so sad,' Allegra said, her heart going out to Gwen. 'It must be hard for her if she was close to your great-aunt.'

'She was,' Max said. 'They were very alike, those two. Davina was, of course, our grandfather's sister, and about fifty years older than Gwen. But, despite the huge age difference, they were like mother and daughter. Davina was a tough cookie and could be very difficult. Gwen could deal with her, though. Davina didn't listen to anyone else. She had this tough surface but I always had a feeling she was soft on the inside. But the way she was brought up meant she never showed her true feelings. It just wasn't done. Stiff upper lip, never complain and all that. I never took to that kind of attitude.'

'Me neither,' Allegra agreed. She couldn't imagine not being allowed to express herself or show how she felt. 'I normally just let it rip when I'm upset. Not in public, though,' she added in case he thought she was the hysterical type.

'I scream into the wind when I'm on my own,' Max said. 'And I find it hard to hold in the tears at funerals. Must be my Celtic side.' He zipped up his jacket. 'But let's get going. It's a grand day and we'd better enjoy it while we can.'

They left the house and headed down to the stables, the leaves crunching under their feet. The air was crisp and cold and the wind played with Allegra's hair, a few wisps fluttering against her face. The mountains rose behind the green fields and she could see the river glinting in the distance as it snaked through the landscape. It was a lovely autumn day of the kind that made one's spirits soar, and Allegra felt a dart of pure joy as she breathed in the clean air. But when the stables came into view and they could hear a whinny from a horse, butterflies started to flutter in her stomach.

Max glanced at her. 'That's just a greeting. Pat is always happy to see me. Don't worry, Betsy will look after you. She has some kind of radar and knows when she has a novice on her back.'

'She won't need a radar,' Allegra said with a nervous laugh. 'I'm shaking all over already.'

'You'll be fine.'

'Easy for you to say, being a pro. I'm just a very unhappy amateur.'

He stopped and looked at her. 'It's okay if you want to drop out. I can ride Pat on my own and you could go for a walk instead.'

'And lose all my self-respect?' Allegra shook her head. 'No, I have to face my fears, my therapist told me.'

'You had therapy?' Max asked, looking at her curiously.

'Yeah, for a while,' Allegra replied. 'But I stopped going when she started telling me how to grieve. It was as if I was supposed to follow a schedule or something. I didn't like the way she looked at me as if I had failed. Except I do think she was right about me facing my fears. But not about grieving according to a timetable.'

'I suppose you can't grieve to order,' Max remarked. 'Or feel the way some people think you should feel.'

'Exactly,' Allegra said, touched by his empathy. She glanced at him. 'You lost a parent too?'

He nodded. 'Yes. My father. When I was a teenager. It was tough. Especially as my relationship with my mother was a bit strained. Still is. But hey, let's not go there right now.'

'Of course not,' Allegra said. 'Not on such a nice day.'

'Maybe another time,' Max said with a look that told her the subject was closed.

'If you ever want to talk, I'd be happy to listen,' Allegra said. 'But now I have to try and be brave enough to ride a horse. I'm going to do this if it kills me.'

Max grinned. 'It won't kill you. Come on, ya big chicken, Betsy is waiting. I think you'll like her.'

'I thought you were going to say you admire my courage,' Allegra remarked.

'You don't need courage to ride Betsy. But come on,' he urged as another whinny echoed through the yard. 'Pat's getting impatient.'

In the stable yard they were greeted by a clattering of buckets from the tack room. Connor stuck his head out and gave them a wide-toothed grin.

'Hi there,' he said. 'I'm just doing the oats here. But I'll feed Pat and Betsy after your ride. No need to upset their stomachs or make them hot for your ride.'

'Good lad,' Max said approvingly as Connor passed them with a bucket. 'Come on, Allegra. Let's find you a helmet and then we'll get you up on Betsy and we'll be off.'

'Okay,' Allegra said, torn between the wish to walk away and the urge to finally be up on that horse and get it over with.

Max selected a helmet covered in black velvet and put it on Allegra's head. 'How does that feel?'

'Fine,' Allegra said when she had wiggled the helmet a bit. She fastened the strap under her chin and smiled at Max. 'I suddenly feel like a real rider.'

Max put on his own helmet and nodded. He took Allegra's arm and steered her out of the tack room and down the line of stables until he came to a stop in front of a stall where a large grey horse stuck its head out, looking at them with huge eyes.

'This is Betsy,' he said.

'Hello, Betsy,' Allegra said and touched the velvety nose. The horse nibbled gently at her hand and Allegra was immediately captivated and stroked the silky neck. 'She's beautiful.'

'I wouldn't go that far, but she's quite a handsome old thing,' Max said affectionately, stroking the horse's head. Then he opened the stable door. 'Grab her bridle and lead her out to that stepladder over there. Then I'll hold her while you get up.'

Allegra did as she was told and led the horse over to the stepladder. Then Max took the bridle while Allegra got up on the stepladder, her knees shaking slightly. But once she was in the saddle, she felt a calm come over her as the horse stood stock-still as if waiting for her to relax.

'How are the stirrups?' Max asked. 'Put your feet in them and I'll adjust the leathers.'

Allegra slipped her feet into the stirrups. 'A little long, I think,' she said.

'Thought so.' Max put his hand on her leg. 'Bend your knee so I can see how much I should take it up.'

Allegra felt a shock wave go through her at the touch of his warm hand through her jeans. Their eyes met for a split second and then she looked away while she pulled up her leg.

'Okay,' she said, her voice oddly hoarse. She bent her knee and then Max pulled at the strap and adjusted it to make it shorter. Then he went around to the other side and did the same.

'How does this feel?' he asked, holding on to the bridle.

'Seems better,' Allegra said. 'You can let go now.'

'Great.' Max dropped the bridle and backed away, his eyes on Allegra. 'Are you sure the stirrups are the right length?'

Allegra nodded. 'They feel fine.'

'What kind of saddle did you use on that old horse in Vermont?'

'We didn't have a saddle. We rode bareback,' Allegra replied. 'This saddle is such a luxury compared to that.'

'Bareback, eh?' Max said, looking impressed. 'Well, in that case you should be fine. Except you might not have done the rising trot.'

'Eh, what's that?' Allegra asked as Max jumped up on his horse without the aid of the stepladder.

'Whoa,' Max said to the skittish horse. 'Calm down, willya?' He tightened his legs around the horse's flanks and seemed to shift his weight, which had the desired effect. The horse settled down and then they walked out of the yard, Betsy following Pat without any urging from Allegra. Then Max turned his head and smiled. 'The rising trot? That's when you meet the horse's movements by rising and sitting in rhythm. But don't worry about it. Try to get into it without thinking. We'll trot down this path and see how you manage.'

'Okay,' Allegra said. 'But don't expect miracles. I'll probably fall off.'

'I bet you won't.' Max touched his heels to his horse's sides and Pat immediately broke into a trot, Betsy following his lead. Allegra found herself awkwardly bobbing up and down for a while until she seemed to automatically find a rhythm and rose and sat as the horse trotted on with a wonderfully smooth gait.

'How are you doing?' Max shouted as Pat surged ahead, nearly breaking into a canter.

'Fine!' Allegra shouted back. 'Betsy's teaching me to ride.'

Max glanced at her over his shoulder. 'You're doing brilliantly. Let's do a little canter.'

'Nooo!' Allegra protested.

'Just sit in the saddle and relax. You can grab on to the neck strap if you feel wobbly.'

Then, without another word, Pat broke into a canter and Betsy wasn't far behind. Allegra found herself sitting down more deeply in the saddle and tried to grip with her legs, grabbing the neck strap for extra security. But there was no need. Betsy's canter was even smoother than her trot and Allegra felt as if she was sitting in a rocking chair. She started to enjoy the motion and let Betsy take the lead, galloping easily past Pat, loving the feeling of speed and the wind whistling in her ears.

'Easy!' Max shouted. 'Pull her in.'

Allegra pulled on the reins and Betsy slowed down before she came to a stop so sudden Allegra was pitched forward and had to put her arms around Betsy's neck to stop herself falling off. Her helmet slipped over her eyes and she couldn't see a thing. Then she pushed her helmet back and struggled to sit back up while Max laughed hysterically. She glared at him while she tried to compose herself.

'Stop it. I was nearly killed there and all you can do is laugh.'

'Sorry,' Max said when he had calmed down. 'But you looked so ridiculous hanging off Betsy's neck. I think you got a little over-excited there.'

Allegra straightened her jacket and sat back. 'Yeah, right. I know. Happy to entertain you. Could we just walk for a bit now?'

'Of course.' Max pointed ahead. 'We can walk the horses along the river and then back to the old tower I showed you the other day. We'll take a closer look at it and then you can see how it can be included in that Christmas fundraiser you're doing with your friend. Great idea, by the way, even if Gwen isn't too enthusiastic.'

'Isn't she?' Allegra asked as she rode beside Max towards the river. 'Why not?'

'I think she's in denial about the house and all its problems. She thinks once the probate is finished, we'll just go back to living the way we were. She'll be running the yard and living in two rooms, with me coming here for the odd break. But there are huge problems ahead. The inheritance tax for a start. That will run into a vast sum because of the value of the land. We'll have to sell most of it off. And then there's the house.' Max sighed deeply. 'We should sell it, but Gwen would be devastated. She grew up here and it's the only home she's ever had.'

'Didn't you grow up here?' Allegra asked as the horses walked side by side down a narrow lane lined with trees and shrubs, the branches of which formed an archway above them.

'No, we only came here occasionally. I grew up outside Dublin in another country house that belonged to my grandmother. Much smaller and easier to run. Then I went to boarding school in England and then came back to study architecture at Trinity College in Dublin. This place didn't mean as much to me or Edwina, my sister, as it does to Gwen. And we weren't as close to our great-aunt as she was.'

'How come your great-aunt owned the house?'

'She outlived everyone else, including both my father and Gwen's. Amazing woman. She went on daily rides until she was over a hundred years old. I can still see her galloping around the place with a cigarette stuck in her mouth. Tough as an old boot. You'd have loved her, except her language might have shocked you. Swore like trooper and didn't suffer fools gladly. But she was dead honest and very loyal to those she loved.'

'Did she love you?' Allegra asked, touched by the warm expression in his eyes. She found it hard to imagine that this chain-smoking rough old woman had once been the young girl who had lost her engagement ring on a beach across the Atlantic.

'She adored me.' Max grinned and gave Pat a nudge with his boots. 'Let's trot down to the river.'

Betsy broke into a trot again, and this time, Allegra found herself moving in perfect time with the horse. 'She moves like a dancer,' she said to Max as she caught up with him.

'Yes, I know. She has a lot of thoroughbred in her, which is why she has this wonderful bounce. Davina broke her in and schooled her to perfection.'

Allegra nodded as they rounded a bend and could see a

view of the river. She pulled Betsy to a stop and stared, awed by the beauty around her.

'Oh, this is beautiful,' she mumbled as she looked across the green field, the blue band of the river and the weeping willows trailing their branches in the water.

She could hear the water rushing over rocks and boulders, and birdsong in the distance, and the cool breeze brought with it the smell of horse, damp earth and grass. They continued down the slope and as they arrived at the riverbank, a heron rose up in front of them and flew along the water with long sweeping movements of its wingspan until it disappeared around a bend.

'Majestic,' Allegra said.

'I always think they look primeval somehow,' Max said. 'Like something from when the earth began.'

'The dinosaur days,' Allegra said. 'Incredible to think that some dinosaurs are related to birds. Did you know that?'

'No, I didn't,' Max said, turning around in the saddle to look at her. 'How come you do?'

'Homework,' Allegra said. 'My nephew Joe did a project for school. I helped him with the research,' she added. 'He's ten and such a great kid.'

'I can tell you're very fond of him,' Max said, smiling.

'Yes, I am. He and Emma, his sister, are like my own children in a way. I get to look after them a lot because my sister and her husband have very busy lives.'

'And you don't?' Max enquired.

'Oh, I do, too, and I live in Boston and they're in New York. But we always go on vacation together. That's when I spend a lot of time with them.'

'So the parents can have some time off and enjoy themselves without worry,' Max filled in.

'Yeah, well, maybe. But I love them so much. I don't mind looking after them at all.' Allegra fiddled with the reins. 'It's true, though, that they use me as an unpaid babysitter. Sometimes I feel like saying no and that I'd like to go off somewhere else on my own.'

'But you did, didn't you? And now you're here all by yourself,' Max remarked.

'Yes. Lucia, my sister, didn't like it much when I said I was coming here for so long, but I promised to be back for Thanksgiving.'

'And will you?' Max asked, looking into her eyes.

'Of course,' Allegra replied, avoiding his gaze. 'I couldn't miss that. The kids would be so disappointed.'

He kept looking at her. 'Do you ever just think of yourself?'

'Not very often. That would be selfish,' Allegra protested.

Max shook his head. 'You're a very unusual girl.' Then he dug his heels into his horse's side and cantered away while Betsy did a little bunny-hop before she started to follow at an easy trot which turned into a canter.

Allegra sat deeper into the saddle, enjoying the motion of the horse, the wind against her face and the feeling of having met the challenge with such ease. Max continued around a bend and up the track until he came to a stop by the tower they had passed two days earlier.

Allegra looked up at the tower, its jagged edge outlined against the blue sky. 'Amazing,' she said. 'I think the kids will love exploring it.'

'I'd say they would,' Max agreed. 'And it's safe and still in good nick. As you can see, the iron door is solid. We could keep the door open and spray it with fake snow as it will lead into the Santa's grotto you'll be creating inside.'

'Great idea.' Allegra looked at him and smiled. 'I have a feeling you played here when you were a kid.'

'Oh, I did.' Max shielded his eyes against the bright sunlight and looked up at the tower. 'With friends from school who thought it so cool to come here and play among these ancient stones. We used to climb the stairs to the top and look out over the landscape and pretend we were knights fighting some enemy force. Great fun if you're ten years old.'

'I'm sure it was,' Allegra said, touched by the wistful look in his eyes.

He was so different today, the arrogance gone and replaced by a warmth she was sure he didn't bestow on many people. She felt privileged to be with him like this, riding this sweet horse and sharing snippets of their lives. He turned his head and their eyes met in a moment of complete complicity – as if two souls were connecting for just a second. It was as if time stood still for a while until the spell was broken by the sound of a car coming up the avenue at great speed, which made the horses shy and step sideways in sudden fright.

'Bloody hell,' Max exclaimed as he steadied his horse. 'You okay?'

'Yes,' Allegra replied, tightening her grip on the reins while Betsy calmed down. 'She was a little startled, but now she's fine.'

'Good.' Max sat back and tried his best to calm his horse, who was still jumping around. 'That's my sister coming up the avenue. She's not the considerate type. I'd better go and see what she wants. Let's get the horses settled first.'

When the horses were in the stables they returned to the house. 'Sorry about that,' Max said. 'But you handled Betsy really well.'

'She handled herself,' Allegra said. 'I didn't really have to do anything. I had a feeling she'd say sorry if she could speak.'

Max smiled. 'Yeah, she's a real lady. Takes one to know one, I should say.'

'Well, I...' Allegra didn't know quite what to say but, as they arrived at the house, the conversation came to an end.

A dark blue Audi was parked on the gravel in front of the steps. A blonde woman dressed in a fur-trimmed camel-hair coat was getting out of the car. But she was not alone. A pretty, dark-haired woman in a wax jacket, tight jeans and knee-high boots opened the passenger door and stepped onto the gravel.

'Hi, Max,' the blonde woman said and gave him a quick peck on the cheek.

'Hello, Edwina,' Max replied without much warmth in his voice. 'What are you doing here?'

'It's... uh... complicated,' Edwina said, glancing at Allegra. 'Hello there. I don't think we've met,' she said and held out her hand. 'I'm Edwina, Max's sister.'

Allegra shook the cold, limp hand. 'Allegra Casey,' she said. 'From Boston.'

'Oh?' Edwina looked surprised. 'Didn't know Max had an American girlfriend.'

'She's not my girlfriend,' Max said, looking irritated. 'Allegra arrived here recently. She works with a fundraising company and they're going to do an event here at Christmas and she wanted to look at the grounds and the house beforehand.'

'In Auntie Davina's boots?' Edwina asked sourly, glancing at Allegra's feet.

'Yes,' Max replied. 'We went riding as it's a nice day and Allegra didn't have any boots.' He looked at the other woman. 'Sorry. I should have said hello.' He held out his hand. 'I'm Max, Edwina's brother. And you are...?'

The woman smiled and shook Max's hand. 'Hi, Max. Nice to meet you. I'm Kate Vanderpump. And I'm actually related to you.'

'What?' Max asked, looking startled. 'Related? In what way?'

Edwina laughed, her blue eyes glittering with mischief. 'Wait till you hear this, Max.'

'Hear what?' Max said, looking even more annoyed.

'You should be sitting down actually, or you might keel over,' Edwina said, her voice bubbling with mirth.

'Please,' Max snapped. 'Spit it out.'

'Okay.' Edwina paused for a moment, looking as if she was going to burst. 'Kate says she's Auntie Davina's granddaughter.'

'What?' Max asked.

'You heard,' Edwina said. 'Kate claims to be Auntie Davina's granddaughter.'

Allegra felt her heart contract as she looked from Edwina to the other woman. Davina's granddaughter? Had she heard correctly? It couldn't be true. Could it?

13

Max gulped and stared at the woman who had introduced herself as Kate Vanderpump. 'Is this one of Edwina's silly jokes?'

'No,' Kate replied. 'It's true. Your great-aunt was my grand-mother. She married my grandfather in Scotland in 1950.'

'I find this hard to believe,' Max said, still looking shocked. 'She told us she was never married.'

'Well, she was,' Kate Vanderpump insisted. 'In 1950. And my mother, their daughter, was born shortly afterwards. Which means I'm your second cousin.'

Allegra felt a shiver go through her as she heard what the woman said. Her hand flew to her chest, where the ring nestled under her sweater. Was this possible? That the resolution was right here in front of her? The answer to all her questions? But if it was all true and this woman could prove it, what would happen now? Speechless, she stared at the woman and then looked at Max, who stood stock-still, his face pale. Something stirred in her memory.

'Vanderpump?' she said. 'Do you have anything to do with *Vanderpump Rules*?'

'No, but we're related,' Kate said. 'We're the Edinburgh Vanderpumps.'

'What's *Vanderpump Rules*?' Max asked, looking even more confused.

'It's a reality show set in a restaurant in LA,' Allegra replied. 'Very popular in the States.'

'Oh.' Max shrugged and turned back to Kate. 'Well, whatever. Let's leave that aside for now. How come you never came forward before? Why did you or your mother not contact Auntie Davina?'

'Because we didn't know who she was.' Kate Vanderpump looked coolly back at Max. 'I see this was a huge shock. I'm trying to take it in myself, now that I'm here.' She looked up at the façade. 'This is some pile of a building. Very nice, I have to say. Early Georgian?'

'Yes,' Max said.

'Should fetch quite a bit,' Kate remarked.

'Possibly,' Max mumbled. 'But we'll never know as it's not for sale.'

'That remains to be seen,' Kate said. 'Now that I'm one of you, it's a whole new situation.'

'Is it?' Max asked. 'I think that remains to be seen, too.'

'Well,' Edwina said after a minute of awkward silence, 'why are we still standing here in the cold? Why don't we go inside and have a cup of tea and let Kate tell you what she told me?'

'Good idea,' Max said.

'I think I'll leave you to it,' Allegra said, feeling she was intruding.

'No,' Max said. 'Stay and have some tea at least.' He started to move towards the back of the house. 'I'll put the kettle on. And pour myself a brandy from Gwen's secret stash in the larder,' he added grimly.

They all followed Max through the courtyard and into the utility room where they took off their coats and jackets while

Max continued into the kitchen and put on the kettle. The dogs, startled by the arrival of the group, jumped up from their beds and started to bark, immediately silenced by Max shouting, '*Sit!*' Buster sat but Lola remained standing, growling at Kate.

'Ignore her,' Edwina said. 'She can be a bit silly.'

'I'm not afraid of dogs,' Kate said but still kept a respectful distance.

Once in the kitchen, they sat down at the table while Max made tea and poured it into mugs that he passed around. Then he joined them and stared at Kate as he pulled up a chair and sat down.

'So,' he said, 'let's hear your story. How on earth did you find us? Or did Davina's solicitor find you?'

'It's a long story,' Kate said, exchanging a glance with Edwina.

'She found me,' Edwina said.

'How?' Max asked.

'Well,' Kate started, 'I was already following Edwina on Instagram. She's an influencer, you see.'

'I know,' Max said. 'Among other things.'

'What kind of influencer?' Allegra asked.

'Fashion,' Edwina said. 'I'm not really a full-time influencer and I don't make much money out of it. I'm a stylist and buyer for Brown Thomas in Dublin. A department store a bit like Saks in New York,' she explained. 'And I help out on the daytime programme on national TV sometimes.'

'I see,' Allegra said. 'I thought you might be into something like that by the way you look.'

'So glamorous,' Kate cut in. 'I love her style.'

'And the car,' Max filled in. 'Not your ordinary little banger, is it?'

'Certainly not,' Edwina retorted. 'Could we get back to the subject?'

'I'm all ears,' Max said, stirring sugar into his tea. 'So, you follow Edwina on Instagram. And then what?'

'What started all this doesn't really have anything to do with Edwina's Insta profile,' Kate said. 'That was just a weird coincidence, actually.'

Max nodded. 'Okay. So what happened to make you think you're Davina's granddaughter?'

'There was an article about Davina Courtney in *House and Garden* about a month or two ago,' Kate said. 'Just before she passed away. I thought it was strange she had the same name as my grandmother, who I had never met.'

'How come?' Max asked. 'I mean, why did you never meet her? The grandmother with the same name, I mean. Do you know why she seemed to have disappeared?'

'Yes, I do,' Kate replied. 'She left my grandfather and went back to Ireland when my mother was a baby and never came back.'

'That's hard to believe,' Max countered. 'How do we know this woman was our great-aunt? I mean, if Davina had a child, why didn't she ever talk about it? Did she just leave her own child behind and then live here for the rest of her life without even mentioning it? That seems incredible to me.'

'It's a little unusual,' Kate replied.

Max let out a snort. 'Unusual? Talk about the understatement of the year.'

Kate glared at Max. 'I have a feeling you don't believe me.'

'That's right. I don't,' Max said, returning Kate's gaze with a cool stare. 'But go on.'

'I had been told she and my grandfather broke up shortly after my mother was born and that they didn't have any contact after that,' Kate continued after a brief pause. 'She left the baby with Sean and went back to Ireland.'

'Sean who?' Allegra cut in, her heart beating faster. 'Was his name Sean Walsh?'

'Yes,' Kate replied. 'I thought I said that already. My grand-father's name was Sean Walsh.'

'Oh,' was all Allegra managed as she tried to take all this in.

'Why did they break up?' Max asked. 'I mean, there must have been a major row for your grandmother to up sticks just like that and leave her child behind.'

'I'm not sure what it was all about,' Kate said. 'All I know is that he then remarried a year later. My mother was brought up by Sean's second wife and thought all her life that she was her real mother. It was only just before he died that Sean told her the truth.' Kate drew breath and drank from her mug. 'That was ten years ago. My mother died of cancer two years later.'

'And she never wanted to get in touch with her real moth-er?' Allegra asked.

'No,' Kate replied. 'She said she couldn't bear meeting someone who'd leave her child like that. Her stepmother, who I called Granny, was the only mother she had, she said. I felt the same, really. She was my real grandmother, not the other one. And I had no idea where in Kerry this woman lived, or if she was still alive.'

Max looked at Edwina. 'So Auntie Davina lived here all this time having left her baby with her ex-husband in Scotland and never said a word or tried to contact her daughter? Hmm.'

'I know,' Edwina cut in. 'I found it hard to believe, too. I mean, Davina was rough and tough and an incredible horse-woman, but she wasn't made of stone. But then, I saw the proof and now I do believe it happened, and that Kate's story is true.'

'What proof?' Max asked.

'My mother's birth certificate,' Kate replied. 'And Sean and Davina's marriage certificate. They were married in a registry office in Edinburgh.'

'Holy mother,' Max said, staring at Kate. 'Can I see these papers?'

'No, they're with the solicitor in Killarney,' Edwina said. 'We just came from there.'

Max sighed and shook his head. 'Incredible. But can we wind the tape back to the beginning and hear how you ended up here, in our kitchen?'

'Of course,' Kate said and put her mug on the table. She sat back, her hands in her lap. 'I hadn't thought about that woman – the woman who is my real grandmother – for a long time. The granny I had always loved died only a year ago, so she was until then the most important person in my life – my rock, if you know what I mean.'

'I'm so sorry,' Allegra said. 'That must have been so hard for you.'

'Thank you,' Kate said. Then she turned to Max. 'As I said, I saw that item about this house in *House and Garden* which was included in a feature a few months ago about lost and forgotten country houses in Ireland. When I read about the old woman who lived here, I realised she had to be my grandmother. This was just before she died, I believe. Everything fitted. Her name, the county, her story...'

'What was in her story?' Max asked. 'I didn't read the article.'

'It said she had travelled to the United States in her youth and also spent some time in Scotland.'

'The States? And Scotland?' Max said, looking at Edwina. 'Did you know about that?'

'I didn't read that article either. But I remember that Davina did mention spending some time in Scotland once a long time ago,' Edwina said. 'But I thought she was there to buy horses or something. She never talked about what she did, did she?'

'Never,' Max said. He turned to Kate. 'Go on. What happened next?'

'I saw this house in a picture on Edwina's Instagram page a few weeks ago,' Kate continued. 'With a photo of Davina and a short little notice that she had died. I waited a little while before I contacted Edwina to tell her my end of the story.'

'Why did you wait?' Max asked. 'Why not come here, or even contact us straight away?'

'I thought I'd wait until after the funeral,' Kate said, putting a hand on Max's arm. 'To give you a little peace and space. I didn't want to upset anyone.'

'How considerate,' Max said with a hint of sarcasm. He pulled his arm away. 'So then, after having respectfully waited a few weeks, you decided to get in touch and claim your inheritance? Which is actually just an old house and a heap of debts plus the death duties, of course.'

'The house is beautiful,' Kate said. 'And it has a lot of potential. But yes, that's what happened. I messaged Edwina on Instagram and then she called me.'

'I nearly fell off my chair when I read the message,' Edwina said. 'And then I told Kate to come here with whatever proof she had. So that's where we are now.'

Max nodded. 'Okay. I'm sorry, Kate, but this has been a bit of a shock. It'll take a while for it to sink in.'

'I know,' Edwina said. 'I still find it hard to get my head around it.'

'What is Gwen going to say?' Max asked. 'She'll have a fit.'

'Where is she?' Allegra asked, looking around the kitchen.

'She went to Limerick with a horse,' Max replied. 'She should be back this afternoon.' He paused and looked at Allegra. 'So here we are. Your story is now making a lot more sense, even if it raises a lot of questions.'

'What story?' Edwina asked, staring at Allegra. 'Does this have something to do with you? Don't tell me you're another granddaughter or something.'

'I'm not,' Allegra protested. 'But the weird thing is that I came here because of a diamond ring I found on the beach on Cape Cod last summer. A ring with the inscription *Sean and*

Davina, 1939. And then I discovered an article in an old newspaper from that year that said a young man called Sean Walsh was looking for the engagement ring his fiancée had lost. Her name was Davina Courtney and they were both from Kerry.' Allegra pulled her phone from her pocket and scrolled to the article she had copied. She read it out loud as Edwina and Kate listened. 'There's a photo of Sean Walsh, but it's a bit blurry.'

'Well, then, there you go,' Kate said, looking at Max with a satisfied air when Allegra had finished. 'Doesn't this prove what I've just told you?'

'Could be just coincidence,' Max countered. 'And it doesn't prove a thing about your story.'

'Give me your phone,' Kate said, holding out her hand. 'I want to see that article and the photo.'

'Okay.' Allegra handed Kate her phone.

Kate stared at the image on the screen. 'Oh yes,' she said after a while. 'Looks like him. Dark hair and eyes. And those eyebrows... Yes, I think it has to be. Everything fits.' She looked back at Allegra. 'Where is this ring?'

Max shot Allegra a warning glance and she stopped herself touching her neck. 'It's in a safe place,' she said.

'And Allegra is the legal owner,' Max filled in. 'She only came here because she felt she should give it to one of Davina's relatives when she had found out if this Davina is our Davina, if you see what I mean.'

'Of course she is – was,' Edwina snapped. 'And I think I should have that ring.'

'Why you?' Max asked. 'Shouldn't it go to Gwen?'

'I think it should go to me,' Kate said. 'As I'm the granddaughter.'

'We have no real proof of that,' Max said, looking coolly at Kate. 'We haven't seen those documents yet. I'm sure our solicitor will look through them and get an expert opinion. Until then, we have no proof. Only your word.'

'My word should be good enough,' Kate said, looking offended. 'I'm an honest person.'

'I'm sure you are,' Max said. 'But I will reserve my judgement until later.'

'Do you think I'm lying?' Kate snapped.

'I don't think anything yet,' Max said. 'All I know is that Edwina wants us to sell the house and the land once the probate is cleared.'

'And you don't?' Kate asked.

'Over my dead body,' Max said hotly.

As the atmosphere grew more tense, Allegra felt more and more uncomfortable. She didn't want to get involved in this conflict that seemed to be escalating as Max continued to stare coldly at Kate Vanderpump, who stared back, looking defiant.

Unable to stand the tension anymore, Allegra cleared her throat and got up. 'I have to go,' she said. 'We can look through the house some other time.'

Max jumped to his feet. 'I'll see you out.'

'Thanks.' Allegra nodded at the two women at the table. 'Bye for now. Nice to meet you both.'

'You're leaving?' Edwina asked. 'But what about the ring?'

'I think we'll sort that out later,' Max said, holding the door open for Allegra, who slipped through, relieved be out of the kitchen.

Max took her jacket from the peg and held it out.

'Thanks,' Allegra said and slipped on the jacket. As something fell out of the pocket, she looked down.

Max bent to pick it up, glancing at it. 'Are you selling lottery tickets?'

'No, they're tickets to the Halloween party in Sandy Cove on Saturday. The proceeds got to St Vincent de Paul.' Allegra took the tickets. 'This nice woman gave them to me and asked me to sell them for her. I don't suppose you'd want to go?' she said in a jocular tone.

'Why not?' he said, smiling broadly. 'Could be fun. I need something to cheer me up after what has just happened.'

'It's fancy dress,' Allegra warned.

'Even more fun,' Max said. 'Are you going?'

'Yes, just because Lucille wants me to. She's the lady who's been very kind to me and has even promised to help me with my research about Sean and Davina. But that won't be necessary now that Kate has turned up.'

'I don't agree,' Max said, glancing at the half-open kitchen door. 'Let's go outside and I'll tell you what I think.' He held the door open and they walked out into the courtyard where Allegra had parked her car.

Halfway there, she stopped and turned to Max. 'What were you going to say?'

'Just that I'm not sure I believe what I heard in there.'

'How do you mean?' Allegra asked. 'Kate couldn't be lying, could she? I mean, she has proof – the marriage certificate and then her mother's birth certificate...'

'Which could be fake,' Max filled in. 'There are ways of faking documents like that, you know.'

'What makes you think she's not telling the truth?'

Max frowned. 'I'm not sure, but for a start I never trust anyone who keeps saying they're honest. But that's just me. Those documents could turn out to be the real thing. But I found it strange that she waited so long before she contacted any of us. Was she waiting for those documents to be made up?'

'That sounds really devious,' Allegra said. 'Wouldn't it be against the law to fake documents like that?'

'Very much so,' Max agreed. 'But let's see what happens. Oh, and just out of curiosity, what kind of research was this lovely old lady of yours going to do?'

'She was planning to drive to Dingle to visit Sean Walsh's family. We have discovered that he came into a lot of money sometime after he returned from America. And he bought his mother a house in Dingle where the family still lives.' Allegra pulled her car key from her pocket. 'Maybe I should tell her she doesn't need to go now.'

'No,' Max said. 'I think she should go. We need to find out everything we can about Sean Walsh and what he was up to during that time. This would be from another angle and could prove that this Kate woman in there is faking it.'

'I suppose it could. Or prove she's not.'

'Either way, it's important. Hey, listen, let me buy a few tickets. How much are they?'

'Twenty euros,' Allegra replied. 'But you don't have to buy any.'

'I want to. I might even turn up,' Max said with a mischievous glint in his eyes.

'As what?'

'It'll be a surprise. I'll take four tickets, please.'

'Four?' Allegra asked.

'One for me and the other three for the good cause.' Max took a wallet from his back pocket and slid out four twenty-euro notes. 'Here you go.'

'Thanks.' Allegra pulled four tickets from the book and handed them to Max in exchange for the money. 'I'm sorry for leaving like that, but I felt a little uncomfortable being there when you were discussing family business.'

'I know.' Max put the tickets in his pocket. 'I was going to show you around the house, but it wasn't the right time. I didn't want Edwina and Kate traipsing around with us poking into Aunt Davina's stuff.'

'That's what I thought,' Allegra said. 'But I would love to see the house another time. And ride Betsy again, if that would be possible. I really enjoyed it.'

'So did I. More than you know.' Max leaned forward and placed a light kiss on her cheek. 'Bye for now. See you soon, I hope. Keep me posted about the trip to Dingle.'

'I will,' Allegra promised as she got into the car, flustered after that light kiss. 'Thanks for buying the tickets. And you absolutely don't have to go.'

'I know.' He smiled and waved.

Allegra drove off, her mind in a whirl and her heart beating so fast she thought she would faint. That little kiss had been just a brush of his lips against her cheek, but still it felt as if it meant something. Then, as she drove through the gates and down the road, she told herself sternly not to be silly. He was from another world, another country, and she was only here for a break. She would go back to her old life in a few weeks and then the memories of this place would fade and she would start to live again and maybe meet someone else, someone she would share her life with and be happy. No need to start flirting with a man with whom she had no future.

But oh, why do I feel like this? she asked herself. *Is it only because I'm looking for comfort?*

But when she thought about Max and the way she felt when he looked at her, comfort was far from her mind.

14

The few days before Halloween went past with astonishing speed. Allegra found that everyone in the village already knew who she was, so she didn't have to introduce herself wherever she went.

The librarian went to a lot of trouble to find books and newspaper clippings about the history of Sandy Cove in general, and the coastguard station in particular, and told Allegra to read the account of the German plane crashing in the mountains above the village during the war. This was around the time Sean had come back from America, and Allegra searched without success for mentions of his name, or even his family. But there was nothing. All she could find was a little notice to say that the post of coastguard was open and to apply at the county council office in Killarney. The cottage was now available to the successful applicant, it said in the issue from 1940. She assumed this was when Sean's mother and siblings were told to leave after his father had died. Allegra felt a dart of sadness as she read it. How hard it would have been to be turfed out like that and find yourself without a roof over your head. And how lucky that Sean had come into money at that precise time. But where had the money come from? Maybe Lucille would find out when she went to visit the Walsh family in Dingle...

Allegra pushed those thoughts away as she walked around the village, exploring the neighbourhood further, spending more time looking around than before. She discovered that the village and its surroundings were even more enchanting than what she had seen on the website. With its lovely old houses all painted in bright tones of red, green, yellow and even pink, the village would have looked strange anywhere else, but perfectly suited the coastal setting. It looked wonderful against the stunning views of the ocean and the islands far out to sea.

She went on long walks up the slopes from the little beach below Starlight Cottages and took a lot of photos that she posted on Instagram, which earned her a lot of likes and enthusiastic comments from awestruck friends in Boston. Despite the cold winds and the ever-changing weather patterns – from rain to sunshine and then back again – Allegra couldn't have been happier. This place was a perfect escape from stress and sorrow and she felt herself healing and regaining some of her lost energy and will to live.

Starlight Cottages were suddenly a lot livelier, as Ella and her husband, Rory, back from Paris, introduced themselves to Allegra and invited her to dinner, along with Lucille, who of course was Rory's mother.

Ella, a pretty and lively brunette with an enchanting smile and a twinkle in her eyes, served a dinner of mussels in a white wine sauce with French fries accompanied by a crisp Chablis, which she declared was 'more Belgian than French'. But as she had bought fresh mussels from the harbour fish stand earlier that day, it seemed the ideal meal for this occasion.

Allegra, who had little clue about the difference between a French or a Belgian dish, declared it was heavenly, to which

Ella blew her a kiss across the table. 'Thank you,' she said, beaming. 'We only just met, but I adore you already.'

Allegra laughed and said she adored Ella, too. But who wouldn't? She was so cute and fun and smiley, chatting a mile a minute and obviously madly in love with her husband who seemed to be just as besotted with her. They were a lovely couple and Allegra smiled as she watched them tease each other and exchange looks that showed they were perfectly in tune. She wondered if she would one day meet someone with whom she would have that complicity.

Then, for some strange reason, Max popped into her mind. She had felt a strong connection to him during their ride through the beautiful countryside, and all his arrogance and haughtiness had been blown away by the fresh, cold air. But the spell had been broken by the arrival of Edwina and Kate Vanderpump. Allegra had gone through the conversation in the kitchen over and over again, trying to decide if Kate was telling the truth, or just playing a very dangerous game. There was something missing in her story, but Allegra couldn't quite put her finger on what it was.

'You look as if you're far away,' Lucille remarked as Ella cleared the plates from the table.

'I was just thinking about that woman who appeared at Strawberry Hill yesterday,' Allegra replied.

'The one with the strange name?' Lucille said as Rory topped up her glass.

'Yes. I was thinking there was something missing from her story,' Allegra said and took a sip of wine.

'Like what?' Ella asked as she passed around little bowls with chocolate mousse. 'Lucille has filled us in on the whole thing, so we're up to date. But you didn't say what this woman's name was.'

'Kate Vanderpump,' Allegra said.

'Sounds Dutch,' Rory said as he sat down and took a bowl from Ella.

'She's from Scotland,' Allegra said. 'And that's her father's name, I think. It's American and she's related to the Vanderpumps of that reality show you might have heard of. *Vanderpump Rules?*'

'I think I've heard of that,' Ella said. 'But it's not shown over here.'

'Her mother's maiden name was Walsh, of course,' Allegra filled in.

'Oh,' Lucille said, looking suddenly a little sheepish. 'I completely forgot to tell you, Allegra. I looked up the Walsh family in Dingle and found they run a bakery and café in that house. And they're open even though it's the low season. So I was wondering if you'd like to come with me on Sunday?'

'Oh well...' Allegra hesitated.

'It's the perfect opportunity to find out about them,' Ella cut in. 'No better place than a country café to pump people for information. The waitress always asks the guests a lot of questions, and then you can do the same about them. Especially if you're from America. They wouldn't suspect any other motive from you.'

Lucille clapped her hands. 'Yes! Of course! We can be undercover and pretend I'm your Irish aunt and we're doing this grand tour of Kerry to find your relatives.'

'Ah come on, Mum,' Rory teased. 'You're getting carried away.'

'I think it's a brilliant idea,' Ella said. 'You don't need to tell that many fibs. Just a hint here and there. I'd say the people who run that café will be very happy to talk about their family. It's the off season so tourists must be thin on the ground right now. Go for it, I'd say.' She sat down and picked up her spoon. 'Dig in. This is my very special French *mousse au chocolat*. Secret recipe passed on to me by my French ex-husband's mother. Bad marriage but the food was good.'

'Contrary to this marriage,' Rory remarked. 'Food a bit iffy but the marriage is amazing.'

'It's extraordinary,' Ella said, smiling at her husband. 'And I got the best mother-in-law in the world, too,' she added, squeezing Lucille's hand.

'Thank you, pet,' Lucille said as she sampled a spoonful of chocolate mousse. 'This is delicious, wherever the recipe came from.'

'Really good,' Allegra said as the chocolate melted in her mouth.

Lucille scraped her bowl clean, then pushed it away and got up. 'I have to leave you now. I promised to help Dominic with his costume for the party and then I have to make up mine. He'll be a wizard and I'm going to be a witch. What about you, Allegra?'

'Oh God, I haven't even thought about that,' Allegra exclaimed. 'Maybe I won't go. I don't have a costume anyway.'

'You don't have to dress up,' Ella said. 'But maybe you could be a zombie like me? That's really easy. Plenty of black eyeliner, a pale face and blood around your mouth and you're perfect. Add some rags and you're done.'

'I'm not sure I can even do that,' Allegra protested. 'I don't have any rags.'

'I'll help you. You have to come,' Ella insisted. 'It's a really fun evening. The kids go around trick-or-treating first and then we all meet up at the library and have a party in the conference room. Food, wine, games, bobbing for apples and all that. It's always great craic.'

'What are you going to do all alone in your house while we're having fun?' Lucille asked.

Allegra had to laugh. 'Oh, okay, I'll come now that you've made it sound so great.'

'Brilliant,' Ella said. 'Come over here first and we'll dress up together.'

'What will I dress up as?' Rory asked.

'You can be a zombie, too,' Ella replied. 'Or maybe a pirate?' She nodded. 'Yes, you'll be a great pirate.'

'Ho, ho, ho and a bottle of rum,' Rory chanted. 'Howzat?'

'Awful,' Ella said. 'But you'll do.'

Allegra smiled. She felt so at home with these people. Ella and Rory were so sweet and friendly, and Lucille had already taken Allegra under her wing. They were all so much older than her, especially Lucille, but here, it seemed that age didn't matter. Nor did looks or status or nationality. It all seemed so warm and welcoming, except for one thing: the divide between Strawberry Hill and the people in the village. Allegra had begun to realise that it was all about the past and also, as Lydia had explained, about ownership of land. Old habits die hard, she supposed. Traditions and prejudices still stuck. The Sandy Cove inhabitants were lively and quirky, far removed from the stiff upper lips of the Courtneys. Would the two worlds ever blend?

She started to look forward to the Halloween party with great excitement. It would be a fun evening. And who knew? Maybe Max would turn up, too. He had seemed keen to get to know the village better – or maybe it was something else that attracted him? Allegra had a feeling that anything could happen in this magical place, far from the stress and pressure of the rest of the world. Anything at all.

15

'Just a little darker red on your lips,' Ella said as she put the finishing touches to Allegra's make-up.

They were in Ella's bedroom where bits of clothing lay strewn all over the large double bed and the dressing table was littered with tubes and pots with lipstick, eyeshadow and foundation. Allegra had arrived earlier dressed in a black T-shirt and leggings as ordered by Ella, who had added a belt with bits of material hanging off it and a ripped black velvet jacket she had found in her wardrobe. 'Some old thing I threw in there ages ago,' she said. 'And now it's coming in very handy. Isn't that what I said, sweetheart?' she shouted through the open door to Rory, who was changing into his pirate's costume in the spare bedroom.

'Any excuse to be messy,' he called back.

'Ignore him,' Ella said. She stood back and studied Allegra, who was sitting on the bed. 'You look a little too pretty, but I've done my best. That wholesome look is hard to erase.'

'Wholesome? Me?' Allegra asked, startled by this comment.

'Yes,' Ella replied. 'You look as if butter wouldn't melt with your cute little nose and sweet smile – until I look into those huge dark eyes... There is something sultry deep down there and I was trying to bring it out. But all could do was make you a little bit scary. Take a look in the mirror.'

Allegra stood up and looked at herself in the tall mirror beside the window. 'Oh, wow,' she said as she saw her image. Her reddish-blonde hair had been twisted into strands that hung around her face, made up with chalky white make-up, black and blue rings around her eyes, making them nearly black, and blood-red lips with drips painted on one side. 'That's scary.'

'Well, I'm an artist,' Ella said. 'And you were my canvas today. How do I look?'

'Awesome,' Allegra replied, taking in Ella's hair with purple and red highlights, her deathly pale face, her black-rimmed eyes and light blue lips. 'You look half dead.'

'Wonderful,' Ella said and did a twirl that made her rags flutter around her slim frame. 'I think we're good to go. Where is that handsome pirate?' she called across the landing.

'Here,' Rory said and stepped out of the spare room, doing a double take as he caught sight of Ella. 'Waah, you scared me for just a second. Excellent costume, I have to say.'

'Thank you,' Ella said, looking pleased. 'But hey, you... My God, you look incredible!'

Allegra had to agree. Rory, with his dark looks and broad frame, made a stunning pirate. He wore a bandanna on his head and a large gold earring dangled from his right earlobe. He had put on a black shirt and tight jogging pants with a colourful scarf around his waist and had somehow managed to adorn a pair of black loafers with big gold buckles.

'I made them with Play-Doh,' he said, lifting one foot. 'And then I used gold paint I found in Ella's studio. The earring is clip-on and it's pinching like mad. I think I might have to take it off.'

'No,' Ella protested. 'You must keep it on. It makes the

whole look. It'll go numb in a little while and then you won't feel it.'

'I'm not sure I can bear it until then,' Rory said with a grunt.

'Of course you can,' Ella said. 'How do you think women survive with all the stuff we have to put on to please you? Those sexy stilettos you love me to wear are pure torture. But I still wear them to parties because they make me look good.'

Rory grinned. 'You women are so brave. But come on, let's go to the party. I think we should go and catch the last of the trick-or-treating and the whole Halloween atmosphere. It's a bit warmer this evening.'

They left the house and walked up the lane, then turned into the main street, where a lot of children all dressed up in Halloween costumes were calling into houses for sweets and other treats. The library at the end was lit in ghostly colours and skeletons and ghosts hung from the branches of the tree in front of the building. And inside, the dimly lit hall was decorated in the same fashion with organ music playing from a loudspeaker.

Lucille, looking cute in a witch costume, greeted them from behind a table laden with all kinds of foods and rows of glasses filled with either red or white wine.

'You can have something alcohol-free too if you want,' she said. 'But help yourselves to sausage rolls or a chicken leg. Or both. And there's a lot of salad and ham and breaded shrimps, and of course my very own brack. I made six, and there is a ring, a stick or a coin in every one of them.'

'Aha,' Rory said. 'You won the battle, then?'

'There was no battle,' Lucille said, shooting him a steely look. 'It's just that the party committee has very good taste.'

Rory smiled and started to heap a plate with food as parents and children began to trickle into the hall. Allegra was introduced to a number of people dressed up in various costumes, mostly witches, wizards, zombies or pirates like Rory, who handed her the plate he had just filled.

'Here,' he said. 'This is for you.'

'Thank you,' Allegra said. 'This all looks delicious.'

'It is.' He took another plate. 'I'll do this one for you,' he said to Ella, who handed Allegra a glass of white wine.

Then they all sat down at a table with a group of other people and their children. Allegra found herself beside two little girls, both dressed in tulle skirts with tiny wings on their backs.

'Are you going to eat all that?' one of the girls asked her. 'Zombies don't eat.'

'I know,' Allegra said. 'But I'm just pretending. Are you a real fairy?'

'No,' the girl replied. 'But I wish I was. Then I could do magic tricks and grant people's wishes. My name is Mandy,' she added, nearly in the same breath. 'What's yours?'

'My name's Allegra, and I'm from America.'

'I'm from Dublin but now I live here,' Mandy said. 'With my daddy and my new mummy and my stepsister, Hannah, who is sitting beside me.'

'Hi, Hannah,' Allegra said to the other girl.

'Hi,' the little girl said and waved her wand at Allegra. 'If I could grant you a wish, what would it be?'

'Oh,' Allegra said, 'in that case I'd wish to have my niece, Emma, here. She's about your age and she would look so cute in one of those dresses.'

'I wish I could magic her over here,' Hannah said. 'Do you miss her very much?'

'I do,' Allegra replied. 'But I'll be FaceTiming with her later and then she will show me her Halloween costume.'

'Can we see it?' Mandy asked. 'We could be on the Face-Time, too, and say hi from Ireland.'

'That's a great idea,' Allegra said, smiling at the two little girls. 'She'd love to say hi to two cute Irish girls in beautiful costumes.'

'Can we do it now?' Hannah asked.

'Um, I'm not sure,' Allegra replied. 'It's still quite early over there in New York. But I can try. I'll text her mom in a little while to see if it's possible. Emma doesn't have her own phone, you see. She's only eight.'

'We're not getting one until we're twelve,' Mandy said. 'So we'll have to wait...' She frowned. 'Five years, I think. 'Cos now we're seven.'

'Good idea to wait a bit.' Allegra looked at the girls. 'So you're the same age? And now you're sisters?'

Mandy nodded. 'Yes. First, we were friends and then I made Daddy fall in love with Hannah's mum.'

'We did it together,' Hannah piped up. ''Cos we wanted to be together forever. And now we are.'

'But we'll have a new brother or sister soon,' Mandy said. 'And she or he will have us as its big sisters.'

'And my little brother will be a big brother to the baby,' Hannah cut in. 'But he's only two so he's not really big.'

'That sounds wonderful,' Allegra said as a heavily pregnant woman came towards them.

'Girls, I hope you're not bothering this nice lady,' the woman said and held out her hand. 'Hi, you must be Allegra. I'm Maura Quinn. I hope the girls aren't boring you.'

'Of course not,' Allegra said. 'We're having a lovely chat.'

'And we're going to FaceTime with Emma in New York,' Hannah said. 'On Allegra's phone.'

'Really?' Maura said, glancing at Allegra. 'Whose idea was that?'

'Mine,' Allegra said. 'Emma is my niece, you see and I had planned to FaceTime with her later. And then Hannah said they wanted to be in on it. But I think it's a lovely idea for the girls to join in.'

'If it's all right with you, that's okay, then,' Maura said, looking relieved. She put a hand on her stomach. 'It's hard to keep up with these two at the moment with the state I'm in.'

'When is the baby due?' Allegra asked.

'In three weeks,' Maura said.

'So then you must be tired. Do you want me to mind the girls for a bit?' Allegra offered as she took in Maura's tired face.

'Would you?' Maura looked relieved. 'Then maybe I could go home and you could keep an eye on them until my husband comes to collect them. He's minding our two-year-old at home, you see.'

'And he's a holy terror,' Mandy cut in.

Allegra smiled. 'Of course I don't mind. We're having such fun, aren't we, girls?'

'Yes, we are,' Hannah said. 'And we'll be very, very good if we can stay with Allegra and do that FaceTiming with Emma in New York.'

Maura nodded. 'Yes, you can. That's so kind of you, Allegra. My friend Maggie and her husband are at the table next door, and they'll take over if you've had enough. And please come and have coffee with me sometime next week. I'll be in touch about that. Bye for now.'

'Bye, and have a good rest,' Allegra said.

Maura shot her a tired smile. 'I'll be asleep as soon as I get under that duvet.' She walked away while Allegra turned to the girls.

'Have you finished your food?'

'Yes, and now you have to get us all a piece of brack,' Mandy ordered. 'We'll wait here and mind your bag while you go and get it.'

'And then we'll call that Emma girl in New York,' Hannah said.

'Yes, ma'am.' Allegra was about to get up when someone sat down on a chair opposite. A man dressed in a wizard hat, dark make-up around his eyes and a cloak wrapped around his shoulders.

'Good evening, Allegra,' he said.

'Uh, good evening,' Allegra replied, faintly recognising the voice. 'Have we met?'

'We certainly have,' he said. 'Only the other day.'

Allegra peered at him and then the dazzling blue eyes and the mellow voice with the clipped accent gave her that familiar jolt.

'Max!' she exclaimed. 'Oh God, I didn't recognise you straight away. That's a great disguise.'

'I stole some of Edwina's make-up, got the hat in a shop in Killarney and the cloak is some of the old things hanging around in the house.' He paused and looked at her. 'Your disguise is brilliant, too. I nearly didn't recognise you but then I saw your tall frame glide across the floor and I knew who you were.'

'I should have crouched a little. Did you just arrive?'

'About twenty minutes ago. How's the party going?'

'Brilliantly,' Allegra said when she had recovered from the shock of seeing him. 'As you can see, I have two gorgeous girls to keep me company.'

Max bowed. 'Good evening, lovely ladies. My name is Max.'

Mandy and Hannah giggled. Then Mandy said, 'Good evening.'

Hannah looked at Allegra and pointed at Max. 'Is he your boyfriend?'

'I wish,' Max said before Allegra had a chance to reply.

'You wish?' Mandy's eyes lit up. She stood up and reached across the table with her wand and tapped Max on the head. 'There! Your wish has come true. You are now the boyfriend of the zombie Allegra.'

'But only until midnight,' Allegra said.

'Of course,' Max said. 'Am I not the lucky fella to be your boyfriend even for a few hours, though?'

Mandy nodded. 'You are, 'cos she's lovely.'

'When are we FaceTiming?' Hannah asked. 'I want to meet that Emma.'

'Me too,' Mandy said.

'I've promised the girls I'll FaceTime with my niece, Emma, in New York,' Allegra explained to Max. 'They're nearly the same age, so I thought it would be fun for them.'

'Sounds great,' he said and got up. 'You do that while I go and get something to eat before it's all gone. Can I get you girls something?'

'Get some brack,' Mandy ordered. 'We want to see who gets the coin and the ring.'

Hannah giggled. 'Or the stick.'

'Okay!' Max walked away, smiling.

Allegra took her phone from her little crossbody bag. 'I'll text my sister to see if it's okay to FaceTime with Emma. And then we might find a quiet corner to do it.'

'We can go into the little reading room at the library,' Mandy suggested. 'That's where we have story time on Wednesdays.'

'Great.' Allegra quickly texted Lucia from WhatsApp asking if Emma would like to FaceTime. The reply came nearly straight away.

Emma is here and would love to show you her costume and chat to the girls. Call in five minutes.

'Okay, girls,' Allegra said. 'We have to call in five minutes. Let's go to the reading room, then.'

The girls squealed with excitement and jumped up, running across the room, and opened a door on the far side, while Allegra followed. Then they settled on a little sofa in the cosy room and Allegra took out her phone and called Lucia's number. Once Emma's face appeared on the screen, she held her phone so the girls could see her.

'Hi, Emma,' she said. 'Here are two lovely Irish fairies to say hello. Mandy is the fair one and Hannah the dark-haired one.'

'Hi, Mandy and Hannah,' Emma shouted. 'I'm a witch and here is my hat,' she continued, holding up a pointy hat. 'I'll be putting on scary make-up in a little while. But I already have my costume on. Mom, hold the phone so I can show them.'

Then Allegra could hear Lucia laugh as she held the phone and Emma did a twirl in a black and purple dress with a black cloak over it. A black plush cat with bright yellow eyes sat on her shoulder.

'It's amazing,' Hannah shouted.

'Thank you,' Emma said graciously, leaning into the screen. 'Are you two sisters?'

'Stepsisters,' Mandy replied. 'My name is Mandy Quinn and she is Hannah Primrose, but her mummy is Maura Quinn because she married my daddy.'

'Before that she was Maura Primrose,' Mandy cut in. 'And before *that* she was called Maura Walsh.'

16

'What?' Allegra said, her heart beating faster as she heard the name. 'Walsh? Was that her name before she got married?'

'Yeah,' Hannah said. 'But that was a long time ago. When she was not married and living with her parents.'

'Like a hundred years ago?' Emma asked on the phone.

'No, but maybe fifty,' Hannah suggested.

'We have to say goodbye now,' Lucia's voice interrupted. 'Emma's friends have arrived and then we have to feed them before they go out trick-or-treating.'

'Bye, Emma,' Mandy said and waved at Emma's face on the phone. 'Have fun scaring people.'

'Bye, Mandy and Hannah,' Emma replied.

They all chanted 'bye, bye' before Allegra hung up at the same time as the door opened and a tall blond man stuck his head in.

'Hello,' he said. 'You must be Allegra. I'm Thomas Quinn, the father of these two. I was told you were in here.'

'Hi, Daddy,' Mandy said and got up. 'We've been talking to a girl in New York.'

'So I heard,' Thomas said. 'That sounds like fun. Nice to meet you, Allegra.'

'It was great fun,' Allegra said and stood up, shaking Thomas's proffered hand. 'Hi, Thomas.'

'Hi, and thank you so much for minding them,' Thomas said. 'Maura was exhausted.'

'So I noticed,' Allegra remarked. She hesitated for a moment, wondering how she could get to see Maura and ask her a few questions. Hearing the name Walsh had given her a jolt and now she wanted to know more about this family. 'Maura invited me for coffee someday next week,' she said. 'So I'm going to take her up on that, if she isn't too tired.'

'I think that's a wonderful idea,' Thomas said. 'I'll be busy in my office and the girls will be in school and little Sean will be in kindergarten. It'd do her good to socialise. I'll tell her to call you, if you give me your number.'

'Of course.' Allegra wrote it down, and then she hugged the girls goodbye before she went back to the hall and her table, where Max was waiting.

'I got you some brack,' he said as he finished his plateful of food. 'And some for those little girls, too. Where are they?'

'They went home with their father,' Allegra replied. 'I think they were getting tired.'

'Then I can come and sit beside you,' Max suggested. 'Let me just take the plates back. I'll take yours, too.'

'Thank you.' Allegra handed Max the plates and then looked at his tall figure as he strode across the room, thinking about what she had just found out.

Maura, the nice woman with the lovely daughters, was related to Sean Walsh in some way. Her little boy was called Sean, too. Did this mean he was called after *that* Sean Walsh? And in that case, what did Maura know about him? Allegra smiled absentmindedly at Max when he came back to the table and decided not to tell him until she had concrete facts. No need to involve him in what could be a wild goose chase.

'You look as if you're miles away,' Max said when he sat down beside her. 'Missing your family?'

'A bit,' Allegra confessed. 'Especially when I saw my little niece Emma just now. But I'm enjoying this evening, though.'

'Me too,' he said, shooting her a warm smile. He picked up the plate with what looked like slices of fruitcake. 'Go on, take a bit of brack. Let's see if you get anything. But bite carefully. You don't want to lose a tooth.'

Allegra smiled, picked up a slice and took a careful bite. As she felt nothing at all, she chewed, enjoying the fruity taste mixed with lemon peel. 'It's quite tasty,' she said. 'And there's nothing at all in mine.'

Max chewed on the slice he had taken and suddenly stopped, picking a small stick out of his mouth. 'Aha, I got the stick. Means my wife will beat me up.' He looked at Allegra, smiling. 'But as you are my girlfriend for the evening, maybe you're planning to beat me?'

'I wasn't, but if it's required, I'll do my best.'

'No need.' Max wiped his mouth. Then he leaned closer to Allegra. 'It's so nice to be here with you and to look at all these happy people having fun. We never mixed much with anyone from the village, so it's great to finally see what it's like.'

'Why not?' Allegra asked. 'Why didn't you mix with the people here?'

'All kinds of reasons,' he replied, looking thoughtful. 'Mainly because we were so busy with the horses. Funny, though, as we can see the ocean from the top windows of the house. I love that view. But the village? I never felt welcome, I suppose.' He shrugged. 'There was a kind of awkwardness from both sides, imagining feelings that were never there.' He looked around the hall at the people chatting and laughing, and smiled. 'I'm getting very friendly vibes here, though. Everyone I've met has been great.' He looked at Allegra. 'Maybe you're the cata-lyst that will bring us all together?'

'Like some kind of chemical reaction?'

'Maybe. In any case this village is lovely. Right now, espe-cially with the main street and all the little houses with the Halloween decorations.'

'I love it already,' Allegra said. 'The village, the people and Starlight Cottages. I feel safe here.'

'That's a great feeling,' Max said. 'Quite unique these days, I think.' He sighed and took another slice of brack. 'It's been a bit tense over at the house. I'd leave but unfortunately I have to stay around as I'm working in the area.'

'Why is it tense?' Allegra asked.

Max swallowed his mouthful. 'Well, Edwina and Kate are still staying there. And Gwen is furious because they're going through everything, including Davina's room.'

'Have they found anything?' Allegra asked. 'Anything that proves Kate's story, I mean.'

'Not yet. And I don't think they will.' He shrugged. 'Davina wasn't the type to write a diary and she was a very poor corre-spondent. They're barking up the wrong tree. And, oh God, I can't stand that woman. She's constantly making snide remarks about me and Gwen. Then she laughs and says she was joking and don't I have a sense of humour?'

'And what does Edwina say about that?' Allegra asked. 'I mean, isn't it strange that they bonded like that so quickly? Wouldn't it be a problem for Edwina that there is another heir to the estate?'

'Edwina wants to sell the house so we can pay the death duties and then share the rest of the money. She wants all the problems solved quickly. Kate is an important ally and would help get this done. I don't think it's all about the money for Edwina, more about closing the chapter on a house she doesn't really love the way I do.'

'But Kate's being mean to you and Gwen. How does Edwina react to that?'

'She finds it really funny. Kate is her new best friend, it seems. In any case, if Kate's documents prove to be genuine we'll have to sell.'

'Why are they so keen on selling?' Allegra asked, puzzled by the worried look in Max's eyes.

'Because they both know the house and land would fetch millions. And once it's all sold and the death duties paid, everyone will get a lot of money.'

'Maybe that would be the best thing for everyone?' Allegra suggested.

'No, not for me. The house would be lost, and Gwen will be without a home, and her business will be gone, too. And her whole way of life, of course. That could destroy her. I can't see her starting up somewhere else.'

'What about you? Where do you stand?' Allegra asked.

'With Gwen, of course.' He sighed. 'I know the house is in a bad state and that it would take a lot of money to restore it. But we can do that bit by bit and then, in a few years, maybe use it as a venue or rent part of it out or something. I don't want the house to go out of the family.'

'But I thought you said it was a money pit and should be pulled down.'

'I know, but that was just me being gloomy. To me, Strawberry Hill is a unique place where I come to relax, ride the horses and get away from stress. The house itself has such a magical vibe. It's old and run-down but there is so much history from bygone days. You'll see what I mean when you go inside.'

'I'd love to see it,' Allegra said wistfully.

'You must,' Max said with feeling. 'Why don't you come one day next week? Edwina and Kate are going to Dublin on Monday. I'll have a bit of work to do on Tuesday morning, but then if I get organised I'll be free later. So if you're not doing anything else, you could come in the afternoon?'

'Oh,' Allegra said. 'That would be awesome. I'll be there whatever time suits you.'

'Two o'clock?' Max suggested.

'Perfect.'

'Great.' Max suddenly looked a lot happier. 'I'm looking forward to showing you every nook and cranny.'

'Gwen won't mind?' Allegra asked.

'Not at all. She knows you're on our side.'

Allegra stared at him. 'I'm not sure I like taking sides. But I do understand how you feel about the house. It's a bit like what I feel about my family's cottage on Cape Cod. My sister owns it now, so it's still in the family. I was so worried she'd sell it, but her husband wouldn't let her. Of course, that's a tiny little beach house, so not at all on the same scale.'

'Places you love have no scale,' Max remarked. 'Could be a cottage or mansion. What matters is what's in your heart.'

'That's true,' Allegra said, touched by the empathy in his eyes.

As they were talking, the party was beginning to wind up and parents were calling their children and getting ready to go home. Max and Allegra got up and started to help with the cleaning up, collecting plates and glasses and putting them in bins for recycling or washing up in the small kitchen off the hall. When they had nearly finished, Lucille, accompanied by a very tired-looking wizard, told them they could go home. The committee members who had signed up for the job of cleaning would take over.

'I have to take Dominic home,' she said. 'He's getting overtired.'

'Not as young as I was,' Dominic said with a wan smile.

'Younger than me,' Lucille quipped. 'But isn't everyone?'

'You have more stamina,' Dominic said.

'I'm a woman,' Lucille said and pulled him away. 'Come on, I'll drive you up the road to your house.'

'Can't believe she's still driving,' Max said, watching them walk away. 'But she seems to be one of those supergrannies.'

'She sure is,' Ella said beside them. She shot Max a smile. 'Hello there, I'm Ella, Allegra's neighbour. You must be Max.'

'I am,' Max said and shook Ella's hand. 'Hi, Ella.'

'Nice to meet you, but I'm heading home,' Ella said. 'My pirate husband is going to the pub with a few wizards and zombies. What about you, Allegra? Do you want to go for a drink with them?'

'No, I think I'll go home, too,' Allegra said. 'I have an early start tomorrow.'

'That's right. The magical mystery tour with Lucille,' Ella said and winked at Allegra.

'Magical mystery tour? What's that all about?' Max asked.

'Oh,' Allegra said, glancing at Ella, 'just an outing that might end in a surprise. I'll tell you about it when we meet on Tuesday.'

'That's fine,' Max said as if he had felt her reticence. 'But now that the party's over, I can escort you ladies home,' he offered. 'I'm not drinking as I drove here, so I won't go to the pub.'

'Terrific,' Ella said. 'Not that we need an escort around here, but a good-looking wizard is always great company.'

Max smiled and took off his hat that had been sitting a little askew on his head. 'I think I can ditch the hat now. You two are the prettiest zombies I've ever seen, in any case.'

'We change into real girls at midnight,' Ella said.

'Pity,' Max said. 'I kind of liked that half-dead look.'

'It takes a long time to achieve,' Ella said as the three of them started to walk down the street. 'So we only do it for Halloween.'

Max didn't reply. Walking beside Allegra, he looked around

as they continued on, taking in the houses with their neat little gardens, the old-fashioned street lights, the quaint shopfronts and the pub where laughter and music were spilling onto the street.

'It's like walking down a village in some old Irish painting,' he said. 'These houses are quite unique and charming. Some of the façades are a lot more elaborate than your ordinary Irish cottage. How interesting. And look at this.' He stopped in front of a two-storey Victorian building that housed the chemist's on the ground floor. 'The plasterwork around the windows is quite beautiful. Never thought I'd see that here.'

'Here where the peasants live, you mean?' Ella asked with a touch of irony.

'No,' Max protested. 'I didn't mean it quite the way it sounded.'

'How did you mean, then?' Ella asked with an edge in her voice. 'And how come you haven't been here that much, living so close?'

'Ah, well,' Max said and started to walk again. 'I didn't live up at the house, we only came for visits and longer holidays. And we were so busy with horses and riding that we didn't...'

'You didn't go slumming around here?' Ella filled in.

'Oh please,' Allegra cut in, annoyed that Ella seemed suddenly so hostile towards Max. 'I'm sure Max didn't mean it the way it sounded. I know how horses and riding can take up a lot of time. And maybe there weren't a lot of horsey people around here.'

'I suppose,' Ella said. She increased her speed and overtook them, looking at them over her shoulder as she passed. 'I'm getting cold, so I'll walk ahead and get home. Bye, Max, nice to meet you,' she said in a tone that said it hadn't been very nice at all. 'See you later, Allegra.' Ella's rags fluttered around her as she carried on, her hair standing up in little spikes.

'Told off by a zombie,' Max said. 'What a come-down.'

Allegra started to giggle. 'I'm sorry,' she said. 'But the two of you looked so funny in your silly costumes, arguing about stupid things. I have no idea what Ella was so annoyed about or why she was so rude to you.'

'It's all about history biting us in the behind from time to time,' Max said, taking Allegra's hand. 'But we won't let it bite us, will we?'

'No,' she whispered, her breath steaming in the cold, still air, the feel of his warm hand around hers making her feel hot all over.

'Are you cold?' he asked, taking off the big black cape and putting it around her. 'Can't believe you went out without a coat or jacket.'

'It was warm earlier,' Allegra said, feeling his clean smell rise from the cape. 'But now the wind has dropped and it's freezing.'

'That's Kerry for you,' Max said, starting to walk again. 'The weather changes all the time. Four seasons in a day sometimes.' He looked up at the dark velvet sky where stars glimmered and sparkled. 'But look at that sky. You'll be able to see the Milky Way very clearly later. That's one thing they have here on the coast. These clear, starry skies. I think it's called the dark sky reserve or something. No light pollution, you see. Quite unique.'

Allegra looked up and discovered how clearly she could see the stars, and how close they seemed. 'It's wonderful,' she mumbled with awe.

'If you see a falling star, your wish will come true.'

'Only if you believe in that sort of thing,' Allegra said as they rounded the corner and started down the lane to Starlight Cottages.

'Of course,' Max said, letting go of her hand as they arrived at the little gate at the front garden of Allegra's house. 'Is this it?'

'Yes,' she said. 'This is the cottage I'm renting.'

'Sweet house,' he said.

'I love it.' Allegra took off the cape. 'Here you are. Thanks for letting me wear it.'

'You're welcome.' He took the cape and swept it around his shoulders. 'You'd better go in. It's getting very cold.'

'I know.' Allegra started to open the door. 'Good night,' she said. 'Thank you for coming to the party.'

'My pleasure,' he said. 'I really enjoyed it. Good night, Allegra.' Then he paused for a moment before he leaned towards her and placed a light kiss on her mouth. 'I never kissed a zombie before,' he said, smiling. 'Sorry if I scared you.'

'You didn't,' Allegra said, wondering if he could hear her heart beating. The light touch of his lips and the heat of his body had made her nearly dizzy. His kiss had been unexpected but something that she had secretly wished for. *Maybe the two little fairies did have magical powers after all*, she thought as she met his gaze. 'It was – nice.'

'Good,' Max said, looking suddenly contrite. 'I wasn't planning to... you know. It was just the night, the stars and the way you look that carried me away. It's as if there is something in the air.'

'I know,' Allegra said. 'The Halloween spirit or something.'

'Who knows?' He backed away, smiling. 'Enjoy the stars. See you Tuesday.' Then he moved away before she had a chance to reply.

With the kiss still burning her lips, Allegra went inside as if floating on air and, without turning on the lights, grabbed her Canada Goose jacket and went out the back door to the terrace, where she stopped to put on her jacket, zipping it up before she sat on the bench and looked out over the starlit waters of the bay. She heard a dog bark far away and the cry of an owl, then all was quiet and she was alone. She looked up at the vast expanse of black sky dotted with stars, and high above her the diamond studded belt of the Milky Way that glimmered and glittered like a million lights turning on and off.

And then she saw it: a streak of light across the sky. A falling star. She followed its path until it died away, and made a wish. She knew it was just superstition, but all the same, it felt as if it was sign of wonderful things to come. She didn't know what or when it would happen, only that the future suddenly looked all sparkly and promising.

She had no idea what the outing with Lucille tomorrow would bring, or what they would find out, but she had a feeling it would take her a step closer to solving the mystery of the ring.

17

With Lucille at the wheel of her ancient Ford Focus, they set off for Dingle early next morning. Allegra had felt apprehensive about being driven by such an old woman, but she relaxed when she realised what an excellent driver Lucille was. With her glasses perched on her nose, she had pulled on a pair of driving gloves and assured Allegra that she knew the road like the back of her hand and that the car had recently been serviced.

'I think I'm the safest driver around here,' she added as she started the car. 'Younger people drive too fast and don't pay attention to the state of the road.' This had proven to be true, and as Lucille mastered the twists and turns, avoiding the worst potholes, Allegra relaxed and enjoyed the views of the beautiful countryside. The road wound itself around the coast, making a detour to Portmagee, a lovely little seaside town where a bridge led to Valentia Island, which was well worth a visit, according to Lucille. Over large cups of cappuccino in a small café overlooking the harbour, they chatted about the previous evening and the party at the library.

'I saw you talking to Maura and Tom's little girls,' Lucille said. 'Aren't they the sweetest?'

'Gorgeous,' Allegra agreed. 'We FaceTimed with my niece, Emma, in New York, who is just a little older. It was so fun.' She paused as she sipped her coffee. 'But you know what I found out? Their mother, Maura, could be related to the Walsh family.'

'Our Walsh family?' Lucille asked.

'I don't know, but I'll find out when I have coffee with her next week. In any case, her maiden name was Walsh.'

'I had no idea she was a Walsh,' Lucille said. 'But then I'm just a blow-in from Tipperary, so there is a lot I don't know about the people of Sandy Cove.'

'What made you move there?' Allegra asked.

'Lots of things,' Lucille replied. 'Mostly loneliness. But also because of Ella. Her mother and I were close friends and we lived together in my house in Tipperary before she died six years ago. And when I came here to help Ella, who was recovering from an accident, I fell in love with the village, the people and the beautiful landscape. And when my son Rory followed me and very quickly fell head over heels in love with Ella, it was as if it was meant to happen. There was a little bit of fighting between Rory and me at first. He didn't approve of me moving from Tipperary. And Ella took my side and that caused some problems between them. But they were so attracted to each other, I have a feeling they enjoyed the fighting in some strange way. But after a lot of arguing we all sorted it out and everything fell into place, so all is well.'

'But you must miss your house in Tipperary?' Allegra said.

'Not really. There were so many sad memories,' Lucille said. 'I was quite happy there when my husband was alive, but after he passed away, it was a lonely place. He died in a horrible riding accident.'

'How terrible,' Allegra said.

'It was,' Lucille said, stirring her coffee. 'And as his family and friends had never really accepted me, I felt so lonely.'

'Why didn't they accept you?' Allegra asked, wondering how it was possible not to like Lucille.

'Oh, it was all about class and where you came from in those days. The horsey set was quite snobby back in the 1950s. Anyone who wasn't born on a horse wasn't good enough in their eyes.'

'But that was a long time ago.'

'Oh yes,' Lucille said, looking brighter. 'That kind of snobbishness is all gone now, thank goodness. Except some people like to think they're better than others. Only most of those families have very little money left to be superior with, if you see what I mean. They do know about horses, though, I have to give them that.'

'Like the Courtneys,' Allegra said.

'I suppose. But I don't know them that well. That good-looking young man you were with yesterday is one of them, isn't he?'

'Yes. But he's not at all superior in any way.'

'Not to you perhaps, as you're such a pretty girl. Ella says he's arrogant. But she knows what I went through, so she's a little biased against someone like that.'

'She was a bit snippy with him last night.'

'Ah, that's just Ella. Her bark is worse than her bite. She might just have been testing him.' Lucille buttoned her jacket and got up. 'We'd better get going if we're to get to Dingle in time for lunch. I want to show you some of the beautiful places on the way there, too.'

They drove on along the road that snaked up the coast, stopping to look at the stunning views of the Atlantic from time to time. Allegra took a number of shots with her phone to post on Instagram. Distracted by all the beauty around her, she nearly forgot why they were there until they drove up the steep narrow street in Dingle town and stopped in front of a two-storey house painted light blue with pink window frames. A sign over the door said 'Walsh's Café' in Celtic letters on a light green background.

'Very bright colours,' Lucille remarked. 'But it suits the street.'

Allegra had to agree. Indeed, the whole town was a riot of colours against the backdrop of the harbour, the green hills and the ocean beyond. There was a fresh smell from the sea mixed with woodsmoke in the air, which added to the atmosphere of a town on the edge of the Atlantic coast. She had asked Lucille to take a shot of her beside the bronze statue of Fungie, the tame dolphin that had lived in the bay for over forty years and then disappeared without a trace.

'They think he probably died,' Lucille had said. 'Everyone was so sad when he was no longer there.'

Lucille switched off the engine and got out of the car while Allegra clambered out of the passenger seat. Then they opened the pink door and entered a large airy room, its walls hung with framed photos of the town and surrounding areas.

Lucille looked around the nearly empty café. 'Where do you want to sit?'

Allegra pointed at a table by the bay window. 'Why not over there? It has nice views of the town and the harbour.'

Just as they sat down, a door opened behind the counter and a tall woman with black curly hair looked at them with a big smile.

'Hello, there. Welcome to Walsh's Café.'

'Thank you,' Lucille said. 'What a nice place you have here.'

'Newly refurbished,' the woman said proudly.

'So you're the owner?' Lucille asked.

'I am,' the woman replied. 'With my husband, Liam, of course.'

'So he's the Walsh?' Lucille asked. 'I mean, he's of the Walsh family?'

The woman laughed. 'That's right. Walsh is my married name.'

'Thought so,' Lucille said, looking satisfied. 'Nice to meet you, Mrs Walsh. I'm Lucille Kennedy and this is Allegra Casey, who's visiting from America.'

'Call me Sheila, please,' the woman said. 'Have you just arrived?'

'Yes. We drove from Sandy Cove this morning,' Lucille replied. 'That's between Ballinskelligs and Waterville.'

'I know where it is. My husband's family came from there a long time ago.'

'Really?' Lucille said in pretend surprise. 'That's interesting. How come the family ended up here?'

'Well,' Sheila started, 'Liam's grandfather moved here with his mother and siblings in the 1940s when their father died. Liam's great-uncle Sean was the one who bought this house for them when they had to leave the house in Sandy Cove.'

'So this Sean Walsh was rich?' Lucille asked.

Sheila shrugged. 'Yes, I suppose he was. But I don't know much more.' She paused. 'But you came here for lunch, so I'll stop blathering.' She picked up two menus from the counter and handed them to Lucille and Allegra. 'This is the winter menu. A slimmed-down version of the summer one. I can recommend the soup of the day. Potato and leek with soda bread. Or the smoked salmon and scrambled eggs. The prawn and mussel salad is very nice, too, also served with soda bread.' She drew breath and looked at them expectantly.

'I'll have the soup,' Allegra said.

'For me, too,' Lucille said and handed back her menu. 'And coffee to follow.'

'And then I'll serve you our special apple crumble,' Sheila said as she took the menus. 'On the house as you're from Sandy Cove.'

'That's very kind of you,' Lucille said. 'And maybe we could say hello to your husband, if he's in?'

'He'll be here soon, so I'll let him know we have guests from Sandy Cove.'

'Hmm,' Lucille said when Sheila had left to get their orders. 'She was nice and breezy. A bit too breezy, if you know what I mean.'

'Not really,' Allegra said. 'I thought she was lovely.'

Lucille nodded. 'She was. But did you notice how she steered the conversation away from Sean Walsh and whatever happened to enable him to buy this house?'

'She just wanted us to order,' Allegra argued. 'Maybe she has other things to do. She said she didn't know anything.'

'That's what she *said*,' Lucille muttered. 'But I think there is something more to this story and it might be something the family want to forget.'

'Maybe her husband knows something?' Allegra suggested.

Lucille opened her mouth to speak, but closed it again when Sheila came back with two steaming bowls of soup and put them in front of them.

'There you go,' she said. 'I'll get you the soda bread that I just took out of the oven.'

'This smells wonderful,' Allegra said and picked up her spoon, sipping the thick, fragrant soup, enjoying the flavours of leek, potato and herbs. Then, when Sheila returned with the soda bread, she spread a still-warm slice with butter and took a bite, amazed at how the slightly salty, buttery taste married beautifully with the newly baked bread.

'Mmm,' she said when she had swallowed. 'This is amazing.'

'The best of Irish cooking,' Lucille said proudly as she dug in.

They chatted quietly about what they knew about the Walsh family so far as they finished their lunch, trying to connect it with Kate Vanderpump's story. Then Sheila came over to clear their plates and announced that her husband had just got home and would serve them dessert and coffee.

'I have to do the school run, so I'll say goodbye now. Lovely to meet you, and enjoy your visit to Dingle.' Then she left as quickly as she had arrived.

'Well, she was nice,' Lucille said.

'Yes,' Allegra said absentmindedly as she looked out the window at the view of the colourful houses lining the street that sloped all the way down to the harbour. She watched a fishing boat coming home from a day out at sea, then turned as a man with dark hair and a rather big nose arrived at their table with two plates of apple crumble that he set down with a flourish.

'Apple crumble for the ladies from Sandy Cove,' he said.

'Thank you,' Lucille said. 'That is so kind of you.'

'We had a lot of it left over,' the man confessed. 'We overestimated the number of guests today, so you're doing us a favour. We don't like throwing away good food.'

'No, neither do I,' Lucille agreed. She looked at the man for a moment. 'Are you Liam Walsh?' she asked.

'I am,' he replied. 'I think you met my wife, Sheila, earlier.'

'We did,' Lucille said. 'Lovely woman.'

'She is,' Liam agreed with a warm smile. 'So who are you, then?'

Lucille smiled and held out her hand. 'I'm Lucille Kennedy and this is Allegra Casey, who is visiting from America.'

'Nice to meet you,' Liam said, shaking their hands. 'Enjoy the crumble.' Then he looked at them for a moment. 'I have a feeling you'd like to hear more about the family. As you've come all the way from Sandy Cove, I mean.'

Lucille nodded. 'We would indeed. Pull up a chair,' she said. 'And tell us about the Walshes and how you ended up here in Dingle in this enchanting house.'

'Oh.' Liam stood there for a moment. 'That's a long story,

but I'd be happy to tell you. I'll bring your coffees and then I'll sit down with you for a bit as we're not very busy right now.'

'Excellent,' Lucille said.

The apple crumble was delicious and they had nearly finished when Liam approached, carrying a tray with three coffee cups, a milk jug and a bowl of sugar.

'I didn't know how you take it, so I brought everything,' he said and put the tray on the table before he pulled out a chair and sat down. 'So,' he said, 'what was it you wanted to know?'

'Oh,' Lucille said airily as she took a cup from the tray, 'just a general question about your family. They used to live in Sandy Cove, so we wondered why they moved here.'

Liam nodded and stirred some sugar into his coffee. 'They moved here in the late 1940s. My great-grandmother and her children had to leave the coastguard station after her husband died. But then Great-Uncle Sean helped her buy this house, which was close to her sister. It was the perfect place for a little café and they also rented out a few of the rooms to earn some extra money. Sean wanted his mother to have an income so she'd be secure in her old age. And her family continued to run the business as we do today.' Liam stopped and smiled. 'That's it, really.'

'So did Sean stay and help run the café and B&B?' Allegra asked.

'No,' Liam replied. 'He actually went to Scotland. He had a friend over there who had a car repair garage and Sean wanted to invest a bit of his money in that. I think he wanted to get away for a while.'

'Why?' Lucille asked.

Liam shrugged. 'No idea. He had been in America before the war, so I'm guessing he liked travelling around.'

'But the family all stayed here, though?' Allegra asked.

'Oh yes. They settled in very quickly and the business took

off,' Liam said. 'Funny, but we're still considered to be blow-ins even after all these years.'

Lucille laughed. 'It takes several hundred years before you'll be a local.'

Allegra nodded. 'That's what Max said. The Courtneys have been at Strawberry Hill since the eighteenth century but they're still considered blow-ins.'

Liam froze, his hand with the spoon in the air. 'The Courtneys?' he said, his face suddenly pale. 'Of Strawberry Hill?'

'Yes,' Lucille said. 'Allegra is friends with one of them, Max. Do you know him?'

'No,' Liam said and got up. 'We don't know any of those people. I'm afraid I have to leave now. I just remembered something urgent I have to see to. Sorry about that... Enjoy the coffee.'

'But we haven't paid for the meal,' Lucille protested.

'On the house,' Liam said. 'Goodbye. Nice to have met you.' He rounded the counter and disappeared through the door to the kitchen.

Lucille and Allegra stared at each other.

'What was that all about?' Allegra asked. 'I thought he was going to faint when I mentioned the Courtneys.'

'I know.' Lucille stirred her coffee, looking thoughtful. 'He practically told us to leave. There is some bad blood there, I think. Something to do with the Courtneys and the Walshes. And that money Sean got. Did it come from the Courtneys? And if so, why? This is getting more and more interesting.'

'But it could be something sad,' Allegra said. 'Something that would cause a lot of pain if we were to reveal it. Wouldn't it be better if we left it alone?'

'Maybe it should come out in the open,' Lucille argued. 'Giving everyone closure, perhaps. And now that there seems to be a dispute about the will and the inheritance, the truth has to come out.'

'I suppose,' Allegra said without conviction. 'But I'm not sure I like it. And if I hadn't arrived with the story and the ring, maybe things would have stayed the same.'

But then I wouldn't have met Max, she thought. And that was something she felt was meant to happen. The ring and the story had both led her to this beautiful place – and that man who pulled at her heartstrings every time they met.

'Things couldn't stay the same,' Lucille argued. 'Not because of you, but because of that woman who arrived out of the blue with her claim to be one of the heirs. That really upset the applecart big time. So you're not to blame at all. In fact—' Lucille leaned closer, muttering under her breath, 'you might be able to save their bacon in some way. Plus, you might get the truth out from another angle, so to speak. We just have to keep digging until we find all the facts.'

Allegra thought for a moment. 'I suppose you're right. And we're looking at it from Sean's side, so if we keep going we might discover what really happened to him.'

'That's right.' Lucille grabbed her handbag and jacket and stood up. 'But we'd better get out of here. I think the mere mention of the Courtneys was like dropping a bomb. Did you see his face? He was as white as a sheet. What on earth did those Courtneys do to poor Sean, do you think?'

Allegra got up and started to zip up her jacket. 'I have no idea. But I intend to find out. I'm going to see the house with Max on Tuesday. I will keep my eyes and ears open while we look around.'

'Don't get side-tracked by that handsome face,' Lucille warned. 'That man could charm an army.'

'I know,' Allegra said. 'But I won't let him distract me.'

'And pigs might fly,' Lucille muttered as they left the café.

18

Lucille's words popped into Allegra's mind as she spotted Max standing outside the front door of Strawberry Hill when she arrived. Dressed in a navy polo neck and jeans with a leather bomber jacket thrown across his shoulders, he was the picture of careless elegance. His eyes lit up as she got out of the car and he ran forward to greet her with a light kiss on the cheek.

'Right on time,' he said as he pulled back to look at her. 'And you're dressed so perfectly for exploring an old wreck.'

'Oh, you're not that old,' Allegra joked. She had dressed carefully in corduroy trousers and a thick grey sweater that wouldn't suffer too much damage if she were to encounter dust and cobwebs.

Max laughed. 'Not old, but a little worn around the edges. I meant the house, not me.'

'I know. Couldn't resist a little tease,' Allegra said, smiling at him, yet again taking pleasure in being with a man taller than her.

'But of course, I wouldn't mind being explored by you,' he added with a wink.

'Could we go inside now?' Allegra asked, trying her best not to be pulled into a flirtatious conversation. 'I'm dying to see the house.'

Max pulled at the massive front door that creaked as it slowly swung open. 'Walk into my parlour, as the spider said to the fly.'

'Yeah, well, I'm no fly,' Allegra said. 'So I'll step inside without fear.'

'You're a brave woman,' Max said as the door clanged shut behind them.

Allegra didn't reply as she found herself in a huge hall with black-and-white tiles on the floor. A big round table stood in the middle and the walls were covered with carved wood panelling. A cavernous fireplace took up most of the wall on the left; above it was a stag's head which seemed to stare at her with its black, glassy eyes. There was a strong smell of damp and cold woodsmoke and Allegra suddenly sneezed.

'Bless you,' Max said. 'The air is a little musty here, I'm afraid.' He walked across the tiles and opened a door to an inner hall, nearly as big again, where a curved staircase with a beautifully carved banister rose to the upper floor. 'Seventeenth-century,' Max said.

'It's wonderful,' Allegra said in awe, looking at the portraits that covered the walls.

'Ancestors,' Max said, pointing up. 'That one there in the powdered wig is my namesake, Max Courtney, who was the squire here about two hundred years ago. He was also the resident magistrate and a number of other things. Quite magnificent, don't you think?'

Allegra stared up at the portrait of the man in a blue silk coat and ruffled shirt, his white, wigged head cocked and his bright blue eyes looking haughtily at her. 'Not a very cosy man, I think.'

'Probably not,' Max said with a smile. 'I was scared of him when I was a little boy. I thought he had cold, cruel eyes. But that's probably just the way he was painted.' Max pointed at a set of double doors. 'Drawing room and dining room through there. And there's even a ballroom. Big, dusty old rooms with no particular interest except for some fine pieces of furniture and a lot more family portraits. We could skip those for now and go straight to the library. My favourite room in the whole house. We use it as the main sitting room these days. Davina spent a lot of time in there.'

'I'd love to see it,' Allegra said, eager to discover more about Davina. She found herself enchanted by this house, despite its dilapidated state. There was something warm and welcoming, as if the house liked her being there and wanted her to be part of its history.

They walked through another set of double doors into a vast room where every wall was covered in bookcases crammed with books, mostly leatherbound volumes but also a mish-mash of hardcovers, paperbacks, art books, maps and stacks of magazines. The oriental carpet, its colours faded with time, was still beautiful despite a few holes here and there. Two chintz sofas flanked the big fireplace where a pile of logs and kindling waited to be lit. Allegra glanced at the mahogany desk by the window with its scarred leather top and wondered if the many drawers might hold some important letters or papers of interest.

Max followed her gaze. 'They went through that the other day. Nothing much except old bills, receipts, some letters and old Christmas cards. Kate was very disappointed.'

Allegra looked out the window at the view of the garden sloping down to the river and the paddock where she could see horses grazing on the sparse winter grass. 'Lovely view from here.'

'Yes,' Max said. 'Davina loved sitting here doing all the paperwork for the yard and writing letters and so on.'

'Did she like to read?' Allegra asked, walking to one of the bookcases, glancing along the row of books.

'Yes, she did,' Max replied. 'Mostly detective stories and biographies. She loved Dick Francis in particular, for obvious reasons.'

'And what are they?' Allegra asked.

'You haven't heard of him?' Max asked, raising an eyebrow.

'No. I'm not into British detective stories, really.'

'Well, Dick Francis was a steeplechase jockey originally before he started writing detective stories set in the world of horse racing,' Max explained. 'All his books centred around horses. That's why Davina loved them. She'd read them all, I think.' Max pulled out a paperback with a horse and jockey against a yellow background on the cover. 'This one was published in the mid-1980s. Davina read it several times. The last time was just before she became ill and had to go to a nursing home.'

'*Bolt*,' Allegra read, taking the book from Max. 'It's about a jockey called Kit Fielding.' She turned the book and read the description on the back. It said the story was about a princess whose invalid husband was being threatened and her best horses were being killed. She turns to a detective called Kit, who is involved in some kind of feud. It all sounded quite intriguing, if a little melodramatic. 'Sounds very romantic.'

'Yes, it does. But Davina was romantic deep down. Loved a good tear-jerker too. And for some reason, this book made her cry.'

'Really? I wonder why,' Allegra mused, turning the book over.

'No idea. Could be that she missed being in that world when she got too old to ride or look after the horses. Gwen had taken over by then. I caught Davina sitting on the sofa over there, crying, with this book in her lap.'

'Did she say why she was sad?' Allegra asked.

'I didn't ask. I backed out of the room to give her some

privacy. She would have hated anyone to see her like that, even though she was over a hundred years old then.'

'Hmm,' Allegra said and flicked through the pages, trying to get the gist of the story. 'Doesn't seem like a sad book.' She gave a start as a piece of paper fell out of the back and fluttered to the floor. 'Oh,' she said, looking at it. 'Something fell out. What is it?'

Max bent down and picked it up, glancing at it. 'A bill? No... it's a letter.' He turned it over and looked at the text. 'No, it's... Oh my God.' His face turned suddenly ashen.

'What is it?' Allegra asked.

'It's a letter from *him*,' Max said in a near whisper.

'Who?' Allegra asked. 'You mean—?'

Max nodded. 'Yes. Sean Walsh. Dated about ten years ago.'

'Just before he died,' Allegra said, remembering what Kate Vanderpump had said.

'Yes.' Max turned the letter again. 'I'll read it to you.'

'Okay.' Allegra's heart beat faster as Max started to read.

'Dearest Davina,

'Many years have passed since I last saw you. Too many years, my dear, since that day when you told me you had to go back to Ireland and that you realised our marriage was a mistake.'

Max paused and looked at Allegra.

'So they *were* married,' she said.

'Looks like it,' Max said and read on. '*I wanted to follow you, to ask you to reconsider, but I knew it would be pointless to try to stick things back together again. So much had happened to drive us apart and I knew it was not possible to go back to happier times or try to recreate them. We were simply not compatible, that's all. I know now that accepting the money from your father was the wrong thing to do, but I had no choice as my mother and my brothers and sisters were homeless. I, as the oldest son, had to* take care of them, and when your father offered me the money on the promise to stay away from you, I had to take it.'

'Oh my God,' Allegra exclaimed. 'So that's where he got the money. Davina's father—'

'Bribed him with money to stay away from her,' Max filled in. 'And he took it. Not very noble of him, was it?'

'No, but he had no choice,' Allegra argued.

'Maybe not,' Max muttered and resumed reading. '*And then, after setting up the business for my mother in Dingle, I left for Scotland to start a garage and car mechanic shop. All that money helped rescue my family and there was enough left over for me to start afresh. I tried to forget you, but it was impossible. I could never get you out of my heart.*

'*That day in 1939, when we met in Boston, was the happiest day of my life. The memory of our few weeks at that little inn on Cape Cod is forever in my heart. And then, when you accepted my proposal, I was overwhelmed. But then, a few days later, when you lost the ring while we walked on the beach, I felt that it was a sign, an omen that we would never be happy together the way we hoped. And I was proven right years later. So many obstacles were in our way. The war, and having to rush back to our families before it got worse, was the beginning of the end of our relationship. Then your father offered me that money that I had to accept – your shock and disappointment and harsh words before I left are forever etched in my mind.*

'*I thought I would start a new life in Scotland and tried to forget you. I had nearly succeeded when you arrived in Edinburgh out of the blue. You came to work for a while at a yard just outside town, training young horses – but you knew I was living there and you looked me up. Just to show there were no hard feelings, you said, when we went out for a drink. But that resulted in us falling in love again and then we were married two months later. But the marriage didn't last. We couldn't forget the bitter-*

ness of the past and you left me for good and we never saw each other again.

'A year later, I met a lovely Scottish girl and remarried and you were back home at Strawberry Hill, where you still live, I've heard. I hope you've had a happy life. I've been quite content here with my family and worked hard to grow my business. But now I'm at the end of my life and I don't think I have much time left. My heart is weak and my kidneys are in bad shape. Not surprising for someone my age.

'I've had a good life and some blissful moments, many of them spent with you. I hope you could find it in your heart to forgive me for all the hurt I caused you. We loved each other but maybe our love wasn't strong enough to endure our differences. So with this letter, I say goodbye and good luck.

'I just wanted you to know that I loved you with all my heart, dear Davina. We are both old, so maybe we will meet in the next life and connect in a spiritual way. I do hope that is what will happen.

'All my love and best wishes, Sean.'

When Max finished reading, they stared at each other in silence before Allegra spoke, her voice hoarse and her eyes brimming. 'That is so sad.'

'Yes.' Max blinked and looked down at the letter in his hand. 'That's what made Davina cry that day. Not the book.'

'I know. How hard it must have been for her to read it.'

'She saved it and read it again and again, I think. She must have felt awful that they never met again and sorted it all out.'

'But, but...' Allegra stammered, 'did you notice that there was no mention of a child? He said he was happy with his family, but he didn't say anything about this supposed baby. That makes me wonder about Kate's story.'

Max looked thoughtful. 'I know. It certainly looks different now.' He stuck the letter into the book. 'I'm putting this back.

It's a good hiding place until it's all resolved. It seems the right thing to do anyway. I don't want to betray Davina.'

'Are there any photos of her when she was young?' Allegra asked, eyeing a table behind one of the sofas. It was crammed with silver-framed photos and it struck her there must be at least one of Davina as a child or a young woman.

'Of course.' Max put the book back on the shelf and walked to the table where he picked up one of the silver-framed photos. 'This one is great. She was photographed at a party in Dublin in the Thirties, I think. She must have been around eighteen or nineteen. Here.' He held out the photo to Allegra.

She peered at the black-and-white photo of a beautiful young woman with dark hair in a white silk dress that clung to her slim body. She wore a long pearl necklace and matching dangly earrings. Her soulful eyes looked into the camera.

'Oh, she was really gorgeous.'

Max nodded. 'So I believe. Not hard to imagine Sean falling for her. I only knew her as an old woman with grey hair who was an incredible rider. Rough, tough, taking no prisoners, that kind of thing. But she had a sweet, gentle side and was kind and generous to us kids. She kept two ponies for me and Edwina to ride when we came here on holiday. Taught us everything about horses and riding.' Max stopped, a sad look in his eyes. 'God, I miss her. She was such fun. And boy, could she argue.'

'I wish I could have met her.' Allegra put the photo back on the table and looked at the others which were mostly of family occasions: weddings, christenings and Christmas parties with a Christmas tree in the hall, reaching up to the ceiling. 'What a huge Christmas tree!' she exclaimed.

Max laughed. 'I know. Davina insisted that it had to reach the ceiling. It's fifteen feet or something and it took a lot of effort to find a tree that tall.' He looked at Allegra across the table with the photos. 'That letter shook me a bit, I have to admit.'

'Me too.' Allegra met his gaze, the sudden spark between them giving her a jolt.

Max seemed to shake himself. 'Do you want to see the rest of the house? The other rooms are quite amazing, actually.'

'Yes, why not?' Allegra replied. The room suddenly felt charged with emotion. That letter had affected her, too, and wandering around the house might defuse the atmosphere and occupy their minds for a while.

But the tour around the big rooms full of old furniture and paintings failed to cool the atmosphere between them. They went through the drawing room to the ballroom, their steps echoing on the parquet floors in the eerie silence and then finally to the large dining room with its tapestry-covered walls, long mahogany table and tall windows overlooking the terrace. Max stopped by the massive sideboard that still held a number of silver dishes.

'This is where the family gathered for breakfast in the old days. And they had some amazing dinner parties and hunt balls here. Way before my time, of course, so I can only try to imagine the grandeur.'

Allegra leaned against the sideboard and looked at him. 'Do you feel sad that those days are all over?'

He laughed. 'God, no. What a bore it must have been. Dressing for dinner every night and no swearing in front of the ladies and all that polite chatter and etiquette. Thank God we're all equals and all living simpler lives. I think Davina hated it. That's why she kept trying to run away. I'd say she was livid with Sean for taking that money.'

'I would've been very disappointed in him, if I had been in her place.'

Max moved closer and looked deep into her eyes. 'In his place, I would never have accepted that money.'

'Even if your family was starving?' Allegra asked, her breath catching in her throat as she looked into those blue eyes. Being so close to him made her suddenly feel faint.

He slowly put his arms around her. 'To hell with my family,' he said softly into her ear. 'To hell with everything. All I want is to kiss you.'

'Me too,' she whispered before their lips met. It was as if she was pulled to him by a magnet and she couldn't stop herself responding in a hot kiss that lasted so long they had to break apart to breathe. 'Oh, God what are we doing?' Allegra panted.

'I don't know but I like it,' he said and kissed her again.

Allegra pressed herself against him and gave herself up to the kissing. She had been kissed before, had a few serious relationships and fallen in and out of love many times. But this was different, this was forgetting time and place and who they were, and what they were doing, and if it was right or wrong. It was true passion that had been building up ever since they first met. It was totally, utterly crazy and impossible. And the most wonderful thing that had ever happened to her.

They finally pulled apart. 'I didn't plan this at all,' Max exclaimed. 'It just happened. You stood there looking so cute and puzzled. And then I tried to imagine myself in Sean's shoes. But then a feeling just came over me and I...'

Allegra laughed, her face hot and her heart beating so hard she thought she would faint. 'I had that feeling, too, just then.' She leaned her head against his chest. 'It's so strange. We have only just met, and here I am feeling as if I've known you a lot longer.'

'Me too,' he whispered, pulling her close. 'Like you've been waiting for me somewhere across the Atlantic and now you're here and we both feel the same thing. That first time when you got out of the car and stood there in front of the house, you took my breath away.'

'Davina brought us together,' Allegra said, 'in some strange way. I wouldn't be here today if I hadn't found that ring.'

'God bless Davina,' Max said. 'I think finding that letter was also a sign. It made me feel sad that those two didn't have the life together they planned.'

'I wonder what happened?' Allegra said. 'Why did they find each other only to part again? What made them break up like that?'

'And why was there no mention of this supposed child?' Max asked. 'So many questions that might never be answered.'

'I'm going to try to find the answers to some of them,' Allegra declared. She pulled away from Max. 'I haven't told you that I went to Dingle on Sunday with Lucille where we met some of Sean's family. The descendants of his mother and siblings to whom he gave money to start a café and B&B. They still run the café.'

'Really?' Max stared at Allegra with interest. 'So what did you find out?'

'Nothing, actually,' Allegra replied. 'The mere mention of the Courtneys made them practically throw us out of the place. They were all smiles at first while we talked about Sandy Cove and the coastguard station, but then I happened to mention the Courtneys. Liam Walsh, the owner, totally clammed up and said he didn't know any of you and then he left.'

'How weird. As if he was holding some kind of grudge against Davina's family.'

'Could be because of where that money came from,' Allegra suggested. 'Not the most gentlemanly thing to do, was it? Either by Davina's father or Sean.'

'No,' Max agreed. 'But it was such a long time ago. Why would they still feel hostile against us?'

'Maybe things like that stay in families,' Allegra suggested. 'Like a legend that they can't erase. Bad feelings can linger for years and years.'

'I think you're right,' Max said. 'It's a bit similar in my family. All that aggro between my parents seems still to be around like a bad smell. It soured things between Edwina and me. We were made to take side between our parents. She sided with my mother and I felt more loyal to my dad. And now she wants to sell this house and I don't. But she might succeed now that she has this Kate woman as her ally.'

'Yes, but those claims might be proven to be fake,' Allegra said.

'I'm not so sure. She looks very determined and might win in the end.' He shivered. 'Sorry. This whole thing makes me feel so weird. Let's get out of this gloom and take a walk outside.'

'Okay.' Allegra took his hand. 'Come on, we'll go and see the horses,' she suggested, thinking it might cheer him up.

Max nodded and started to walk across the room to the tall windows, pulling her with him. 'We'll go out this way so you can see the terrace. It has lovely views even on a cloudy winter's day.'

He opened the tall French windows and they stepped onto the terrace that had a stone balustrade and planters dotted around the perimeter. They stopped at the edge and gazed across the lawn that sloped down to the river gushing noisily over rocks and boulders. 'It's quite wild right now because of all the rain,' Max said. 'But in the summer it's just a trickle. I love this view.'

'It's very nice,' Allegra said softly, touched by the obvious love he had for the house and the land.

Suddenly a crunch of tyres on the gravel could be heard from the side of the house. 'Someone's here,' Max said and let go of Allegra's hand. 'Maybe Gwen's back.'

But it wasn't Gwen who had alighted from the Audi that had just pulled up in front of the house. It was Edwina and Kate, both dressed in down jackets, jeans and boots. They smiled as Max and Allegra rounded the corner. Then a tall, elegant man in a Barbour got out of the back seat and stood looking around while he took a notebook out of his pocket.

'What's going on?' Max asked, looking at the man.

'Hello,' he said, holding out his hand. 'You must be Max Courtney.'

'Courtney-Smythe,' Max corrected, ignoring the man's hand. 'And who are you, if you don't mind my asking?'

'This is Jonathan O'Reilly,' Edwina cut in, walking to the man's side. 'From Sotheby's International real estate.'

Max stiffened. 'Real estate?'

'Yes,' Jonathan O'Reilly replied. 'We buy and sell houses. Mostly country houses with great potential like this one.' He looked up at the façade. 'Quite impressive, I have to say.'

'Is it?' Max said sourly. 'That's nice to hear. Except it's not for sale and never will be.'

'That's not what I heard,' Jonathan O'Reilly countered. 'I've been told it's only a matter of time before the probate is sorted, isn't that right?'

'Yes, so far you're correct,' Max said, shooting Kate a stern look. 'But not the rest of it. There's a claim to the property that needs to be proved before the fate of the house can even be discussed.'

'But we have some news,' Kate said. 'We just heard from the solicitor.'

'You did?' Max asked, looking startled.

'Yes,' Edwina cut in. 'He'll be contacting everyone as soon as he finishes the paperwork. Kate's documents have been examined and been declared valid. There is only the official report to come.'

'Which is just a formality. So I'm a legal heir to this estate,' Kate said, beaming a broad smile at Max. 'We're officially cousins and co-owners of Strawberry Hill.'

19

Kate Vanderpump's announcement and the subsequent phone calls to the solicitor, which confirmed her story, had pierced a hole in Allegra's happy mood, and the afterglow of what had happened between her and Max quickly faded as she drove home in the late afternoon. They hadn't had a chance to exchange so much as a glance after that bombshell and, feeling she was intruding, Allegra had left quietly without saying goodbye.

Everything seemed to have been put on hold; even the plan for the Christmas event was now looking as if it wouldn't happen. If the house was put on the market and would be shown to prospective buyers, the estate agents weren't likely to agree to such an event. The house could even be sold by then, Allegra thought glumly. She was so sad for Max that she hardly noticed the gorgeous landscape bathed in a golden light from the sun sinking into the sea or the soft breeze as she arrived at the cottage. She had begun to understand his deep love for the house as they moved through the big, dark rooms. Despite the damp patches on the walls, the peeling wallpaper and crumbling plaster, she had been captivated by the beauty of the interior. The graceful proportions of the rooms, the high ceilings, the sunlight streaming in through the tall sash windows, were all unique and wonderful. A true architectural gem, but also a home that, despite its size and dilapidated state, should be allowed to stay in the family. Turning it into a hotel or conference centre seemed like a sacrilege.

Allegra sat in the car for a moment and looked at the cottage. She felt as if she had been here for months instead of the eight days that had passed since she arrived. She had been pitchforked into a world she had not known existed before she came to this little seaside village. So much went on under the calm, peaceful surface and she had learned so much about the history and the many layers of society that still existed today.

Max was part of a family that was not quite accepted here, and the barriers of class still lingered, making a natural and relaxed relationship difficult between the once privileged so-called 'upper classes' and the people who lived and worked in the village. Ella's reaction to Max came very much from those old conflicts that shouldn't exist today, but still did. Allegra's heart ached for Max because she knew how honest and true he was, and how he loved the house that had been in his family for so many generations. But that could be seen as arrogance and a wish to cling to old values instead of simply loving a beautiful old house and wanting to help his cousin Gwen to keep living and working there.

The letter they had found was confusing, even though it confirmed the fact that Sean and Davina had been, if briefly, married. But there was no mention of them having had a child, which, to Allegra, seemed strange as that would surely have been a strong bond between them. But Kate Vanderpump's documents appeared to be genuine, so that was possibly the end of the argument. So sad for the two cousins who wanted to keep the house, especially for Gwen. And Max? Her thoughts drifted yet again to what had happened between them and she wondered if it had meant as much to him as it had to her. Maybe kissing a woman he found attractive was just a habit to him...

Allegra gave a start as her phone pinged and she picked it up, finding a message from Max with a YouTube link. She clicked on it and found it was a jazz number sung by Louis Armstrong with the title 'A Kiss to Build a Dream On'. With a slow smile, she listened to the soft gravelly voice singing the lovely lyrics, her heart soaring as she remembered the touch of his lips and his arms around her. She knew then that the moment had been as blissful for him as it was for her, and that there was now something special between them. He had been distracted by the arrival of Kate Vanderpump and his sister, but they would eventually be able to continue what they had started. Allegra smiled and put the phone away, but it rang almost immediately, making her jump. Startled, she pulled it out of her bag again and answered, hoping it would be Max. But she was disappointed.

'Hi,' a breathless voice said. 'Maura Quinn here. How are you?'

'Oh hi, Maura,' Allegra replied, trying to pull herself together. 'I'm fine. And you?'

'I'm okay. Getting heavier by the minute. I'd love to see you if you have the time to pop in for a coffee. How about tomorrow morning? Thomas is going to be stuck in his study practising and the kids will be in day-care and school.' Maura drew breath. 'Sorry,' she said with a laugh. 'That sounded a bit needy. But I thought you looked like someone nice to chat to and I'm in need of company before I push out this baby. I won't do that while you're here, I promise.'

Allegra laughed. 'That's a relief. I wouldn't know what to do.'

'Of course not. In any case my aunt lives next door, so I can yell for her should something happen. But it won't for a while, my doctor tells me, more's the pity. I might ask her to come anyway, just to meet you. Eleven o'clock okay for you?'

'Perfect,' Allegra said. 'That gives me time for a run beforehand.'

'Oh, you're the fit and healthy type? That's something we have in common. I'm a yoga freak myself when I'm not pregnant.'

'I love that, too,' Allegra said, smiling. Maura was a real tonic. 'How do I find your house?'

'It's the big white one with the green door at the end of the main street. The front garden has a tall cabbage palm and a clump of pampas grass. Easy to spot.'

'I think I know where it is,' Allegra said.

'Great. See you tomorrow. Bye for now,' Maura said and hung up.

Allegra smiled and put her phone back in her bag. Maura was such a fun, friendly woman and she looked forward to the coffee the next morning. It would give her an opportunity to ask about the Walsh family connection and perhaps get another clue to the mystery of Sean and Davina, and what had happened between them. But it might not be quite correct to pump Maura for information, so she would have to be casual and not appear too inquisitive. She would do her very best to find anything out that would be useful to Max. Kate Vanderpump had to be defeated somehow. There was something that didn't quite hang together in her claims, but she couldn't quite put her finger on it.

Something was missing. But what?

Maura's house was easy to find as Allegra had passed it a few times on her way to the main beach. It was a nice two-storey house with a white stucco façade and green window frames matching the front door with its big wrought-iron knocker. Allegra lifted it and banged, and the door was opened a few seconds later by a beaming Maura.

'There you are!' she exclaimed. 'Right on time, too, and with a nice glow from your run. Lovely day, isn't it?'

'Gorgeous,' Allegra agreed as she squinted against the bright sunlight. 'I had a great run on the beach about an hour ago.'

'That makes me jealous,' Maura said. 'But I'll be able to run in a few months myself. I'm so looking forward to not being like a stranded whale like right now.' She opened the door wider and stepped aside. 'But come in. I thought we'd sit in the sunroom so we can look at the view while we have coffee. I have it all ready and my auntie Dee is joining us a little later.'

Allegra walked into a bright hall where she hung her jacket on an antique hallstand crammed with coats and hats. Then they entered through a door into a bright kitchen with a sunroom at the end that had amazing views of the bay and the islands beyond. The table in front of the light green velvet sofa was already laid with cups and a plate of cookies and slices of cake and the room smelled of coffee and vanilla. Faint piano music echoed softly from another part of the house.

'Sit down and I'll get the coffee,' Maura said.

Allegra sat on the sofa and looked around the bright room where a doll's house and a toybox took up the far corner. She glimpsed swings and a trampoline in the large back garden. Even though it all bore the marks of a family with small children, everything was neat and tidy.

'Your house is lovely,' Allegra said. 'Is that your husband playing the piano?'

'Yes. He's a composer and pianist. That's one of his own pieces he's working on. A lullaby for the new baby.'

'What a beautiful thing to do,' Allegra said, feeling herself relax as she listened to the music and nibbled on a cookie.

Maura poured coffee into the china cups on the table just as the door opened to admit a chubby woman with grey curly hair and a dimply smile.

'Auntie Dee,' Maura said, 'say hello to my new friend Allegra from America.'

'Hello, Allegra from America,' Auntie Dee said and shook Allegra's hand. 'Welcome to Sandy Cove. Are you here long?'

'I've been here a little over a week,' Allegra said. 'And I'll be going back home in ten days or so.'

'She's already the talk of the town,' Maura said. 'And she's been going to Strawberry Hill to ride with the Courtneys as well.'

'How did you know that?' Allegra asked, startled.

Maura winked. 'Jungle telegraph. That's what we call gossip around here. Spreads like wildfire. Someone tells someone and then it's out there. Or they might guess by the way you dress or something. There are no secrets in this village.'

'That sounds scary,' Allegra said, wondering how on earth her riding with Max had come out.

'I find it comforting,' Maura said. 'Like being part of a huge family. Sit down, Auntie Dee, and help yourself to the cookies I baked this morning.'

Auntie Dee nodded and sat down, taking a cookie while Maura pushed a coffee cup towards her. 'You're a devil for punishment, Maura. Nearly giving birth but here you are baking and entertaining guests.'

'Ah well, you've always said I was hyperactive,' Maura retorted light-heartedly as she joined them on the sofa.

'So you went riding up at the big house?' Auntie Dee said, focusing her twinkly eyes on Allegra.

'Yes. With Max Courtney-Smythe. He's Gwen's cousin.'

'And Davina's favourite great-nephew,' Auntie Dee filled in. 'She doted on that boy.'

'Auntie Dee was friends with Davina during her last years,'

Maura cut in. 'Despite all the aggro between the Walshes and the Courtneys.'

'Oh?' Happy that the conversation had taken the turn she wanted, Allegra smiled at Auntie Dee. 'So you knew Davina well, then?'

Auntie Dee swallowed her bite of cookie. 'Yes. Very well. I was working as a nurse at the GP practice about twenty years ago. Before Bridget, who's the nurse there now. Davina needed a bit of help when she was recovering from an injury and I visited her as the district nurse was on holiday. And after that I fell into the habit of calling in for a cup of tea and a chat whenever I was passing. She was in her eighties then and still very active, riding and looking after the horses and so on. Just like young Gwen is doing now.'

'Did you talk about the Walsh family during that time?' Allegra asked, taking a sip of coffee. 'And about Sean Walsh?'

Auntie Dee sighed. 'Oh yes. Sad story, that. I don't think she told anyone else exactly what happened, but I think she felt I would be discreet being a nurse and all. And she was right.'

'So you didn't tell anyone?' Maura asked, putting a cushion behind her back.

'Not a soul,' Auntie Dee said. 'I didn't think it was my secret to tell.' She looked thoughtfully at Allegra. 'You're not related to them, are you?'

'No,' Allegra said and put her cup on the saucer. 'But it's because of Davina and Sean that I'm here.'

'Really?' Maura asked, looking excited. 'In what way? I have been wondering what brought you here at this time of year.'

'Did the jungle telegraph not tell you that?' Allegra asked with a cheeky smile.

Maura smiled back. 'Only some of it. Of course, people are talking but everyone has a different take. Maybe you could tell me the real story of your connections with them?'

'Lydia and Ella know. And Lucille, who is looking into it and trying to find the truth.'

'They're not good at the old gossip,' Auntie Dee cut in. 'Lydia is far too sensitive to spread any kind of rumours and Ella doesn't like it much either because she's married to a solicitor. And Lucille keeps any story to herself until she has all the facts. They are all annoyingly good at keeping quiet about things like that.' She leaned forward, fixing Allegra with her eyes. 'But go on. You were about to tell us what brought you here and why it's connected to both our family and the Courtneys.'

Allegra laughed. 'Okay, as the story is out there in different versions, I'll tell you what brought me here, and also all the complications that have arisen lately at Strawberry Hill.'

She paused for a moment, taking a swig of coffee before she launched into her tale, starting with the ring on the beach, the newspaper article, and then went on to her visits to Strawberry Hill and the claims by Kate Vanderpump that had now been proven true.

Maura and Auntie Dee looked intently at Allegra while she finished her story. There was a long silence as she came to the end.

'So this woman claims to be Davina's granddaughter?' Auntie Dee asked.

'That's right,' Allegra replied. 'Her mother's birth certificate has been examined by the solicitor handling the probate. And they found it to be genuine.'

'Really?' Auntie Dee said, looking startled. 'But that's not possible. That woman couldn't have been Davina's daughter.'

'Why?' Maura asked.

'Because I know what caused Sean and Davina's divorce and why she left Scotland.'

'She abandoned her baby?' Allegra asked.

'No, of course not,' Auntie Dee said vehemently. 'She

would never do that.' Auntie Dee paused for a moment. Then she drew a deep breath before she spoke. 'There was no baby to abandon, you see.'

'What?' Allegra and Maura both stared at Auntie Dee while the piano played in the distance.

20

Auntie Dee's words hung in the air as Allegra tried to take in what she had just heard. This was completely unexpected. But could it be true?

'No baby?' Maura finally said and put her hand on her bump.

'She had a miscarriage,' Auntie Dee said.

'When?' Allegra asked.

'Just after they were married,' Auntie Dee replied. 'She hadn't told a soul, and even Sean had to promise not to tell anyone.' She shifted on the sofa, turning to Allegra. 'Sean and Davina's love story started in America just before the war, and ended ten years later. They did love each other desperately, but I have a feeling it wasn't meant to be, that the stars didn't align in their favour or something.'

'Why not?' Allegra asked.

'Maybe their different backgrounds played a role as well?' Maura suggested. 'That would have been important, then.'

'Possibly,' Auntie Dee said. 'But what happened when they met again was probably what broke them apart. When Davina and Sean met in Scotland they fell in love all over again, Davina told me. And this time it was even more passionate. So much so that Davina got pregnant. Then they married in a hurry, of course, like anyone would back then. Sean had never stopped loving Davina and she loved him, even if she was very angry with him for taking money from her father...' Auntie Dee paused and looked at Allegra. 'I won't go into the details, if you don't mind.'

'I know the circumstances of the money,' Allegra said. 'Go on.'

'Well, anyway they were married at a registry office in Edinburgh and then moved in together into the little house Sean was living in then. But only a month after that hasty wedding, Davina lost the baby. She had been out riding at the yard where she was working training young horses. She had a bad fall and not only lost the baby but also fractured her pelvis and was in hospital for a long time. Sean couldn't get over the fact that she had been riding horses when she was pregnant and accused her of killing his child. She couldn't cope with his anger and accusations, so they broke up and filed for divorce. Davina went home to start up her own yard that her grand-niece Gwen is still running to this day.' Auntie Dee drew breath.

'That is so sad,' Maura said, her eyes glistening with tears. 'I can't imagine how she felt having lost her baby and then her husband accusing her like that.'

'I think it hardened her,' Auntie Dee said. She sighed and reached to take a slice of cake from the plate. 'This looks lovely.'

'Oh God, I forgot all about my manners,' Maura exclaimed. 'I got lost in the story. Please help yourselves.'

'This is really good,' Auntie Dee said, through her bite. 'Is this your mother's recipe?'

'Yes,' Maura said. 'From her secret recipe book that I inherited.'

Allegra's thoughts drifted as Auntie Dee and Maura chatted. It all seemed to fit now that she had heard Auntie Dee's story. The series of events from Sean and Davina's engagement on Cape Cod, their return to Ireland at the beginning of the war, the break-up caused by Sean taking the money and then them meeting again ten years later, followed by their divorce, was like a long, sad story of a love that ended in tragedy. The beautiful young woman with the soulful eyes in the old photo had been hardened by what had happened between her and Sean, and she had turned into someone completely different at the end of her life. But who could blame her?

After her return from Scotland, she must have been devastated to have lost both her baby and the man she loved. The sad memories must have been lingering all through the rest of her life and could have made her bitter and disillusioned. No wonder she cried reading that letter. Allegra knew she should lose no time telling Max what she had learned. He had to find out as soon as possible. She started to get up.

'I think I should go now. I need to talk to Max.'

Maura's gaze turned to Allegra. 'Of course you do. The family must know that this woman's claims are false.'

'If you need me to talk to them, I'll be happy to help,' Auntie Dee said. 'I don't mind telling them what happened now that poor Davina is dead. She would want the truth to come out and the rightful heirs to get what they are entitled to.'

'I think she would,' Allegra agreed. 'I never met her, but I'm getting to know her by what those nearest to her have told me. Thank you so much for telling me what Davina told you. This needs to go to the solicitor so they can look up hospital records in Scotland.'

'Of course, it was seventy years ago, but I'm sure there would be some record of it,' Auntie Dee said.

'Has to be,' Maura said.

'I hope so.' Allegra grabbed her bag and her phone. 'Don't get up, Maura, I'll see myself out. Thanks for the coffee and cookies. They were delicious.'

'Thanks for coming. Let's stay in touch,' Maura said and waved from the sofa. 'The girls will be sad they missed you today, so we'll have to do this again with them. They told me all about you and FaceTiming with Emma in New York.'

'That was fun,' Allegra said, smiling at the memory. 'I'll see if we can do that again. Bye for now, Maura. And... Auntie Dee, if I may call you that? It was so lovely to meet you.'

'Of course you may call me that,' Auntie Dee said, showing her dimples. 'Everyone does. Bye, dear girl. Let me know if there is anything I can do.'

'I will,' Allegra promised.

She walked out of the house while the lullaby Thomas was composing for his new baby played softly, deep within the house. What a wonderful, welcoming home it was with two parents still so in love with each other, and the little girls now stepsisters as they had wished ever since they became best friends.

Will I ever have such a family? Allegra wondered, thinking fleetingly of Max and their budding relationship that seemed destined to become something stronger and more durable. That thought was like a happy little flame that burned warmly in her heart. The fact that they were from different countries and would have problems sorting out what they might do seemed far away in the distance. It was something she didn't even want to contemplate at this moment. They would sort it out somehow.

All kinds of thoughts whirled around in Allegra's mind as she returned to Starlight Cottages. The stiff breeze whipping up waves in the bay and the clouds scudding across the sky barely registered as she planned what she was going to say to Max. He would be happy to hear what Auntie Dee had said, and then he could give the information to the lawyer who was in charge of the will and it would all eventually be resolved. The fact that Kate Vanderpump would be exposed was a worry, but not something that made Allegra feel any kind of pity for the brash woman who had arrived out of the blue with her false claims.

Allegra took out her phone when she arrived home. Sitting on the sofa, she dialled Max's number and smiled as she waited for an answer. What a pleasant surprise it would be for him to hear what she had to say. But the phone rang and rang without an answer and then went to voicemail. Allegra hesitated for a moment and then left a brief message saying she had some good news and to call her as soon as he could. She hung up feeling disappointed, but assumed he would call back soon. Then she made herself a light lunch and called Lucille to see if she was in. She was and would be calling in to see Allegra during the afternoon so she could hear the great news.

After lunch, Allegra called Max's number again but hung up when she heard the voicemail. Where was he? Why didn't he call her back? Maybe he was busy working or driving from the building site he was involved with. He'd call her back that evening, she assumed, and tried her best to occupy herself. She pushed away the niggling worry that was beginning to form in her mind. It wasn't like him not to call her back. Or was it? She suddenly realised how little she knew about him. But the memory of what had happened between them was still vivid, and she was sure they were on the cusp of something special and real. She knew he had felt it, too, by what he had said to her, and the look in his eyes. She finally tried Gwen's number and was told Max had had to leave for a few days for work and would be back at the end of the week, which didn't help at all. It only made Allegra more miserable and worried. Then Gwen hung up before she had a chance to relay any of what Allegra was about to tell her.

Allegra tried to stop fretting and, when Lucille dropped in later that day, she repeated the conversation with Auntie Dee nearly word for word, which left Lucille speechless for a moment before she reacted.

'Holy saints in heaven,' Lucille exclaimed from the depths of the sofa where she was enjoying a cup of tea. 'That's going to put a stop to all those claims.'

'If there is proof,' Allegra remarked.

Lucille sat up. 'What did your Max say about it? He must have been over the moon.'

'He would be if I could talk to him,' Allegra said. 'But he hasn't answered any of my messages.'

'Is he away somewhere?'

Allegra shrugged. 'Yes, but I don't know where.'

'Maybe you could call Gwen?' Lucille suggested.

'I did, but she just said he was away and then she hung up before I had a chance to tell her anything.'

'Typical,' Lucille said, putting her cup on the coffee table. 'Those people can be so rude sometimes. They don't mean to be, but they simply have no manners. We'll just have to go and tell her in person.'

'I don't want to go there if I don't hear from Max first,' Allegra said.

Lucille peered at her. 'Is there something going on between you two?'

Allegra blushed and sighed at the same time. 'I thought there was. But maybe I was mistaken.'

'Maybe you weren't,' Lucille said.

'But he just left without saying anything to me, and he's not answering my calls.'

'Something must have come up.' Lucille paused. 'When I want to find out what people are doing, I usually check their Facebook page to see if there are any posts. Are you on Facebook?'

'Yes, but I don't use it that often,' Allegra replied. 'I prefer Instagram.'

'Check both,' Lucille suggested.

'I don't know if he actually uses social media,' Allegra argued.

'Well, find out, then.' Lucille struggled to get up and held out a hand. 'Please, dear, help me out of this very squishy sofa.'

Allegra gently pulled Lucille up. 'There.'

'Thank you.' Lucille straightened her cardigan, fluffed up her hair and grabbed her large handbag. 'I have to go. Must do a little shopping and then I will drop in to my friend Dominic to see if he needs anything. Thank you for telling me everything. Now, we have to make sure that the family gets the story and acts on it. And do try those social media sites and see if you can find your young man. Fortune favours the brave and all that.'

'Okay,' Allegra said. 'If you say so.'

'Good girl. Bye for now. And don't worry. Everything will work out in the end. It always does, even if for the worst.'

'That's a cheery thought,' Allegra said with a laugh.

Lucille waved on her way out of the room while Allegra straightened the cushions and collected the cups to bring back to the kitchen.

She sat down again as the front door slammed behind Lucille and grabbed her laptop. She'd take a quick look on Facebook, even if she didn't believe she'd find anything...

She quickly logged into her Facebook profile and put the name Max Courtney-Smythe in the search box. There was only one profile with that name and she clicked on it. His cover picture was of horses grazing in the field by the river at Strawberry Hill. And his profile photo was of him wearing sunglasses, his white teeth gleaming with that gorgeous smile that never failed to make her heart race.

She scrolled a little further down the page and froze as she saw a photo he had just been tagged in. Dressed in a tuxedo, Max was clinking champagne glasses in some fancy bar with a black-haired beauty in a red dress. He looked into her eyes with delight, and his smile revealed an unmistakable intimacy between them. The text said:

> *Look who's finally back in the big smoke, Caroline and Max, the glamorous duo together again. How we have missed you!*

Rigid with shock, Allegra stared at the couple in the photo until it was blurred by tears welling up.

A kiss to build a dream on, she thought. *What did he mean by sending me that song? And what was he doing in some champagne bar in Dublin with this woman, looking at her that way?*

21

The image of Max and the beautiful woman in the red dress was burned into Allegra's mind all through the rest of the day. She tried to pull herself together when Lydia called in after dinner to discuss the Christmas fundraiser event, but her monosyllabic answers were revealing enough to make Lydia stop and look concerned.

'Are you feeling sick?' she asked, touching Allegra's cheek as they sat on the sofa. 'You're so pale.'

Allegra pulled back. 'I'm fine. Just a little tired. It's been quite a busy day. And all this stuff with Strawberry Hill and the research into Sean and Davina's history is getting complicated.'

'Because of the dispute about the inheritance?'

'Something like that. I'm just a little tired of it all.' Allegra leaned her head against the back of the sofa. 'I never thought it would get this messy. I had imagined something completely different and lovely. I thought I'd just come here, find the couple or their descendants, and give the ring to them as a memento of two young people who were in love a long time ago.'

'The reality is never as beautiful as the dreams,' Lydia said.

'Dreams,' Allegra said with a touch of bitterness. 'Yeah, I know about them. And falling for...' She stopped and turned her head away.

Lydia touched her hand. 'Is it Max?' she asked softly.

'I don't want to talk about him.'

'Okay,' Lydia said and picked up her notebook from the coffee table. 'Then let's talk about the Christmas event. Apparently, it's still on, Gwen told me today. Even if the house is going to be sold, it won't be until after the holidays. But we have decided against doing an app. That was Helen's idea. She's my partner in the fundraising firm and very astute. She said she thought an app wouldn't work because many of the children taking part wouldn't have phones yet. We were wondering if you could help us with the website and social media? I'd like to have a Facebook group especially for this event. Would that be something you could help us with?'

'Facebook?' Allegra said, staring at Lydia.

'Yes. Is there something wrong with that? We thought we'd ask the parents to log in and...' Lydia stopped. 'What's the matter?'

'I...' Allegra started. Then she picked up her phone and logged into her Facebook app and went to Max's profile. 'I saw this post on Facebook today that upset me. Hang on, I'll find it...' She scrolled down his page but the photo was gone. She sat up and stared at the phone. 'What? Where is it?'

'Where is what?' Lydia asked.

'The photo of Max and this woman,' Allegra replied. 'It was there earlier. He was with some bimbo in a red dress drinking champagne...'

'Are you sure?'

'Of course I'm sure,' Allegra insisted. 'I saw it clearly. Someone tagged him. *Caroline and Max*, it said. *Back together.*' She stared at the screen. 'Oh God, this is driving me nuts.'

'*He* is driving you nuts, you mean,' Lydia said, her eyes full of sympathy. 'I knew he was trouble the minute I saw him and the way he looked at you that day. Did he... Have you fallen for him big time, then?'

'Yes,' Allegra whispered. 'Stupid of me, but I couldn't help it. He was so nice to me. We went riding and then later on he showed me around the house and then he kissed me and... it was so amazing.'

'I bet it was,' Lydia said scathingly. 'I'm sure he's very good at that kind of thing. Did you search his friends list to see if this woman is there?'

'No, I didn't,' Allegra protested. 'That would be spying on his private life.'

'What's private about it?' Lydia asked. 'If he has set his page so that nobody can see the posts, then, yeah, that would be spying. But if it's all out there in public anyone can take a look. I bet he doesn't use Facebook that much and hasn't bothered with the privacy settings.'

'Oh,' Allegra said after a moment's consideration. 'If that's the case...'

She got up and fetched her laptop from its bag beside the small desk at the far end. Then she sat down again and logged into Facebook as soon as it had started up. She quickly looked up Max's profile again and clicked on his friends list. He had a little over 200 friends, she discovered. Then she put the name Caroline in the search box, but nothing came up.

'No Caroline here,' she said, scrolling through the friends list that consisted of an equal number of men and women in all kinds of walks of life.

'She's probably some old flame he bumped into at that party, then. Or it's an old photo,' Lydia suggested. 'Maybe someone – or this Caroline – was trying to annoy him, or play a joke or something.'

'Could be,' Allegra said, her spirits rising slightly, even though the image of Max's eyes on the woman was still upsetting her. 'But that doesn't explain his behaviour to me. Why he just disappeared and why he hasn't replied to my messages.'

'No, it doesn't, of course,' Lydia agreed. 'But he could be busy with something to do with work.'

'It's so strange, though,' Allegra said. 'And upsetting. I wanted to tell him about what Maura's auntie Dee told me. Such a strange story about Sean and Davina that could change everything for him.'

'What story?' Lydia asked, looking intrigued.

'Maura's aunt was friends with Davina and she told Auntie Dee something nobody else knows.' Allegra proceeded to tell Lydia a shorthand version of what had happened between Davina and Sean in Scotland.

Lydia's hand flew to her mouth. 'Good Lord!' she exclaimed. 'What a story. How very sad for them both. But as you said, this would prove this Kate Vanderpump woman to be a fake and the house will be safe.'

Allegra nodded. 'Yes, and I wanted to tell Max but he has gone away somewhere and wasn't answering his phone. I've texted him so many times without a reply. But then I saw that photo,' she ended, as tears started to roll down her cheeks. Once she started to cry, she found she couldn't stop. 'We only just met,' she sobbed. 'But I thought it was the start of something incredible, something that would last forever. I've never felt like that before with anyone else. It was like being hit by lightning. Love at first sight, isn't that stupid?'

'Oh, darling,' Lydia said and put her arms around Allegra, 'I know what you mean. It is perfectly possible to fall in love with someone even the very first time you meet. And maybe he felt the same.'

'I thought so,' Allegra said, comforted by Lydia's arms around her. 'But he just disappeared, and didn't get in touch or answer his messages, and then I saw that photo he was tagged in on Facebook. He looked at that woman as if she was the love of his life.'

'Are you sure?'

'Oh yes, I am,' Allegra insisted. 'There was no mistaking how attracted he was to her. He was only having a bit of fun with me.'

'I don't know about that.' Lydia looked doubtful. 'That photo doesn't tell us anything except that he met her in a hotel bar during some kind of event. We don't know when that was, do we? He seemed fascinated by you at the Halloween party. Couldn't take his eyes off you.'

'Oh yeah, well, he was probably drunk or something.' Allegra pulled away from Lydia's arms and pushed her hair from her face. 'But I'm not going to let him make me miserable. In any case I'm going home at the end of next week and that will be that. Except I don't know who I should give the ring to.'

'Why don't you keep it?' Lydia suggested. 'It's legally yours after all.'

'I don't want it after all this,' Allegra protested. 'It'll only remind me of all the misery with *him*.'

'In that case, why don't you give the ring to Gwen?' Lydia said. 'I have a feeling she was the one who was closest to Davina. They were really alike, I've heard.'

'I don't think she even likes me,' Allegra muttered as she took a tissue from her pocket and blew her nose.

'I'm sure she does,' Lydia argued. 'She's actually very nice behind that gruff exterior, I've discovered. And she really wants to do the Christmas fundraiser. She's even said she'd love to help out with other events at the house to raise money for charity. We're talking about an egg hunt at Easter. I'd say the ring would make her very happy.'

'Yeah, I suppose I should give it to her,' Allegra agreed. 'And I have to tell her about Auntie Dee. That feels right, somehow. And she should know about what happened to Davina in Scotland so they can search the hospital records or whatever it is they need to find.'

'Exactly.' Lydia patted Allegra's shoulder and got up. 'Gwen is coming to see me tomorrow to discuss the arrangements for the Christmas event. Why don't you join us? Your help with the website would be great. And you can then tell her the story and give her the ring then if you want.'

'Oh.' Allegra thought for a moment. 'That would be perfect, actually. I won't have to go back to Strawberry Hill at all then.'

'No,' Lydia said, 'and you'll be able to spend the last few days enjoying this place before you go back. Really see the area and have a bit of fun. Come to the pub with me and Jason and Ella and Rory for the trad night on Friday. Always good craic.'

'What's that?' Allegra asked.

'Traditional Irish music and dancing. Everyone has a go at playing something or singing a song or dancing.'

'I'd love that,' Allegra said, feeling a lot more cheerful. 'I've always loved Irish music.'

'Great.' Lydia hovered in the doorway, looking thoughtfully at Allegra. 'I know you can't forget him, but do try to turn your mind away and enjoy yourself before you go home. We're all so fond of you, you know. And this village is the best place to mend a slightly dented heart.'

Allegra smiled. 'I think you're right. I'm glad I came here despite what happened with – him. And I'm going to do my best to have a lot of Irish fun before I go. So don't worry. I'll be fine. Eventually.'

'Of course you will. You're made of strong stuff,' Lydia declared. 'See you tomorrow, then? Gwen is coming around at ten thirty-ish.'

'I'll be there,' Allegra promised.

As the door closed behind Lydia, Allegra began to feel a lot better. The lingering pain and disappointment of the way things had ended with Max would be there for a long time. But she would occupy her mind with other things and then slowly forget what he had done to her. And maybe, one day, she would remember the sweet moments with him as a beautiful dream that would never have become reality. There was a lot more to life than romance. She had a job to go back to. Her own apartment in a nice part of Boston, family and a lot of friends who would welcome her back with open arms.

Allegra nodded to herself. Yes. She would go back home and start living again. She just wanted to hand over the ring to Gwen and close the chapter.

And, in the unlikely event that she bumped into Max before she left, she would be cool and distant, and not show how much he had come to mean to her. If she managed to pretend.

22

As her stay at Starlight Cottages drew to a close, Allegra packed her bags on her final Saturday, preparing for her drive to Shannon airport where she was staying at a hotel before catching her flight back home on Sunday morning. She felt, in some strange way, that she had been there for months rather than a few weeks, and the events of the last fortnight went through her mind as she stacked her clothes in neat piles on the bed ready to put into her suitcase.

The coffee at Lydia's with Gwen had gone off well and Gwen had seemed to soften towards Allegra as she heard with astonishment what Auntie Dee had said about Davina and Sean's baby. Gwen had immediately excused herself to call the solicitor, who had said they had decided to reinvestigate and would examine the documents again. But now, with new evidence, they were beginning to think it was all lies. It looked increasingly like Kate Vanderpump was in big trouble.

Then Allegra gave Gwen the ring she had found on the beach. Gwen stared at it for a moment and then slowly put it on the third finger of her right hand. 'Thank you,' she said softly. 'You have no idea how much this means to me. Davina and I were very close. I still can't believe she's gone. But now I feel I'll be wearing a little part of her.'

'I'm glad,' Allegra said. 'It felt right to give it to you.'

'Max will approve,' Gwen said. 'I'll show it to him when he comes back.'

'Back from where?' Lydia asked, glancing at Allegra.

'I don't really know,' Gwen said. 'He took off suddenly. Said he got an email about something urgent and that he'd be back on Saturday.' She looked at Allegra. 'Will you still be here?'

'On Saturday? Well, I'll be packing and then I'll be off,' Allegra said, trying to look unconcerned even though her stomach flipped at the mere mention of his name. 'I'm thinking I might drive to Limerick and stay the night as my flight is very early on Sunday morning. So I probably won't be here.' She cleared her throat. 'Tell him I said hi.'

'I will,' Gwen said, looking puzzled. 'But I thought you were in touch. I mean... it looked as if he was getting... that you and he...' She paused, looking slightly embarrassed. 'I have a feeling I'm stepping on some sore toes here. Tell me to stop.'

'It's okay,' Allegra cut in. 'Nothing really happened between us. Just a bit of flirting that didn't mean anything. I've forgotten about it already,' she added to emphasise her lack of concern, even if it hurt to dismiss what had been a very deep emotional connection. For her, anyway, even if it had been just fun and games to Max.

'He can be a bit of a flirt sometimes,' Gwen said. 'He doesn't mean to hurt anyone, it's just the way he is.'

'I suppose.' Allegra had nodded and then quickly turned to the matter of the Christmas event and what could be done with the website and Facebook group. The subject of Max was dropped.

The trad evening on Friday night had been huge fun and she had even joined in with the Irish dancing, trying her best to learn the steps to everyone's amazement. Dancing, laughing and drinking pints of Guinness with the locals had made her feel part of the village as everyone made her promise to come back very soon. *An evening to remember*, Allegra thought as she folded her clothes and put them in her suitcase. It had helped her put the hurt of Max's behaviour in perspective and now she could move on and enjoy the happy memories. Even those that included him.

She had spent the rest of her time walking around the area, out to the headland and hiking up the slopes of the mountain above Sandy Cove and discovered even more glorious views. The fresh salt-laden wind, the ever-changing light, the birds soaring high in the sky and the sight of dolphins playing far below in the bay never failed to take her breath away. It was possibly the most beautiful place she had ever visited and she promised herself she would come back during the summer months so she could enjoy swimming and surfing and catching up with all the friends she had made during the past few weeks.

Allegra picked up the grey sweater she had worn the day that Max showed her around the house. The day when they kissed and he had seemed to be falling in love with her. And when he had sent her that song. *A kiss to build a dream on*, she thought. *Well, that was all it was, a dream that dissolved in the daylight*. She pressed the sweater to her cheek as every minute of that moment went through her mind. A memory laced with sadness that she would never forget. She had misread the signals and now she felt foolish for having seen something in his actions that wasn't there.

She sighed and folded the sweater before she put it into the suitcase. There. Nearly all packed up, the house tidy and the hotel at Shannon booked for tonight. All she had to do was to give the key back to Lydia and Jason and say goodbye. Then she was off home to Boston and back to work and a new life.

Lucia had promised to pick Allegra up at the airport and then she would spend Sunday with them in New York before she caught the flight to Boston to be back at work on Tuesday. Allegra felt a dart of happiness at the thought of seeing Joe and Emma again and telling them all about this amazing place and all the adventures she had had while she was here. What a vacation it had been. Despite the heartache.

Allegra's phoned pinged and she went to pick it up from the bedside table, smiling as she checked to see who had sent her a text. Probably Ella saying goodbye. But when Allegra saw the message, the smile died on her lips and her eyes widened in shock.

It was from the airline:

Flight cancelled. Blizzard closes all airports on the east coast. Check airline for details.

Allegra stared at the message, trying to take it in when her phone rang.

'Hi,' Lucia said. 'I suppose you've heard. All airports over here are closed from tonight. The blizzard has just hit New York. It's wild here.'

'I know,' Allegra replied, trying not to burst into tears. 'I just got a message from the airline. Are you okay?'

'We're fine,' Lucia shouted as the signal seemed to weaken. 'Schools are closed and we're staying home. Try not to...' Then the connection broke.

Allegra sank down on the bed and tried to sort out her feelings. She had been ready to go home and pick up her life again. She had been looking forward to getting back to a job she loved, and turning the new apartment into her home. Going out with friends and maybe even dating again, which would be good for her, she had decided. But now here she was, unable to travel and not knowing when the airports would be open again and when she would get a seat on a flight. So many people would be stranded – she was lucky not to have to spend the night at the airport.

Allegra quickly phoned the airline's Irish number and was put on hold for nearly half an hour before someone replied to tell her she could expect to fly home 'towards the middle of next week, weather permitting'. They would send her an update as soon as they had some news. But they also warned that the storm might be tracking across the Atlantic, which might mean closures at airports in the west of Ireland, which would delay her flight yet again.

Allegra threw the phone on the bed and lay down, staring at the ceiling. She could be stuck here a lot longer than she had thought. All because of the weather. Maybe it *had* been crazy to come at this time of year, but the compulsion had been too strong to resist. But now that she couldn't go home, she started to regret ever coming here. She was suddenly hit with a wave of homesickness so bad she started to cry. She turned over and hugged a pillow, sobbing into it as she realised how much she missed Lucia and the children.

What am I doing here so far away from home? she asked herself. *Why did I come to this place instead of spending my break with the only family I have? And why did I have to go and fall for that man who just tossed me away when he had more important things to do? Like drinking champagne with that woman in a fancy hotel in Dublin...* She started to cry again, her body shaking with violent sobs, until she was exhausted. Then she lay there like a rag doll, wondering if she would ever be happy again.

A sudden noise from downstairs made her sit up. Someone knocking at the door. Could it be Lydia having heard the news? *Oh God, and I'm such a mess*, Allegra thought. She got off the bed and tried to tidy herself up by smoothing her tangled hair, quickly dabbing her red, swollen eyes with a cold facecloth. She still looked awful but Lydia would understand how upset she was.

'I'm coming,' she shouted and walked slowly downstairs to let Lydia in. It would be nice to see a friendly face. She would explain that she would be staying an extra week, she thought, opening the door and squinting against the bright sunlight at the figure before her, who was taller and broader than Lydia, she saw to her astonishment.

'Hi,' Allegra started, shielding her eyes with her hand. Then she stopped as she saw who was standing there.

23

'Max,' she said, backing into the hall.

'Yes, it's me,' he said. 'I heard about the storm over there, so I came to see if you were still here. Gwen said...' He stopped as he looked at her. 'You look awful. Are you okay?'

'Of course I'm not okay,' she snapped. 'And I'm not in the mood for visitors. Please, Max, go away. I really don't want to talk to you.'

Mortified that he was seeing her like this, and still seething at the way he had treated her, she started to close the door.

Max pushed the door open. 'Please. I need to talk to you...'

'Well, I don't want to talk to you,' Allegra said between her teeth. 'I don't want to hear your lies.'

'They won't be lies,' he protested. 'Allegra, I need to explain. I didn't mean to... It's not what you think.'

Allegra felt herself turn rigid with anger. How dare he stand there looking so handsome and pretend he was sorry for what he had put her through? How dare he even look at her like that when she was a total wreck? But what did her appearance matter anyway?

'Explain what?' she asked, her voice cold. 'That you forgot

to tell me you were leaving? Or what the *hell* you meant by playing around with me and sending me a song about kisses and dreams and then just disappearing without a word? And then you were drinking champagne with...' She stopped and glared at him. 'Is this some kind of weird sport for you?'

'No, that's not at all what happened.' Max stepped inside the hall, and tried to take her hand. 'Could you please just listen for a second?'

Allegra snatched her hand away. 'I don't want to hear your lame excuses. Just leave, please.'

'I will when you've heard what I have to say.'

His blue eyes were so contrite she nearly gave in. But no, she had to stay strong and not fall for his tricks again.

'It's no use, Max. I won't believe a word of it.'

'Why not?' he asked in a near whisper. 'Why are you so hostile all of a sudden? I thought you had feelings for me.'

'Oh yes, I do,' she snarled. 'I hate you.'

'Why?' he asked, sounding confused. 'Because I didn't tell you I had to go to Dublin in a hurry?'

'Yes, that, too. But then I also saw the photo. The one on Facebook of you and... whatshername,' she explained, unable to say the name.

'Caroline?' he said, looking suddenly furious. 'That photo was three years old. I was afraid you'd see it for some weird reason so I deleted it. Edwina put it there just to annoy me. And you.'

'Me?' Allegra asked. 'Why would she want to annoy me?'

'Because she was miffed that you didn't give *her* the ring. And because she feels that you're trying to wreck Kate Vander-pump's case by digging into Sean and Davina's relationship. Which I now hear has revealed some new evidence that might blow everything out of the water for her. I should say a huge thank you, but first I want you to hear what I have to say.' He paused and pushed at the door again. 'Please, Allegra, let me in and listen to me.'

Allegra met his pleading eyes and suddenly softened. She was still angry but it seemed unfair not to at least hear his side of the story.

'Okay,' she said and backed away from the door, folding her arms across her chest. 'I'm listening. But don't think it'll change anything between us.'

'Thank you.' He hesitated for a moment and then stepped further into the hall, closing the door behind him. 'I want you to know exactly what happened and why you didn't hear from me for so long. No lies, I swear.'

Allegra nodded. 'Go on, then.'

'That day, I got a text message from my office in Dublin followed by an email from a client about the work that was being done on his house. A big extension costing a lot of money. Part of the new roof had fallen in and he threatened to sue if this wasn't seen to. Someone had messed up somewhere, and I had no idea what had actually happened. It turned out to be a builder who used substandard material. So that had to be corrected and redone. And the builder had to be fired and we had to find someone else. It will mean taking down nearly the whole roof and starting from scratch. My assistant was off sick so I had to go up there to inspect the damage and see what could be done. And also see if I could talk to the client and calm him down a bit.'

'I can see that was an emergency,' Allegra said. 'But why didn't you contact me or send a text or something?'

'I left my phone behind by accident,' Max replied, looking sheepish. 'It was in my jacket that was hanging in the utility room at Strawberry Hill. I have two phones, one private and one for business, you see. I was in Dublin before I realised what had happened. I was about to call you when I discovered that I hadn't brought my phone with your number.'

'You could have called Gwen.'

'I was about to do that when all hell broke loose and I had to sort out an almighty mess with the contractors and the builders. That took a couple of days. You'll forgive me if you and everyone else kind of receded into the background during all this. I sent a message to Gwen asking her to explain it to you, but she didn't see it in time.' He shrugged. 'She's not very reliable when it comes to text messages. Doesn't check her phone that much.'

'She didn't seem to have a clue where you were or what you were doing.'

'I know. I should have realised.'

'I thought you had forgotten all about me. I thought you had just been fooling around with me for fun. Especially when I saw the photo.'

'I'm sorry.' A look of annoyance flashed through his eyes. 'I'm really mad at Edwina for doing that. I can imagine how hurtful that must have been.'

'Yes. It was.' Allegra looked at her feet. 'I thought... Oh, never mind.'

'I can imagine. I could wring Edwina's neck. But I came here as soon as I could after everything was sorted so I could explain to you.'

'Will you be sued?' Allegra asked.

'I hope not. We're redoing the roof and paying for it ourselves so it should be okay. We'll take a bit of a financial hit but that can't be helped.'

'At least your firm is safe.'

'For the moment. I was going to call you yesterday but I was afraid you were so mad at me you wouldn't want to talk to me. I thought it would be better to see you face to face so I drove down from Dublin this morning and came straight here to see you and explain. I didn't stop anywhere on the way. Gwen finally saw my message and said you would already have left for

Limerick. But then I heard about the storm on the east coast on the radio, so I was hoping you'd still be here. And thank God, you were.' He drew breath and looked at her for a reply. 'So now you know.'

'Yes.' Allegra didn't quite know what to say. She fumbled in her pocket for a tissue as she felt tears welling up.

'You've been crying.' He pulled a white handkerchief from his pocket and handed it to her. 'Here,' he said.

Allegra took the hankie. 'Typical,' she said, halfway between tears and laughter. 'Of course you'd have a clean hand-kerchief in your pocket. Who even does these days?'

'I find it very – handy,' he said, beginning to smile. 'I'm so sorry I upset you.'

'It wasn't just you.' Allegra dabbed at her eyes and then blew her nose noisily. 'Everything seemed so hopeless suddenly when the flight was cancelled and I couldn't get back home to my family.' She had wanted to make him suffer for all the pain his silence had caused but now she realised it wasn't really his fault. All the anger against him slowly receded, and as their eyes met, she couldn't stop herself smiling. 'Okay,' she said. 'I see what happened. I can understand that you forgot everything under the circumstances.' She wanted to say it was all right and that she wanted them to talk about what was going on between them. She wanted to fall into his arms and kiss him the way they had that day. But she couldn't get the image of him and that beautiful girl out of her mind. 'Tell me about Caroline,' she said.

'Why?' he asked, looking confused. 'I haven't seen her for three years. That photo was from a New Year's Eve party just before we split up.'

'You didn't look as if you wanted to break up with her.'

'I might have been a little sloshed then. She was a fun girl but we were never really compatible. Caroline is a party princess with attitude. Rich, spoiled, selfish.'

'And very beautiful.'

'Yes, that's true. But there is one thing wrong with her.'

'What's that?'

'She isn't you.' Max's eyes were tender as he looked at Allegra. 'She would never get up on a horse even though she was terrified, or make friends with dogs and old ladies,' he said softly. 'She wouldn't dress up as a zombie and spend the evening having fun with two little girls.' He stepped closer. 'She wouldn't try to help me keep an old wreck of a house by researching into my great-aunt's past.'

'She wouldn't?' Allegra whispered, looking deep into his blue eyes.

'Not in a million years,' Max said, slowly putting his arms around her. 'No way would she do that. Or stand there looking like a waif with her hair all mussed up around her face and her eyes red from crying.'

'A waif?' Allegra's voice was full of laughter. 'Is that like a homeless person?'

'More like a slightly bohemian girl who is beautiful dressed in anything. And classy and smart and totally irresistible,' he mumbled, his mouth against hers.

'Oh,' she said before their lips met in a long, slow kiss full of pent-up emotion. Allegra felt herself melt into his embrace, responding to his kisses with a fervour that surprised her.

'Do you still hate me?' he asked between kisses.

'No... yes... I'm not sure,' she said and kissed him again.

They finally pulled apart. 'I assume you have forgiven me?' he said, his eyes gleaming.

'Maybe,' she mumbled against his chest. 'I'll think about it.'

'While you do that, how about something to eat?' he asked. 'Don't kill me, but I'm suddenly very hungry after that long drive.'

'I haven't got much,' Allegra said, looking up at him. 'In fact, I have no food at all in the house. I was supposed to drive to

Limerick just now. I was just going to close up and give Lydia and Jason the key before I drove off.'

'Lucky I caught you.'

'I wouldn't have gone once I heard about the flight being cancelled.'

'That's true,' he said, still holding her tight.

'I suppose you'll find my text messages on your phone later,' Allegra said, laughing softly. 'I sent about fifteen.'

'Oh God,' he said. 'It'll make me feel awful to see them.'

'Sorry.'

'That's what *I* should be saying. Are you hungry?'

'Starving,' Allegra said, realising she had forgotten to eat since her very early breakfast.

'Come with me to the pub in the main street and have a late lunch,' Max suggested. 'Not exactly The Ritz, but I think they do a good Irish stew there.'

'I don't want to go anywhere looking like this,' Allegra protested.

'Can we call for pizza?'

'I don't think there is a pizza place open around here at this time of year.'

'Okay,' Max said, resting his chin on top of Allegra's head, his arms still around her. 'Let me think. How about I go to that little shop up the main street and get something? I'm sure I can put together some kind of lunch for us and then we can eat here.'

'That would be great,' Allegra said. 'And I can fix myself up a bit in the meantime.'

'You don't have to,' Max said and kissed her nose. 'I love you the way you are.'

Allegra froze. 'Did you mean that?' she asked. 'The "I love you" that you just said? Or was it an "I love you" as in "I love spaghetti"?'

He looked at her and blinked. 'I... it just came out.' His eyes softened. 'But yes, I do love you. I really do. Much more than spaghetti. A real, true love. Would I have driven for four hours without stopping if I didn't?'

'No,' Allegra said. 'You wouldn't. And I feel the same about you.'

Max smiled. 'That makes me very happy.' Then he kissed her cheek and stepped away, opening the door. 'I'll be back in a minute or two. And that's a promise,' he added with a wink.

Allegra laughed. 'I'll hold you to that.'

'You should. I'll go and get us a feast to celebrate our reconciliation.'

And that you just said you love me, Allegra thought as she watched him leave. *And I love you*, she thought, her heart skipping a beat. She had known it for a while. It was stupid and crazy and impossible but she did love him with all her heart and soul in a way she had never loved anyone before. But how on earth were they going to manage a relationship? It would be very complicated. Max couldn't possibly leave Ireland to go and start afresh in Boston. And she couldn't imagine leaving her job and her friends and her family and live in Ireland for good. A long-distance relationship, and then...? That didn't seem very attractive as right now she didn't want to be away from Max for longer than a few minutes. One of them would have to emigrate, if they were to last.

Allegra sighed. Why was life always so complicated? She pushed away all those thoughts and went upstairs to tidy herself up, floating on clouds as she remembered the look in his eyes as he said those three little words: *I love you*.

24

By the time Max came back, Allegra had splashed cold water on her face, applied blusher and mascara and changed into a soft blue sweater. She brushed her hair and tied it back in a pony-tail. Feeling refreshed and happy, she laid the table in the sunroom so they could enjoy the views while they had their lunch.

'What a gorgeous place,' Max said, walking into the hall carrying a paper bag. 'This village is a true gem. Couldn't help chatting to a few people on my way. Everyone knew who I was and they seemed to think I'm also your boyfriend.'

Allegra grinned. 'They know what you're doing even before you know it yourself.'

'Scary.' He smiled and shot her an appreciative glance. 'You look nice.'

'I freshened up a bit.'

'Lovely. Where's the kitchen?'

'Through there,' Allegra said, pointing to the half-open door. 'It's state-of-the-art, so you have to dig out your techie skills to use everything. What did you get?'

'A true Irish feast,' Max replied as Allegra followed him into the kitchen. 'But it's a surprise, so stay out of the kitchen until it's ready.'

'Okay, I'll wait in the sunroom. I set the table there. Straight down the corridor and through the living room. Hard to miss.'

'See you out there in a bit, then,' Max said. He pushed her out of the kitchen and closed the door.

'Let me know if you have problems with the equipment!' Allegra shouted.

'I won't!' he shouted back.

Allegra decided to leave him to it. Just as she was about to go through to the sunroom, someone knocked on the front door. Allegra opened it and found Lydia on the doorstep looking worried.

'Hi, Allegra. We just heard about the blizzard. I hope you're not too upset.'

'Not really,' Allegra replied. 'Just disappointed that I couldn't go home as planned.'

'Yes, you must be. I'm so sorry,' Lydia said, her voice full of sympathy. 'But Jason just said to remind you that you paid for the full four weeks, so there is no extra charge. You can even stay longer if you want. We have no other tenants until the spring, anyway.'

'That's very kind,' Allegra said. 'And that reminds me to call about the car and prolong the rental agreement. I hope that won't be a problem.'

'I'm sure it won't be,' Lydia assured her. She hesitated. 'Look, if you feel lonely, come and have dinner with us tonight. I'm going out now, but I'll be back later in the afternoon.'

'Thank you, Lydia, but I...' Allegra started before her face broke into a smile. 'Max is here, cooking lunch for me. And...'

'Oh,' Lydia said, looking startled. 'I was wondering about the other car outside. So he's here? But I thought he... I mean, you seemed so upset with him earlier.'

'Not anymore,' Allegra said, laughing. 'He came here about

an hour ago and... We've had a talk and, well, now we're – getting on a lot better,' she ended, knowing her happiness shone through her eyes.

'I see,' Lydia said, smiling. 'That explains your glow and that sparkle in your eyes. Hey, I'll leave you two alone. We can talk later. Or not,' she added with a wink. Then she leaned forward and kissed Allegra's cheek. 'I think it's wonderful,' she whispered. 'I know I shouldn't approve but it's really none of my business. Just be happy.'

'I will,' Allegra said. 'Thanks for everything.'

'You're so welcome.' Lydia smiled, waved and left while Allegra closed the door thinking how lucky she was to have friends like Lydia and Jason.

She settled on a chair in the sunroom and gazed out at the view of the wind-ruffled water of the bay, the clouds drifting across the sun and the islands shimmering in the distance. It was such a magical place and she suddenly wondered what it would be like to actually live here. Max seemed to be seeing it with fresh eyes, having turned his back on it for so long. How strange to be so close and never discover the wonders of this stretch of the coast.

She turned as Max came in carrying two steaming plates with something that smelled heavenly. 'What did you make?'

'Colcannon with pork sausages,' he replied, putting a plate in front of her. 'So Irish it'll give you an urge to burst into "Danny Boy". Usually served on St Patrick's Day, but that's months away and you won't be here then.'

Allegra looked at her plate. 'Green mashed potatoes?'

'Mash mixed with kale and scallions and a big lump of butter,' Max replied. He put the other plate on the table and sat down only to shoot up again. 'Forgot the soda farls. You dig in. I'll be back in a sec.'

Allegra did as she was told, finding the mashed potatoes with kale and scallions absolutely delicious. The sausages were better than any she had ever tasted, and she closed her eyes as she ate, thoroughly enjoying the food. Then she opened her eyes as Max returned with a plate of some kind of triangular bread. 'What's that?'

'Soda farls. Just soda bread, really, but cooked on a griddle,' Max replied, handing her one. 'Doesn't really go with the meal but I love them so I couldn't resist.'

Then they ate the meal in silence except for smiling at each other and uttering sounds of delight at the food. Finally, Max wiped his mouth and drank some water. 'Well, that was good. I'm feeling much restored. How about you?'

'I'm stuffed,' Allegra said and pushed away her plate. 'You're a good cook.'

'Chef, if you don't mind,' he corrected, looking at her haughtily.

Allegra giggled. 'You look just as arrogant as when we first met. You were looking down your nose at me just like that, as if you were lord of the manor and I was just some lowly little scullery maid.'

'I was trying to look cool.' He took her hand. 'I thought you were utterly gorgeous, but I was trying to hide it. With your huge brown eyes and reddish-blonde hair and the freckles across your nose and that dimple...' He stopped and gave her a look full of love. 'And then, as we got to know each other better I discovered that your beauty is not really on the outside but on the inside. You came here because you had found that ring and discovered a story of two people in love. Most people would just have kept the ring, but you didn't.'

'It didn't seem right,' Allegra said. 'It had to belong to the woman who lost it – or someone in her family.'

'You came here on a quest.' Max squeezed her hand. 'And then you stole my heart.'

Allegra smiled. 'Do you want it back?'

'No, I want you to keep it. I know you'll be gentle with it.'

He looked at her thoughtfully and then kissed her hand. 'I haven't felt this happy for a very long time. Or ever.'

'Neither have I,' Allegra said and touched his cheek.

'That's lovely to hear,' Max said. 'But there is an elephant in the room that we have to tackle.'

'I know.' Allegra pushed away her plate. 'But do we have to tackle it today?'

'Maybe it's too soon.' Max got up and went to the window, looking out at the view. 'This is incredible.'

Allegra got up to join him. With their arms around each other they watched the sun dipping behind the Skelligs, the sky a riot of red, orange and pink. 'I love this time of day here,' she said.

'I can see why. I'm standing here wondering why we turned our backs to this village and this incredible view.' Max sighed. 'The arrogance of land and wealth, I suppose. There is no more wealth now and the arrogance is slowly going as well.'

'You seem a lot less arrogant than when I met you,' Allegra remarked.

'All because of you.' Max smiled and kissed her cheek. 'Would it be terrible if I told you I bought a bottle of wine? And that I now feel very tired and need to lie down? With you.'

Allegra smiled as it hit her what he was hinting at. But she wasn't offended. She wanted it, too, with every fibre of her body. The physical attraction between them had been strong from the start but now it seemed to vibrate at even the slightest touch. She stood on tiptoe and put her mouth to his ear.

'There is a very soft double bed upstairs, where the views are even more spectacular. Do you want to come and watch the sunset with me?'

'I thought you'd never ask.' He pulled her with him towards the door.

They forgot about the wine and walked up the stairs, kissing and laughing as they went and finally landed on the bed, where they lay for a moment, looking at each other before they started to undress in a hurried, messy fashion that resulted in more laughter.

'This is the best fun I've had in a long time,' Max said and kissed Allegra's bare shoulder.

'Me too,' she said.

Then they were quiet and as the sun set and dusk fell, made love, and finally fell asleep under the duvet.

Later, much later, they drank the wine and talked.

'Can we do this?' Max asked, sitting up in bed, cradling his glass, the pillow behind his back. 'Me here and you over there... How is that going to be? I mean, a long-distance relationship, I don't think that's going to work. Do you?'

'Not really.' Allegra sat up beside him and bunched her pillow behind her head. She stared out into the dark night where stars twinkled in the black sky and the crescent of a new moon rose over the bay. They hadn't bothered to pull the curtains, wanting to see the stars. 'I think,' she said slowly, putting her head against his shoulder, 'that we have to be together. I can't bear the thought of not being with you.'

'Neither can I,' he said and kissed her hair. 'So maybe I could close down my firm and come to work in Boston. I'm sure I could get a job there.'

'No, you couldn't,' Allegra protested. 'Because I won't let you. And also because of the way I feel, not only about you but about the house.'

'This house?' he asked, confused.

'No, you fool. Strawberry Hill.' She sat up and looked at him. 'I've been thinking about this for a while. Well, until you left without telling me. Then I tried to get it out of my mind and move on. But now...'

'Yes?' he said and put his glass on the bedside table. 'Now

things are different, aren't they? We know how we feel and we have to work out a plan.'

'We do,' Allegra said. 'And I know what we're going to do.' She paused for a moment and smiled at him. 'You know I've fallen in love with you.'

'Yes, sweetheart, I do,' he said, stroking her cheek.

'But I'm also in love with that old wreck of a house.'

'You are? Why?'

'Because it's old and beautiful and mysterious and full of history,' Allegra explained. 'Why can't we live there? I could easily work online once I've talked to my boss and you can do a lot of your office work there, can't you?'

'Well, yes, but...' Max looked thoughtfully at her. 'You really want to live in that old house?' he asked, staring at her. 'It's a complete and utter wreck.'

'No, it's not,' Allegra protested. 'It's a bit broken and unloved but we can bring it to life again while we live there. We can do it up little by little over several years. Oh, Max, I think it would be fantastic.'

'Are you serious?' Max asked. 'You mean you want to stay in Ireland and then come and live in the house with me? And Gwen?'

'Yes!' Allegra exclaimed. 'How many times do I have to say it? I think,' she said, looking through the window at the view, 'that I'm beginning to put myself first and listen to a little voice inside that tells me I should do what makes *me* happy and not worry about other people all the time. And Gwen won't have to move, of course. What do you think of that?'

'That sounds good,' Max said, softly touching her hair. 'So, your sister will have to look after her own kids from now on?'

'I suppose. Except I will always be their aunt who loves them. But in a different way.' She turned and smiled at Max. 'I do so want to live at Strawberry Hill with you, I really do.'

'You might be sorry once you've seen the bedrooms.'

'We can do them up. I think it would be like a great adventure. And...' Allegra stopped and laughed, 'don't think I'm completely nuts but I want to keep riding Betsy. And have our own dog.'

Max grinned and ruffled her hair. 'I knew it wasn't just my pretty face that made you want to do all this. Horses and dogs, eh? Isn't that what it's all about?'

'Not all of it,' Allegra said. 'But a big part of it, yes. And this village where people are so amazing and the beaches and the mountains and the pubs and the laughs that people have here. I want my sister and her family to come next summer to see it all.'

Max gathered her in his arms. 'Okay, I'll buy all that. It'll be a right royal mess at first but we'll sort it.'

Allegra kissed his cheek. 'Of course we will. But I have to go back home for a bit first,' she continued. 'To sort things out, get an Irish passport and then...'

'How can you get an Irish passport?' Max asked.

'My grandmother was born here,' Allegra replied. 'And I've read somewhere that if one of your grandparents was born in Ireland, it gives you automatic right to an Irish passport. All you have to do is apply with his or her birth certificate.'

'Oh yeah, that's right, I had forgotten about that. I even had a friend from California who did it.'

'It'll make it easier to live and work here,' Allegra stated.

'Great idea, sweetie.'

'So that's all sorted, then. Except for the matter of the probate and Kate Vanderpump and all that.'

'I know, but Gwen was looking after that and our solicitor will do all the necessary investigations. It could become quite ugly if it comes out that Kate has been falsifying documents.'

Allegra shivered. 'I hope not. Maybe she could just have been mistaken?'

'That's not very likely.'

'I suppose not.'

'I just want her to disappear, to be honest,' Max said.

'Me too,' Allegra said, sighing.

Max lay down in the bed and pulled the duvet up to his chin with a huge yawn. 'Enough about her. I'm getting sleepy. Can we leave everything until tomorrow?'

Allegra curled up beside him. 'Yes, we can. Let's sleep on it.'

'Okay,' Max mumbled.

'Good night, Max,' Allegra whispered.

There was no reply. Allegra smiled and cuddled up beside him.

She drifted off to sleep herself while the stars twinkled and glimmered in the dark sky.

Early on Sunday morning, loud knocking on the front door woke them up.

'What's that noise?' Max asked drowsily.

Allegra sat up in bed. 'Someone's at the door.'

'Tell them to go away.' He turned over and put his pillow over his head.

Allegra looked at her phone. 'It's ten o'clock.' She got out of bed and put on her dressing gown. 'I'm going downstairs to see who it is.'

'Okay,' he mumbled. 'I'm going back to sleep.'

Allegra ran down the stairs as the knocking started again. 'Coming,' she shouted. Then she opened the door and stared at the person standing there. 'Edwina,' she said. 'Hi... err...'

'Good morning,' Edwina said, looking sourly at her. 'I believe Max is here?'

'Max?' Allegra stammered.

'My brother,' Edwina said. 'I'm sure you know who I mean, and I'm also sure he's here because that's what I heard.'

'From whom?' Allegra asked.

'People coming out from mass. I asked them and they said

he was here with you and that he arrived yesterday. In any case, I can see his car, so there is no use denying it.'

'Why would I deny it?' Allegra stepped aside and opened the door wider. 'Why don't you come in? Max is asleep, but I can wake him if it's important.'

'It is,' Edwina said and swept past Allegra into the hall. Then she marched ahead straight into the living room and looked around. 'Cute place.' She moved to the door of the sunroom and looked out. 'In fact, it's pretty fab, I have to say, for a small house.'

'Yes, it is,' Allegra agreed as Max entered the room, fully dressed but unshaven.

'Hello, Edwina,' he said. 'What are you doing here?'

'I came to tell you something,' Edwina said. 'Something important.' She sat down on the edge of the sofa and looked from Allegra to Max. 'So you two are together, then?'

Max put his arm around Allegra. 'Yes, if that's what you want to call it.'

Edwina shrugged. 'Whatever. I was hoping you and Caroline would patch things up, actually. But, hey, whatever floats your boat.'

'Allegra certainly does,' Max said. 'And a lot of other things as well. But let's not go into that.'

'No,' Edwina said, making a face. 'Let's not. I didn't come here to discuss your love life anyway.'

'Why are you here, then?' Max asked.

'To tell you that Kate Vanderpump has disappeared.'

'What do you mean?' Max asked. 'I thought you and she were close friends and allies. And that together you would get the house sold and we'd all be rich.'

'Yeah, that was the plan.' Edwina sniffed. 'But something happened yesterday that scared her away. The solicitor called Gwen to say they have checked her documents again and they seem not to be genuine.'

'How did they check them?' Allegra asked.

'The solicitor asked the authorities in Scotland to send her mother's birth certificate so they could compare it to the one she had given them. And then when it finally arrived, it was discovered that Kate's certificate was fake.' Edwina sighed and looked at Max. 'I thought she was the real deal.'

'I never did,' Max said.

'And then there was that story about Davina having lost her baby,' Edwina continued morosely. 'That turned out to be true as well. They checked the hospital records and got a call yesterday to say it really happened. Then they told Gwen she could have Kate accused of fraud or something. I tried to call Kate to tell her, but she didn't answer. And she had checked out of the hotel in Killarney.'

'What about her Instagram account?' Allegra asked. 'Couldn't you send her a message there?'

'She has disappeared from there, too,' Edwina said. 'Either she blocked me or she took down the account.'

'My wish came true,' Max said with a glint of amusement in his eyes. 'I said I wanted her to go away, and then – *pouf* – she did. Maybe I have magical powers?'

'Stop it,' Edwina said. 'It's not funny.'

'No, it isn't.' Max folded his arms, glaring at Edwina. 'It's not funny having your sister going against you, or have her trying to destroy her cousin's life. Or siding with a complete stranger so she could sell a house that has been in the family for over two hundred years. What the hell got into you?' he thundered.

Edwina looked at him and suddenly burst into tears. 'I don't know,' she sobbed. 'I just thought it would be better not to have the problems of the upkeep and repairs of that old pile. I know you love it there, but I never did. Not the way you and Gwen do anyway. And in any case, I wasn't there that often after

Mummy and Daddy's divorce. That split us apart and it wasn't my fault.'

Max sighed and sat down beside Edwina, putting his hand on her shoulder. 'Please stop crying, Edwina. I know the house didn't mean that much to you and I never blamed you for that. But why didn't we discuss it? Why did you have to go and start plotting and scheming with that woman?'

'I didn't,' Edwina protested. 'It was just that she made it all seem so easy. She made me believe it was the best thing to do for everyone.' Edwina wiped her eyes with her hand and fished a tissue from her Hermès handbag. She blew her nose and sat back in the sofa, looking at Max. 'I'm sorry,' she whispered. Then she looked at Allegra. 'And I'm really sorry about that Facebook picture. It was a mean thing to do.'

'Yes, it was,' Max agreed. 'But we've sorted that one out. And everything else.'

'Oh, good,' Edwina said with a sigh.

Allegra sat down on her other side. 'It's going to be okay,' she said.

'Is it?' Edwina asked. 'But what about the death duties and all the repairs and everything? Kate said if we kept the house, we'd end up with huge debts. That's why the house had to be sold, she said.'

'She was wrong,' Max protested. 'We can work it out by selling a lot of the land and letting the rest, which will give us some money to pay the tax and do up the house slowly. In fact,' he continued, 'we might even be able to buy you out in the end.'

'Really?' Edwina dabbed her eyes with the tissue, looking a little brighter.

'If that's what you want, yes,' Max said. 'It could be enough for you to buy your own house or invest in something.'

'That would be fabulous,' Edwina said. 'And Gwen can stay on and keep running her yard?'

Max nodded. 'She can, I'm sure. And Allegra and I plan to live there, too, and do up the house bit by bit.'

'What?' Edwina stared at them wildly. 'You and—?' She shot a dark look at Allegra. 'You mean this is for good?'

'I certainly hope so.' Max reached out and took Allegra's hand.

'But you only just met,' Edwina protested. 'How can you know if it's going to last?'

'I don't,' Max said. 'But I feel that I have met the woman I want to share my life with.'

'I feel that too,' Allegra said. 'Hard to explain, but when it happens you just know.'

'Well, congratulations, then,' Edwina said without much conviction. 'But did I hear right? Did you just say that you're going to live in that cold dark place? Are you mad?'

'No, but maybe a little too romantic,' Max replied, smiling. 'We're just building a dream at the moment. So much to do and plan before it can happen.'

Edwina laughed. 'You are both insane. But hey, who am I to judge? Look at what I did. I believed in some con-woman and nearly made us lose that house.'

'But it didn't happen,' Allegra said.

'All thanks to you,' Edwina said, looking at Allegra with more warmth. 'I see that now. You came here at exactly the right time. How amazing is that?'

'Truly amazing,' Max agreed.

'It is.' Edwina got up. 'But now I'm going to leave you. I'm off to Dublin to go back to work tomorrow. I'll drop in on Gwen on the way and say sorry about everything. She'll tell me off big time, I'm sure, but I deserve it.'

'Don't go all saintly on us,' Max protested. 'The hair shirt doesn't really suit you. There's no need to call in to Gwen and apologise. I'll talk to her.'

'You will?' Edwina asked. 'That's so kind of you, Max. Not quite like you, though.'

'It's the Allegra effect,' Max said. 'She's turning me into a better person. You'd better be on your way, or she'll do it to you, too.'

Edwina laughed. 'I can see you want to be on your own.' She leaned down and kissed Max and Allegra in turn. 'See you soon, darlings. Keep me posted on everything, okay?'

'We will,' Max promised, as he got up from the sofa. 'I'll see you out.'

'No need,' Edwina said. 'I'll let myself out. Bye for now. And thanks for not punishing me.'

Max heaved a huge sigh when the front door slammed behind Edwina. 'Thank the Lord and all the saints for that.'

Allegra smiled up at him. 'She seems to have reformed.'

Max laughed. 'Reformed? Nah, she'll be back to her old ways in no time. Except I think we'll get on better from now on.' He took Allegra's hands and pulled her up. 'Strange family you're getting into. Do you still want to move in with me and live in that old wreck? Or maybe you should just say "weird to know you" and run for your life?'

Allegra smiled. 'No chance. You think your family is strange? Wait till you meet mine.'

'I can't wait.' He pulled her into his arms. 'I think this is a match made in heaven. We'll drive each other crazy.'

'Bring it on,' Allegra said and kissed him.

EPILOGUE

The wedding was the talk of the village when, eight months after Allegra's arrival in Sandy Cove, she married Max in the rose garden of Strawberry Hill.

Nearly everyone in the whole village was there and all the shops and pubs were closed for several hours while Allegra and Max said their vows in front of Father O'Malley. The sun shone from a clear blue sky as Allegra, in her mother's wedding dress, and Max, in his grandfather's morning suit smelling faintly of mothballs, were finally married. Gwen had found an antique lace veil in a cupboard and had it mended and cleaned for Allegra, and the flower shop in Killarney had made a beautiful bouquet and also a wreath of wildflowers for Allegra to wear on her head.

There had been a communal gasp among assembled guests as Allegra walked down the path with Emma, Mandy and Hannah in matching light-blue dresses skipping ahead carrying tiny bouquets. Joe followed behind with the rings on a red velvet cushion. Max's eyes filled with tears as he looked at his beautiful bride, and she could hear Lucia let out a little sob as she took the bouquet from Allegra. She looked into Max's lovely blue eyes as she said her vows and felt her heart contract with joy and love for this man who had never left her side since the day he'd told her he loved her.

He had insisted on coming with her to Boston once the snow cleared and stayed until Thanksgiving when they travelled together to the farm in Vermont. Lucia, Phil and the children had taken to him immediately and he had soon become a very popular uncle to Emma and Joe. In Boston, Max had stayed with Allegra while she sorted out her job situation and put her apartment on the market. After a little persuading, Allegra's boss, Annie, had agreed to Allegra working for them remotely as a web designer and developer. In fact, Annie had realised that getting into the Irish market was a good thing as there were many business opportunities with Irish firms, and even American ones, that had relocated from London to Dublin after Brexit.

Then Lucia and her family had come over to Sandy Cove for Christmas. Lucia, Phil and the children had stayed at Jason's house at Starlight Cottages while Max and Allegra camped in Strawberry Hill, where the Christmas fair a week before had been a huge success. They had all celebrated Christmas at Strawberry Hill. Edwina had joined them for the festivities and the following days, before going on a skiing trip with friends for New Year. They had put a huge Christmas tree in the library and spent the day there in front of a blazing fire, opening presents, playing games and drinking champagne. Gwen and Lucia had cooked an American-Irish Christmas dinner with traditional food from both countries.

And the next day, Maura and Thomas had invited them all to lunch, which had been noisy and lively with all the children running around. Maura's baby girl had been only two months old, but Maura managed to look wonderful, which Lucia had declared 'very annoying'.

Lucia had been bowled over by the beauty of Sandy Cove and declared it 'nearly as lovely as Cape Cod', which was a huge accolade coming from her. Allegra secretly thought Sandy Cove far superior but wasn't brave enough to argue.

The following months had been spent settling into life in a huge draughty house, which had been more than a challenge for Allegra, used to all the comforts of modern life. They had installed themselves in the master bedroom which had a big four-poster bed and a dressing room next door. But the only bathroom was down the corridor and, although lovely with a Victorian bath and basin, it was very cold on a winter's day. Max installed an electric heater that helped make it a little warmer. The water that was never more than lukewarm felt soft on Allegra's skin and the views from the large window were so stunning that she forgot her shivers. But she added 'new bathroom' to the long list of improvements they were planning for the coming years.

During the week after Christmas, there had been many fun parties in the evenings, and Irish music nights at the pub in the village with singing and dancing which Max, and even Gwen, had attended. Max quickly became quite good at Irish dancing, charming all the women by asking them to dance in turn. Amazed, Allegra had watched the two worlds finally come together and put all their hang-ups aside.

Lucille declared it was all thanks to Max and Allegra, and that Allegra had been the one to bridge the gap and brought everyone together. 'You're the dove of peace,' she had said, having downed a pint of Guinness with amazing speed, which, she confessed, always made her emotional. Even Ella had finally buried the hatchet and admitted that Max was a true blue and that Gwen was actually good company, especially after a few drinks. Allegra had to smile when she watched Gwen and Ella chatting and laughing and seemingly becoming new best friends. 'Talk about chalk and cheese,' Rory had muttered in her ear while they were dancing a jig. Even Edwina had joined in the festivities and Allegra had slowly begun to discover Max's sister wasn't all bad now that she had accepted that Strawberry Hill would stay in the family. 'She's just a little lost and lonely,' Lydia had remarked, which puzzled Allegra. Smooth and polished Edwina lost and lonely? Could there be some issues hiding behind that perfect exterior? Allegra promised herself to get to know Edwina better and maybe bring brother and sister closer together. That would be good for Max, and for the whole family.

Max had proposed on New Year's Eve and had gone down on one knee holding out a scuffed velvet box with a ring that had been in the family for generations. Not Davina's lost ring, which Gwen wore with pride, but a ring set with amethysts and diamonds in rose gold. Allegra had burst into tears and wrapped her arms around Max's neck, nearly choking him, whispering, 'Yes, yes, please.' Then they had started planning a summer wedding which seemed too far away, but here they were at last, in front of the priest promising 'to have and to hold, from this day forward, for better, for worse, for richer, for poorer, in sickness and in health, until death do us part.'

Then they exchanged rings, and when Father O'Malley said, 'You may kiss the bride,' fell into each other's arms and kissed long and hard while everyone in the rose garden applauded and cheered.

Max's mother and stepfather had attended the ceremony, his stepfather dark and serious, his mother a glamorous blonde in a designer dress and several rows of pearls. Both of them seemed a little out of place at this happy event and not very pleased to be there. Allegra felt a dart of pain for both Max and Edwina, who had been brought up in what seemed like a dysfunctional family with much money but very little love. She was relieved when they left before the reception and she saw that Max felt the same.

The party lasted into the small hours of the following day, spilling down to the village where the pubs were offering free drinks and a live band played traditional Irish music and everyone danced all along the main street. Max and Allegra sneaked off around midnight but nobody noticed as the party was in full swing.

They were just getting into Max's car when Lucille caught up with them. 'So you're off, then?' she asked.

'Yes,' Max replied. 'Better to leave quietly and let everyone enjoy the party.'

'Where are you going?' Lucille asked.

'Dingle,' Max replied. 'I wanted to go to the Seychelles, but Allegra insisted we go and see another part of Kerry. So we're going to tour around Dingle and stay in a lovely little B&B in Castlegregory. The forecast is good and we're going to relax and swim and surf and stuff like that.'

'Excellent,' Lucille said. She stood on tiptoe to kiss Max on the cheek. 'Good luck. Love each other and never go to bed angry.'

'I promise,' Max said.

Lucille hugged Allegra. 'Be happy. And you know where I am if he's difficult.'

'I don't think he will be,' Allegra protested.

'Of course he will,' Lucille said. 'All men are. But what would they do without us?'

'We'd never manage,' Max said. 'Where is Dominic?'

'Asleep in my car. I'm taking him home. I think the conga line was too much for him. But he'll be fine after a night's sleep.' Lucille waved. 'Off you go. Have a wonderful time.'

'We will,' Max said as he opened the passenger door for Allegra.

Then they drove off, laughing as boots and cans that had been tied to the back of the car clanged behind them. Max had to stop at the gates to remove them. Then he got back in and, as the sun set, they continued down the road that stretched ahead, full of promises of happiness and a bright future.

A LETTER FROM SUSANNE

Thank you for reading *The Lost House of Ireland*, which I so enjoyed writing. If you want to keep up to date with my latest releases, just sign up at the link below. Your email address will never be shared and you can unsubscribe any time.

www.bookouture.com/susanne-oleary

I hope the book swept you along to the beautiful south-west of Ireland that I love so much. While I wrote this story, the pandemic was still with us, but there was a light at the end of the tunnel on that front at least. Right now, there is war in Europe, something we never thought we'd see again. I do hope that by the time you read this there will be some kind of peace. In any case, I hope reading my book cheered you up, wherever you are in the world.

I would really appreciate it if you could write a review as I love feedback from readers. Your take on my story is always so interesting – and even surprising sometimes. Your comments might also help other people discover my books. Long or short, a review is always helpful.

I also love hearing from my readers – you can get in touch on my Facebook page, through Twitter, or my website.

See you soon again in Sandy Cove!

Susanne

KEEP IN TOUCH WITH SUSANNE

www.susanne-oleary.co.uk

 facebook.com/authoroleary
twitter.com/susl

ACKNOWLEDGEMENTS

Huge thanks to my wonderful editor, Jess Whitlum-Cooper, for her never-waning support and hard work to make my book shine. Also all at Bookouture – always such a delight to work with.

My husband, Denis, deserves an extra-enormous hug and thanks for all he does for me, and my family and friends who are there for me. With all these wonderful people in my life, I feel incredibly lucky.

Last but not by any means least, I want to thank my readers for your kind messages and comments. You are the reason I keep writing and your enthusiasm is my best inspiration.

THANK YOU!

Made in the USA
Columbia, SC
08 August 2022

64865266R00150